The Whirligig of Time

Charles Tabb

Gifted Time Books
Beaverdam, VA 23015

ISBN- 9781086182293

DEDICATION

For Roger - I hope this one pleases you, too.

ACKNOWLEDGEMENTS

Thanks once again to my BETA readers: Chuck Shelton, Trisha Shelton, Sue Schorling, and my wife, Dee, who is my most ardent critic, but always critiques with love. They seem to be right every time with their suggestions. Thanks also to my editor, Kristine Elder. What a joy it was to find you for this task. Your suggestions have made this a considerably better book.

Books by Charles Tabb

Literary Novels

Floating Twigs
Finding Twigs
Canaries' Song

Detective Tony Pantera Novels

Hell is Empty
The Purger
The Whirligig of Time

Coming in 2022

Scattered Twigs

And thus the whirligig of time brings in his revenges.

--William Shakespeare
Twelfth Night, V, i

Beware the fury of a patient man.

--John Dryden
Absalom and Achitophel

ONE

Detective Tony Pantera was too busy to deal with crap like this. A guy that had become known as Crazy Carl had come into the station yet again to confess to some crime or other. It was always the same thing. He'd come in, dressed in his insane choice of outfit for the day, confess to a crime he'd read about in the newspaper or seen on local TV, and leave reluctantly when they refused to arrest him. He invariably knew little about the details of the crime. He was just a sad person who needed to confess for psychological reasons.

The reason Pantera was so busy was that the city had been experiencing a rash of burglaries. The clues were mostly nonexistent, and the people at the top of the mountain were pushing the shit downhill toward Pantera and his partner, Harry Overmeyer. A friend of the mayor's had been one of the victims, so the heat was on to stop the criminals before they were caught by the homeowners and the outcomes became much worse.

They suspected these were being done by the same gang of thieves, but this gang was not the ordinary drugged out guys on street corners who decided to break into a home or business out of boredom. These guys were professionals.

There had been five break-ins in the past month, and so far not a single clue had been left behind, not even shoe prints. These guys were able to disarm the security systems, get in, get out, and not leave so much as a hair behind. It was frustrating as hell, but Pantera had to hand it to these guys. They were good. So good, he wondered if they would ever find them without an amazingly lucky

1

occurrence, like finding one of their wallets that had dropped out of a pocket, which of course was never going to happen.

Pantera wanted to solve them as well for that reason alone. Dealing with a typical breaking and entering was one thing. Dealing with a dead body was something entirely different. But now Pantera was forced to deal with Crazy Carl instead.

Pantera had once asked a police psychologist about people like Carl and was told it was probably because the confessor felt he needed to be punished for a list of things he'd done wrong as a child.

"Is there some way we can make him stop?"

"Does he confess to crimes that you aren't investigating? You know, like another department is in charge of the investigation?" the psychologist asked.

"No. They're always recent crimes in our purview."

"My guess is he might be confessing to other crimes to other detectives in and around the city."

"So we can't get rid of him."

"Oh, you could bar him from the station, but it's probably helpful for him, psychologically, to have something to confess to. If he doesn't have such an outlet, there's no telling what he might do—harm himself or others, for instance."

"He doesn't appear to be harmful," Pantera said. "Quite harmless, in fact."

"The human psyche is an odd thing. If in need of a release mechanism and denied it—. Well, to use the technical term, he could go bat-shit crazy."

Pantera had laughed at the words coming from someone who, in normal circumstances, would anger at such a term.

"So, we just let him come in and confess? It's a waste of time."

"Consider it a duty that helps others. I would recommend finding lower echelon officers to handle the interviews, if at all possible."

Usually, that was indeed possible, but Crazy Carl had decided to come in this time during graveyard shift, which Pantera was working because he'd pissed off Chief of Detectives Childers for the umpteenth time. Childers had demanded that Lt. Gariepy punish Pantera for what Childers termed insubordination. Pantera preferred to call it being too busy actually solving crimes to come to a meeting Childers had arranged to ream him out. Pantera had sent an email instead requesting Childers reply to that email to yell at him to save everyone the time.

Okay, Pantera thought, *maybe that was a bit over the line*.

Now, though, he had to deal with Crazy Carl, who wasn't named Carl at all, in fact. His name was Lenny, which Pantera had always associated with the guy on the old Laverne and Shirley TV show. This Lenny, however, looked nothing like the actor who had played Lenny on the show. That Lenny was at least funny. This one was, well, Crazy Carl.

"Okay, Lenny," he said, stopping himself at the last second before calling him Carl. "What did you do this time?"

"You people never take me seriously. I'm here to tell you, I robbed that store on Cannon Avenue."

A bodega downtown had been robbed two nights ago. The news had appeared in the Richmond Times-Dispatch the next morning. The only thing Lenny had going in his favor was that he fit the general description of the perp, just without the odd way he dressed. This time Lenny wore a long-sleeve wool shirt despite the warm temperature outside and cargo shorts. The shirt had every button buttoned. He also wore a tie that looked as though it had been new twenty years ago.

"About what time did you rob it?" Pantera asked, searching for the fact Lenny/Crazy Carl didn't know so he could end this charade.

"Around 9:30," Lenny said.

Pantera jotted that down in the fake report. "Okay, why did you lock the old man who was working that night in the store's cooler. He practically froze in there. That's something the public didn't know."

This hadn't happened. In fact, it was a young man at the register that night, and the robber had demanded the money, scooped it from the counter, and ran.

"Yeah, well, I'm sorry about that, but I didn't want him calling the cops before I could get away. If they cornered me, they might shoot me. By coming in and confessing, nobody gets hurt."

Pantera wadded up the paper he'd been writing on and tossed it in the wastebasket. "Lenny, Lenny, Lenny. It wasn't an old man. It was a young guy, and the robber didn't lock him in the cooler."

"Oh?"

"Listen, Lenny, why don't you try to get some help? There are agencies that can help you with this. Every time you come in and confess to something, it takes time we just don't have."

"I'm sorry, Detective Pantera. Really, I am. I just, well, I just can't help it."

"Yeah, I know. That's what I mean. You should seek some counseling for this. It's not all that rare. Guys turn into habitual confessors all the time." This wasn't exactly true, but he wanted to make Lenny believe his affliction wasn't rare.

"So, I guess you're not gonna arrest me for this?"

"Nope. Tell you what I will do, though," Pantera

said. "I'll buy you a Coke. How's that?"

Lenny, who had trouble looking anyone in the eye just glanced around the squad room, his eyes darting here and there as if gathering images the way a squirrel gathers acorns.

"Yeah, okay."

After buying a Coke from the machine and giving it to Lenny, Pantera went back to the real work. He had that robbery to solve, for one thing, along with the string of break-ins around the city.

He looked at the clock and noticed the day shift would be in soon. He was more or less working with his friend Harry Overmeyer on the B & E cases. Harry did the leg work during the day, and Pantera did the paperwork at night, along with handling other crimes committed in the overnight hours. That night, no violent crimes had been reported, so he'd had time to get quite a bit done, especially given the speed with which he'd managed to get Crazy Carl back out the door of the squad room.

At 6:57 Harry walked through the door and said, "Mornin', Tony! How'd you sleep?"

"Like a baby," Pantera said. "A colicky one."

"Well, now you get to go home and get some sleep-the-day-away rest."

"I have trouble sleeping in the daytime. Sun keeps making the room too bright, even when it's cloudy."

"Get a blindfold. Or better yet, buy some of those curtains that don't allow the light to get inside. What d'ya call 'em? Blackout curtains."

"Thanks for the advice, Harry, but I'm supposed to get off the hell shift at the end of the week."

"Just tryin' to help," Harry said, pouring himself a cup of coffee.

"Actually, I was thinking of going by The Watering

Hole after trying to get some sleep to see if Dean or Pete have heard anything about the bodega robbery." The bodega was just down the street from Pantera's favorite bar, known as The Watering Hole.

"You're off duty in the afternoon," Harry said, as if Pantera had to be reminded.

"Yeah, well, once I'm awake, I gotta do something. Might as well stop in for a drink and a chat with my friends there. After all, if I'm officially off-duty, I can have something stronger than a Coke to wet my whistle."

"In that case, have one for me. I'm a scotch man. My favorite is twenty-one-year-old Glenlivet."

"Too expensive," Pantera said.

"It is for me, too, but since you're buying."

"I'll have a whiskey to toast your health, but that's all. He stocks Writers Tears Irish for me now, so that's what you'll get—it'll just go down my throat."

"Oh, well. Enjoy," Harry said before changing the subject. "Did you manage to get much paperwork filed on the B & E?"

"All caught up, despite having Crazy Carl drop by."

"Oh?"

"He stopped in to confess to the bodega robbery."

"How nice of him. Did you give him my regards?"

"Yeah. Told him you were taking him to Ruth's Chris for Father's Day."

"Sure. We can bring you along to pick up the tab."

"Ha! In your dreams," Pantera said. "Well, I'm leaving now. As much as I love this place, I have to get home. Later!"

With that, Pantera walked out and drove home. Sleep came more easily than it had been the past few nights. He set his alarm for 4:30 and actually slept in until then.

He showered before heading to The Watering Hole. He'd met Dean Ackerman, the owner, and his permanent barfly, Pete, who was also his brother-in-law, when he was investigating the murder of a young prostitute about a year ago. She had been a victim of a serial killer, and Pantera had wondered if the killer might have stopped in for a drink or to use the bathroom.

According to accounts from the scene, it was clear the killer had walked through an alley where the murder was committed to Cannon Street where The Watering Hole sat. It was the only place that had been open on that block at that time of night.

Arriving at The Watering Hole, he called out to Dean, "Hey, ya ol' bastard! What's cookin'?" It was a standard greeting by the regulars in the place.

Dean came back with his usual response. "My nuts on summer days!"

Pantera took a seat next to Pete. "How they hangin', Pete?"

"Doin' well enough, I guess. How you been?" he said in his raspy, smoker's voice.

"Hangin' in there. Trying to keep my head while doing the graveyard." He'd already shared the news of his punishment by Childers the day it was handed down.

"When does that shit end?" Pete asked.

"This Friday night."

"You off any before that?"

"Nope."

"Well, just two more then. You'll live."

"Oh, I know I'll live. I just hope I don't lose my head and punch Childers on the jaw when I see him next time."

"Just keep in mind things could be worse, and he'd figure out a way to do that."

"Oh, yeah. He'd have my freakin' badge if I did

that, so I won't. Doesn't keep me from thinking about it, though."

Dean set his Writers Tears and Coke on the counter. "Add it to your tab?"

"Yeah, and give Pete here another on me."

Pete raised his beer. "Thanks, friend."

"Don't mention it."

Dean asked, "So you're workin' again tonight?"

"Yep. Not off 'til Saturday. Then I go back to my day shift starting Monday."

"You catch that guy who robbed the bodega down the street?"

"A man came in and confessed last night around midnight."

"No shit?"

"Yep. Of course, the guy also came in and confessed to a dozen other crimes over the past several months."

"Really? You mean there's a guy who comes in and confesses to crimes he didn't commit?"

"It happens," Pantera said. "These people feel a need to be punished. At least that's what the police shrink told me."

"Well, let me know if someone legit confesses or you catch the guy who did it."

Pantera raised his glass. "Will do." Pete clinked the glass with his fresh beer and they drank.

TWO

B lanton stood in the darkness of an alley across the street from The Watering Hole. He was known only by his last name to almost everyone he knew. He'd been called Blanton since his days playing high school football, and he knew people who'd known him for years who had probably never heard his first name. Only his family could be assured of knowing it, but he'd not seen most of them since leaving home eight years ago.

Now it was dark, and Blanton could see inside the bar through the plate-glass window. He watched as Detective Tony Pantera enjoyed his drink.

Pantera knew these men in the bar well, and it showed. Their shared laughter and interactions suggested good friends coming together for drinks. This did not bother Blanton. In fact, it made him smile. If Pantera had a drinking problem, then all the better. Alcohol numbed the brain even when those who imbibed were not drinking. It had lasting effects, and the fact that most cops drank made him wonder how they ever solved a crime.

Blanton intended his own crimes to be completely unsolvable. All criminals did, but he would accomplish it. He had planned the perfect murder over the past ten years. He would get his revenge, and he would see to it that Pantera ended up on the case. In fact, that would be the easiest part of his meticulously considered plot.

He wanted Pantera because Pantera was considered by many in the city to be the best detective on the force. Blanton had asked around, nonchalantly of course, in the bars where most of the cops hung out. This wasn't one of them, and Blanton admired Pantera for frequenting a bar few cops used. This suggested the detective was an individualist, someone who didn't go with the crowd. Blanton liked that.

He'd seen Pantera in The Watering Hole with only one other cop—another detective named Overmeyer who worked with Pantera at his precinct. As far as he could tell, those were the only two cops to ever patronize The Watering Hole, probably because it wasn't big enough for a gaggle of cops to gather and have room to do more than cram themselves into the few seats and booths. The place wasn't much bigger than the bodega down the street that had been robbed a few nights ago.

He knew the cops would catch whoever had done that because there was a witness. Only one, but one was enough. The robber would hold up another place, and soon after there would be a composite in the news that someone would recognize and phone in a tip. Blanton was surprised one hadn't been generated already.

Rather than committing high-risk armed robberies, Blanton had been breaking into homes over the past month without being seen or even caught on camera, but that spree was over now. Those break-ins had been a test of his methods to see if any clues were found beyond the missing items, and of course there had been none, mostly because he'd not left any. Every move, every step had been planned with precision. He'd known everything he needed to know about each home and had used that information to his benefit.

Now, the murder Blanton had planned for a decade was ready for commission. He couldn't afford to have such painstaking preparation go for nothing, so as time passed, his level of care increased. The killing had a motive, but the distance in time between the spurring events and the murder would prevent anyone from suspecting him. He'd been only seventeen when the first thought about killing his high school math teacher had occurred to him. Now, the long wait was nearly over. That distance in time was part of the plan, and Blanton knew that patience was necessary when committing the perfect crime, especially the perfect murder. After all, as they say, patience is a virtue. Blanton thought about this pithy little saying whenever he considered the time it was taking to kill the man he hated most in the world. Another favorite was, "Vengeance is a dish best served cold." It had been used in an old sci-fi movie, but it was actually nineteenth-century French.

Now, he watched the man who would be his adversary in this drama of his own creation. He had nothing against Pantera. From what he could see, he was a fairly nice guy who went about his job the best he could. However, Blanton intended to win this chess match of wits. In order to do that, he would need to know everything he could about his adversary. It was all part of the plan to have his revenge and enjoy his lifelong freedom at the same time.

In his preparation, he had discovered that Pantera had an ex-wife and two daughters, though so far he didn't know where they lived. He would have to find out in case he had to resort to more drastic measures to ensure his continued freedom. He didn't think that would happen, but being sure his stratagem would work even if things didn't go as planned was crucial.

He had also found out where Pantera lived. He would go there the next evening if the detective was at work and break in, mostly to get the layout and leave a few items behind. He would leave no clues though, not even a hint that someone had been there. Again, it was a dry run of sorts. He would be doing the same at his

11

victim's home next week and needed to make sure he could break into a house and leave those items behind while leaving no hint that he'd even been inside. The police investigated the rash of breaking and entering jobs, but this time he needed nobody to look into the crime, not to notice it at all. Blanton figured the best detective in Richmond would recognize something was amiss if the break-in wasn't as undetectable as Blanton thought. If that went well, then the plan would move into full-speed-ahead mode. Then nothing could stop him, not even a detective as good as Pantera.

He also intended to follow Pantera on his days off to see if he visited his ex-wife and kids. Even if the kids were delivered to Pantera, he could follow whoever dropped them off, probably the ex, and find out where they live. All he had was time anyway. His trust fund paid his bills.

Yes, Blanton's former math teacher, Mr. Grant Davis, would be dead within two weeks.

And Blanton himself will have gotten away with murder.

THREE

Pantera drove home from The Watering Hole after only two drinks. He had a few things to do before going in for what would be his penultimate graveyard shift. He couldn't wait for Saturday morning for more reasons than ending that last shift from hell.

Nancy, his ex, would be bringing the girls for the weekend. She would deliver them, and he would take them home Sunday evening. He was working hard to repair the fraught relationship he had with his daughters. Andrea was fifteen, soon to turn sixteen, and had come out as a lesbian just a couple of months ago. Beth, who was twelve, adored her father, and he was doing his best to be worthy of her love.

Arriving home, he called Nancy.

"Hey," he said when she'd answered.

"Hi, Tony. I hope you're not calling to cancel the weekend."

Part of him couldn't blame her for thinking he might cancel—he'd done it too often before—but another part wondered when she would start believing he was doing his best to change. Because he was already angry that he had to work the graveyard, he lashed out before thinking it through.

"Why do you always draw that conclusion? I'm trying my best, Nance. No, I'm not canceling."

"Sorry, Tony, but it's hard not to believe the worst when it comes to you spending time with the girls. Your work tends to get in the way too much. Always did."

"I'm doing my best, okay? I was calling to make

13

sure nothing had happened on your end to cause a cancelation. So you see? I'm looking forward to the weekend with them."

"Sorry, okay? Sorry. Yes, I will be bringing them. You'll bring them back Sunday night?"

"Of course. They have school Monday. I wouldn't interfere with that." He paused a second. "Remind me when school's out. I want to plan something with them for a getaway. Maybe spend a week at the beach."

"June 7. I think they'll enjoy that. In fact, I know they will."

"I just need to coordinate the dates with you."

"Okay. So I'll see you Saturday around three?"

"Sounds good."

An hour into his shift, a call came in about another armed robbery. When he heard where it had happened, a shudder passed through him.

The Watering Hole had been robbed, and someone had been shot. As he drove to the scene, he prayed Dean and Pete were okay. Arriving, he rushed in, maneuvering around the ambulance with its bubble lights giving the scene an eerie red glow. An officer was already there.

As he entered, he saw the medics working on a man who was lying on the floor. Stepping to the side, he saw Pete's pale face looking up at the medics. He was conscious.

Pantera leaned over him. "Pete! Pete!"

"Huh?" Pete said, his voice weak.

"Where's Dean?"

A voice rang out from a booth. "Over here, Tony."

Pantera glanced over and saw Dean with a uniformed officer. He looked shell-shocked but otherwise okay.

Turning back to Pete, he said, "You're gonna be okay. Hang in there."

14

"Course I will. It's just a shoulder."

The medic interrupted. "Lie still, Mr. Bray. We'll get you to the hospital and get you into surgery so the doctor can take that bullet out and make sure the wound doesn't get infected."

Pantera suddenly realized he'd never known Pete's last name. The name Pete Bray rang a bell, but he wasn't sure from where.

"Jus' give me a beer, and I'll be fine," Pete said.

"Can't do that, sir. But in a week or so you'll be back here having a cold one," the medic said.

"A week, my saggy ass. A day."

"Well, I wouldn't count on it," the medic said and looked at his partner. "You ready?"

"Yeah," said the other medic.

The first guy looked down at Pete. "You think you can walk, Pete, or should we get you on the gurney?"

"I can walk."

As Pantera straightened up, he sighed. If they were letting him walk to the ambulance, Pete would be fine.

Pantera turned to Dean. "So, what happened?"

"Got robbed, but I think I may have hit him."

"Hit him?"

"Yeah. I keep a gun behind the bar. He pulled his and I pulled mine. That's when his gun went off and Pete fell. A wild shot, I guess. I shot at him, and he ran, but he was limping, like he'd been hit."

"You didn't notice if he reacted to getting shot?"

"No, sorry. Happened too fast. I was barely lookin' in fact. I mighta closed my eyes, but I saw him run out. He wasn't limping that I saw when he came in, and a limp that bad I woulda noticed."

"Did you see which direction he went?"

"Nope. I was checking on Pete."

Pantera excused himself and went outside. The

ambulance was pulling away from the curb to take Pete to the hospital to have the bullet removed. Pantera didn't doubt for a moment that Pete would be back at the bar again tomorrow.

He went to his car and took out his flashlight then walked west along the street, looking for blood drops on the sidewalk. After going about thirty yards, he came to the bodega that had been robbed just a few nights before and wondered if it might have been the same perp in both cases. If so, he might live nearby.

He turned around and walked along the street to the east, passing The Watering Hole and continuing for another thirty yards or so. He saw no blood drops.

Then he stood and looked around, trying to figure out if there might be another direction the perp had gone.

Crossing the street, he walked to the west, passing the business across the street from the bar and continuing until he was across the street from the bodega. Nothing.

Turning around, he started back toward The Watering Hole when he thought about the alley. An alley emptied onto the street just across from The Watering Hole. It was the same alley where the prostitute who went by the name Carlotta had been murdered by the man who called himself the Purger, which had led Pantera to meeting Dean and Pete in the first place.

Walking toward the alley, he shone his flashlight into the darkness and found what he was looking for. A few feet into the alley, a drop of blood lay on the cracked pavement. He stepped into the alley, shining his flashlight at the ground. Every few feet, another drop of blood waited like markers dropped to prevent getting lost in the woods.

Pantera followed these to the street where Carlotta had been murdered just a few feet inside the alley. Upon coming out of the alley, he saw another hooker strolling the street. She was maybe twenty-five, with an olive complexion.

He followed the blood drops, but they ended at the edge of the street. He looked around but saw no more blood drops, which had become more frequent as he walked the alley.

He walked up to the girl and said, "Excuse me."

She must have figured him for a cop and said, "I ain't doin nothin' but walkin' home."

"I'm not here to arrest you or give you any problems. I'm just wondering if you saw a guy come limping out of that alley maybe an hour ago."

She eyed him. "What's in it for me?"

"No phone call to vice."

She heaved a sigh, as if everything in the world was against her, and for all Pantera knew, maybe it was. He just needed to know if she'd seen the guy and if she knew where he went from there.

"Okay, yeah. I saw him. He was bleedin'. He got in a car and drove off. That's all I know."

"What kind of car?"

"A car. I don't know. I don't pay attention to that."

"What color was it?"

"Jeez. Dark. That's about all I know. Lighting ain't good out here, you know."

"What did the guy look like?"

She crossed her arms and stuck her hip out to one side. "A guy. Dark hair. He was limping like crazy."

"How tall?"

"Jeez, man! I didn't take no picture. He was average. Kinda thin."

"So you didn't recognize him? If you did, you should tell me now. Later, and it won't be good for you."

"No! I never seen the dude before."

"You're sure?"

"Yes!"

Pantera thanked the girl, but before leaving to return to The Watering Hole, he handed her ten dollars. "You don't have to tell Bam-Bam I gave that to you." Pantera knew Bam-Bam was the pimp who worked the girls in this area.

She looked shocked and stuck the money into the pocket of the tight shorts she wore, struggling to get the money into the tight space.

Returning to The Watering Hole, Pantera spoke briefly to Dean. "You hit him. He ducked down the alley to where he was parked on the next street, literally feet from where Carlotta was murdered."

"You think you can find him?" Dean asked.

"I think so. He'll need a doctor, and they have to report a gunshot wound."

"What about if a friend works on his wound?"

"He seems to have been hit bad. He might need surgery beyond just removing the bullet."

"You think he'd be dumb enough to go to a hospital? He's gotta know the police are looking for him."

"Dean, guys who walk into a bar and try to hold it up without knowing the bartender keeps a gun behind the bar aren't very smart to begin with. Yeah, I do."

"Good luck," Dean said, and Pantera left. He drove to VCU's emergency room. When he walked in, he showed the admitting clerk his badge and asked if any gunshot wounds had come in that night.

She rolled her eyes at him. "This is the gun and knife club, you know." He'd heard that before.

"So, have there been any? I'm looking in particular for a young man with dark hair who's been shot in the leg or maybe the hip."

The woman pointed at a doctor. "That's the person you want to talk to."

Pantera introduced himself to the doctor and repeated what he was searching for, noting her name—Dr. Suddath.

Dr. Suddath smiled and said, "Come on back. I think he's back here. We're about to admit him for surgery, but he's not being the most cooperative patient about that. Just wants the bullet removed. I guess he thinks this is the wild west and we can just use a probe and *bingo*, the bullet just pops out."

As they entered the treatment area, Pantera noticed a young man with dark hair propped up on a gurney. He was facing them, and when he saw Pantera, he did his best to run, tumbling off the narrow bed and onto the floor before struggling to stand. His leg, however, wasn't cooperating. It crumpled beneath his weight, and he did his best to stand again to no avail.

Several male nurses went to him, initially thinking he'd fallen from the gurney, but when he tried to fight them, they managed to subdue him. Both the nurses were bigger than the man with the bum leg, so they had no trouble.

Pantera walked up casually and introduced himself, finishing with, "And you're under arrest for attempted armed robbery and assault with a deadly weapon. Maybe even attempted murder during the commission of a violent crime."

After filling out the proper paperwork, Pantera called in to arrange for a police guard to be stationed at the man's door once he was moved to a room, a job that typically went to rookies.

He learned the perp's name was Ronaldo Arillas. A quick check revealed he'd been arrested before for various small-time felonies, but nothing this major. He'd be going to prison for several years for this one, especially since he'd shot a man during the attempted armed robbery.

Returning to the precinct, he completed the paperwork on Arillas and finished his shift by poring over the paperwork on the B & E's. He wanted to catch these guys because they were obviously professionals and would do more damage if not taken off the streets.

By the time his shift had ended, he was exhausted. He went home, stripped down, and climbed into bed.

He noticed nothing amiss in his home, despite the fact someone had been inside for several hours that night.

FOUR

Blanton sat at his computer and listened as Detective Pantera entered his home. He'd spent the night installing "bugs" in Pantera's home. From long experience, he knew how to place them in locations nobody ever looked. For instance, the device in the kitchen was taped securely to the underside of the small dining table. He'd also bugged his phones, of course. Pantera might find them in time, but by that time, they wouldn't be necessary anymore.

He listened to the sounds of a man going to bed and signed off. He had also placed a computer in a corner of the attic that was sound activated to record whatever it "heard" to make constant monitoring of the sounds in the house unnecessary. He could link up with that computer any time to listen to whatever it had recorded.

Of course, listening to Pantera wasn't the goal. That was just part of the dry run to ensure the equipment worked the way it should before moving on to his true target, Grant Davis. A decade of preparation gave birth to such meticulous details.

Blanton was tired as well and set an alarm for two o'clock that afternoon. He didn't want to sleep the day away, just get enough that he wouldn't be wide awake all night.

When Pantera arrived for his final graveyard shift, Harry greeted him by wrapping an arm around his shoulders. "Tony! The bodega guy ID'd the fellow you caught last night as the man who robbed him! You got a two-for-one!"

21

"Great," Pantera said. "I'm glad he's caught." He stepped away from Harry and sat at his desk. "Any news on the B & E's?"

"None. The break-ins were happening like clockwork, then nothing. It's weird. Not that I'm complaining, but it makes me wonder if it's a gang that moves on after a few jobs. It definitely would help prevent being caught."

"Yeah, that's true. Or they could have hauled in what they wanted and are enjoying the fruits of their labor. It was mostly cash, along with some jewelry, which they'd have to fence somewhere," Pantera said. "I'd think they were looking for someone to sell the jewelry to, but something makes me think these guys already had that arranged. These aren't amateurs."

"If they were, they'd have been caught by now," Harry said before leaving for home.

During his shift, Pantera investigated a domestic incident where a wife shot her husband in the leg. The bullet had gone through the soft tissue near the man's crotch, fortunately missing any major blood vessels as well as her intended target. He also investigated a hit and run that left a man dead on the side of the street. The biggest question there was whether it was intentional or accidental where the driver panicked and drove off. The victim was a known smalltime drug dealer, so Pantera strongly suspected the former.

But fifteen minutes into his shift, he also had another visit from Crazy Carl, who had read about the breaking and entering spree and wanted to confess. Pantera didn't have time for his games, so he ended the conversation two minutes into it when Crazy Carl claimed to have entered the home by using a glass cutter to make a hole in a window, which he unlocked to enter the latest house.

He had asked the shrink if they couldn't just ignore Carl, but the doctor said doing so would only cause the visits to increase, or worse. After Carl had left, Pantera fumed for a while over the lack of help for those suffering from mental issues. Carl was only the tip of the iceberg and harmless. Others were like powder kegs waiting for a match.

In the end, it somehow became the responsibility of the police to deal with the fallout of the constant cuts to funding to take care of those with mental health problems. It was a waste of time and manpower because it only dealt with the symptoms, not the causes.

The next morning Pantera went directly home again and crashed. It had been a long final shift, and the paperwork had kept him at the precinct until nine. He wanted to be rested enough to spend time with the girls that weekend before having to take them home Sunday evening. It would only be a twenty-four hour stay, and he wanted to make the most of it.

Before crashing, though, he poured some orange juice in a glass, along with a splash of vodka. He didn't like to drink in the mornings, but he wanted something to help him sleep, as well as to provide some kind of celebration for reaching the end of the shifts from hell.

He also called Nancy to make sure the time hadn't changed for their arrival. In response to his question, Nancy said, "I'm more punctual than you, Tony. We'll be there at three on the dot." He ignored the dig, mostly because he was too damn tired to care.

His alarm went off at two, giving him a grand total of four hours of sleep. It would have to do. He took a shower, dressed, and had downed two quick cups of coffee before Nancy arrived with the girls.

He greeted his daughters with hugs and a kiss on the cheek for each. Beth, for one, looked thrilled to be spending the time with him. Andrea was her usual self, excited to be there but reluctant to show it. It had been a month since they'd last visited, despite the divorce papers saying every other weekend. Unfortunately, despite Pantera's desire for a more regular visitation, his work got in the way too often.

Nancy said, "So, you'll have them home by six tomorrow evening?"

"Six," Pantera said. "On the dot." He could see she understood the dig at her response that morning, but she ignored it, just as he had done earlier.

Nancy left and drove back to her house in Charlottesville, just over an hour away. She and her husband, Phil, had plans for the evening since they rarely had the house to themselves. He had stayed home to clean the grill and buy some steaks for dinner along with a good bottle of wine. As she drove, she thought about the evening ahead. With her thoughts on that night and with the abundance of traffic on I-64 between Richmond and Charlottesville, she wasn't aware of the car following her, barely taking notice even when it drove past her as she pulled into her driveway and went inside.

Blanton drove past the house as Pantera's ex stepped out of her car and walked to the front door. He turned onto the next street and turned around. As he sat at the stop sign, he read the number on the mailbox and wrote the address on a pad, using a small piece of cardboard beneath the paper he wrote on to prevent indentations from marking the next sheet.

Removing the sheet with the address, he folded it and placed it in his shirt pocket. He had memorized it already but never trusted his memory in such instances. He folded the cardboard and tucked it in his pocket as well. He would burn it and replace it with another fresh piece of cardboard once he was home so he would have that new piece in the car when he needed it.

You can never be too careful, he thought to himself. *Never.*

He drove back to his home in Richmond, stopping for gas and a bottle of water. The drive felt more pleasant than usual. He wanted to thank Pantera and his ex for making the phone call, but of course, he couldn't. Still, the call had allowed him to know exactly what time to be at Pantera's to follow the ex back home.

And now he had the address where Pantera's daughters lived. They provided some very valuable insurance in case anything went wrong, which of course was unlikely. He'd created the perfect crime—and found the perfect insurance as well.

FIVE

That night after dinner, Pantera put the dishes in the sink for cleaning later. He didn't want to waste the time that his daughters were awake washing dishes. He started to make himself a Writers Tears and Coke, but Andrea stepped in.

"Can I make it, Dad?"

He looked at her, dumbfounded for the moment. "You thinking of becoming a bartender when you grow up?"

"I'm mostly grown up already, Dad. I'll be sixteen next month."

He chuckled. "Honey, being sixteen doesn't make you grown up. It just gets you a year closer."

"Well, to answer your question, no, but Mom lets me be their bartender some nights. It makes me happy to do that for them."

"I know how to make my drinks."

"I'm not offering to do something for you because I think you're incapable. I'm offering because I want to do something nice for you."

He chuckled again. "Well, who am I to take away your desire to do something for your dad? By all means. Do you know how much of the whiskey I take?"

"I've only watched you make your drinks since I was seven," she said, taking the bottle of Irish whiskey out of the cabinet.

"Well, then, I'll just go have a seat in the living room with your sister and you can bring me my drink when you're done."

She smiled at him. "No prob."

He laughed. "You're not planning on slipping me a Mickey so you and Beth can go out on the town, are you?"

"Dad, I wouldn't even know how."

He went to the living room, where Beth had already turned on the TV. He had something else in mind, though.

"You mind if we don't watch TV right now? I want to ask you girls about something."

"Sure," Beth said, turning off the TV.

Andrea came into the room carrying his drink and a coaster, setting them on the table beside his chair.

"Have a seat," he said. "I want to ask you something."

After Andrea sat beside her sister, Pantera began.

"Did your mother mention anything to you about taking a short vacation with me this summer?"

They both shook their heads.

"Well, I was wondering if you would like to go to the beach again. Not Florida this time, but maybe the outer banks of North Carolina."

They grinned. He knew they loved the beach. "Are you kidding?!" Beth asked.

"We'd love it!" Andrea said.

"Great, I'll let you know a few weeks in advance so you know when we're going."

"Dad?" Andrea said.

"Yeah?"

"Would it be okay if I brought a friend?"

"Who?"

"Her name's Dani."

Pantera glanced at Beth. "Should we talk about this in private?"

"Oh, she knows."

"Knows what?" Beth asked.

"That I'm gay."

"Oh, yeah." Beth looked at her dad. "It's kinda obvious when she's with her girlfriend, Dad."

"And Dani's your girlfriend?" Pantera asked.

"Yes."

Pantera sat back and took a deep breath before continuing. This hadn't occurred to him before. For a straight girl, a sleepover was just a sleepover. For a gay one, it could mean something else, and probably did. He wasn't so naïve that he thought all girls Andrea's age were virgins. But for Andrea and her girlfriend, virginity was something different. He knew teenagers would engage in sexual activities when the opportunity arose, at least a large percentage of them would. He recalled his own teen years and how preoccupied everyone his age had been about sex.

He felt amazingly uncomfortable talking about this with Andrea, especially in front of Beth, but he also knew he would have to do it whether he wanted to or not. Besides, what he was about to say would also apply to Beth when the time came.

"I'm not sure that's a good idea, sweetheart," he began. "It would be like bringing your boyfriend along on a vacation. With a boy, you'd already know the ground rules, but with another girl, you might be expecting to sleep in the same bed."

Andrea blushed. Her reluctance to talk about bringing her girlfriend had extended to not wanting to talk about the elephant in the room, namely that she might be having sex with Dani.

"We won't do anything."

"Maybe you won't, but I can't allow you to sleep together anymore than I would if you were straight and wanted to bring your boyfriend."

"But, Dad! I have friends who are allowed to bring their boyfriends on vacations!"

He thought for a moment. This was true.

"Okay. Tell you what. I'll allow it as long as we handle it the same way. I don't want to treat you differently because you're gay, so I'll treat you like the normal teenager you are. Dani can come, but you two can't sleep together."

She considered it. Pantera could tell she didn't love the idea. Still, he could see she understood he was doing his best to treat a girl-girl relationship between teenagers the same way he would treat a boy-girl relationship.

"It's as good a deal as I'm going to get, huh?"

"It's the only deal you'll get. It's all about setting limits, which at sixteen, you still need."

"Okay."

"So that's settled?"

"Yeah. As long as you don't mind if we kiss each other goodnight."

"Just observe some decorum when you do."

"Decorum?" Beth asked.

Pantera said, "Yes. In this case, it means no making out at a bedroom door, just a brief kiss goodnight."

"Oh," Beth said.

"Now, how about a game of Clue?" Pantera asked, wanting to move on from the discussion.

"Sure!" the girls said.

"Can I be Ms. Scarlet?" Beth asked.

"Sure," Andrea said.

When the girls went to bed, he cleaned the kitchen. He would take them to Lewis Ginter Botanical Garden, or the Richmond Science Museum the next day, depending on where they wanted to go.

Late that night, Blanton listened to the recorded

conversation that had taken place about the older daughter bringing her girlfriend on a vacation to the Outer Banks. He was surprised the girl was gay but even more surprised that Pantera knew and was okay with it.

Blanton knew some parents would disown a kid who turned out to be gay. He himself certainly would. Pantera was more liberal than Blanton had thought. He smiled as he realized Pantera's love for his daughter could be used against him given the right circumstances.

SIX

The weather had cooperated for the past few days. Sunny days had allowed the ground to dry. That Monday morning, Blanton sat outside the home of Grant Davis and fantasized about killing him for maybe the thousandth time. He'd considered the method in every way imaginable—strangulation, stabbing, drowning in the bathtub, electrocution. All of them held appeal. He had plans on what he wanted to do with the corpse once the deed was done, and that would require time. Nothing disgusting, just posing the body in such a way as to make the hounds sniff in many directions.

As he sat staring at the house, he thought about why he was there in the first place. He remembered how his math teacher, Mr. Davis, had ruined his life—the life he had planned for since he was ten.

The memory came back in the same startling detail that it always did.

It was Blanton's senior year of high school in Alexandria, and life was good. He had been courted by numerous universities to play football. He was a star running back considered to be one of the nation's top recruits. All the major programs had come knocking—Alabama, Ohio State, Clemson, LSU—all of them. He'd chosen Alabama because they were known for producing NFL level running backs. Blanton had dreamed of playing in the NFL since he was in peewee football and heard others talking about how he was like a man playing against children, even at that age. Whichever

31

team had him would win the league championship, and he knew he would one day be the best NFL running back in the league.

When he ran, it was as if everything slowed down. Sometimes, he could see holes opening in the defense a full second before it did, and he had the power, speed, and cutting ability to dominate at every level. He would do the same at Alabama, which had won the NCAA National Championship last year and placed in the top five in the nation every year as if it were a given. The reason for that, of course, was that the program was able to recruit the best of the best.

His prowess on the football field led to popularity with everyone at school, especially the girls. Some of them were willing to do damn near anything to go out with him, and he took full advantage of their willingness.

Yes, life was good.

As he sat in math class listening to Mr. Davis drone on about mathematics as if everyone loved it, he did his best to stay awake. He'd been up late last night having fun with Heidi Edwards.

He'd dozed off in class, and when he woke up, Dipshit Davis, as his students called him behind his back, was tapping Blanton's desk with a yardstick.

"Welcome to the land of the living!" Davis had boomed when he'd awakened. A few snickers from the guys who were jealous of him sounded around the room. Blanton turned to look at the faces of those guys, but they wisely shut up before he could see them.

"Would you mind answering my question, Mr. Blanton?" Davis said, smirking.

"Sorry. I didn't hear the question."

"Of course, you didn't. You were snoring." Davis turned back to the front of the room. Walking to the white board, he pointed with the yardstick at a problem they'd been working on in class.

"What is the solution?" he asked.

Blanton stared at the problem, which contained the symbol for pi in several places, among other Greek symbols. He seized on this one aspect and said, "I don't know, Mr. Davis. It looks like Greek to me." A few of his football buddies laughed this time.

Davis stared at him. Blanton hated Davis, of course, but why Davis hated him was beyond his ability to understand. For a student to hate a teacher was almost expected, especially one as distasteful as Davis. But for a teacher to so obviously loathe a student was anything but expected, at least not as much as Davis obviously hated him.

Davis glared for a moment, his eyes narrowing into slits as if trying to figure out whether or not Blanton was being a smartass, which Blanton took as a sign of how dense Davis was.

Finally, Davis went to the board and finished working out the problem, explaining as he did. Then turning to the class, he said, "Take out last night's homework and have it on your desk for me to check. While I'm doing that, complete the even numbered questions on page 249. It will be due at the end of class."

When Davis came to Blanton's desk, he saw that Blanton did not have his homework out. "Blanton, did you hear me tell you to take out your homework?"

"Yeah."

"So, where is it?"

"Didn't do it."

"And why not?"

"I was busy last night." A few snickers from his buddies on the team rippled through the room. They knew all about the night before because he'd told them

33

in detail that morning about his fun with Heidi.

"Well, Blanton fans," he announced. "Another zero for your idol."

Davis marked the zero in his grade book and moved on.

Such interactions had been common between Blanton and Dipshit Davis, Blanton thought as he sat looking at Davis's house where the man had moved to after divorcing his wife and taking a teaching job in Richmond.

These encounters were bad enough, but it was what Davis had done the next day that had sealed his fate.

The drug dog had visited the school for his quarterly hunt for illegal drugs in the lockers. There would be an announcement that all classes should remain in place until further notice to prevent a class change from occurring while the drug dog did his thing.

While Blanton was fond of smoking a joint or drinking beer with friends, he stayed away from the hard stuff because he knew it would get in the way of success in the NFL. He didn't need an addiction, nor did he need the more intoxicating drugs to have fun. He had girls like Heidi for that.

When they heard the dog barking, signaling he had found drugs, Blanton ignored it since he knew it didn't concern him. Yes, he would smoke a joint, but bringing drugs to school was asking for trouble. He could lose his scholarship to Alabama for something like that.

A moment later, a knock at Davis's door was followed by Mr. Nelson, one of the assistant principals, sticking his head in and signaling Davis to step outside. After that, Davis came back in, a smirk on his face that he made no attempt to hide.

"Mr. Blanton, could you step out here, please?"

Blanton looked up in disbelief. There had to be a

mistake. But when he walked out, he was met by Mr. Nelson, the cop, and the police dog, who was seated in the hallway. The two men stared at him as if blaming him for everything bad that had happened to them in the past week. Blanton looked back at Davis, who looked ready to burst into gales of laughter.

"Is this your locker?" Mr. Nelson asked, indicating what was, indeed, Blanton's locker.

Blanton hated that question, as if Mr. Nelson didn't have the list of all the locker assignments on his phone.

"Yeah."

"Would you mind opening it?"

"What for?" Blanton wasn't sure why he was stalling, which of course everyone knew he was doing. It wasn't as if they wouldn't open the locker themselves.

This was another thing Blanton hated. They always made students open the locker instead of using the key they all had to open the locks using the keyholes in the back. Hell, they could use bolt cutters if they needed to. As it had been pointed out numerous times, the lockers were the school's property and subject to being searched without warning by an administrator or a teacher. Being forced to open the locker was like having to get your own switch so your parent could mark your butt and thighs with red welts.

"The 'what for' is simple," Nelson said. "The dog says you have drugs in there."

"Well, I don't."

"Then open it up and let's see," Nelson said, sounding as if he were asking Blanton to show him a favorite passage in a book.

Blanton stepped to the locker and opened the combination lock. He rarely used the locker other than to store his lunch, a few rarely used textbooks and his letterman jacket.

35

What he saw on top of the stack of books made him feel faint. Lying there in plain sight was a baggie with a white powder inside, along with a few rocks of what he recognized as crack cocaine. He'd never done coke before of any kind, but it wasn't as if he'd never seen any before.

Looking at the bag, he guessed it held at least an ounce of cocaine or some other very illegal drug. He was shocked to find what amounted to a small fortune placed inside his locker.

He had no idea where the bag came from until he looked at Davis and his smirk.

He wondered where Davis had managed to get his hands on so much coke, but it was obvious to Blanton that Davis had been the one to plant the drugs in his locker. He had been the teacher who'd issued him the locker, so he had access to the combination. The baggie was too thick to be pressed through the tiny grates that decorated the locker door, so the person who had placed the drugs inside the locker would have to be able to open it.

Blanton lunged for Davis, wanting to knock the smirk off his face and possibly kill him with his bare hands for doing this to him. Blanton knew finding these drugs would cause him to lose his scholarship, his future—everything.

Nelson and the cop grabbed Blanton, but not before Blanton landed a hard punch below Davis's left eye. The dog began barking aggressively, as if giving him two seconds to stop before he tore out a chunk of Blanton's leg.

"Whoa! What are you doing?" Nelson said as he and the cop pressed Blanton against the lockers, holding him there to prevent further violence.

"He did this! He framed me! He planted the drugs!"

"On my salary?" Davis said. "Anyway, why would I do that?"

"Because you hate me almost as much as I hate you!" Blanton screamed.

Several doors along the hallway opened and teachers stuck their heads out. Blanton figured they either wanted to see if they could help or, more likely, to watch the end of Blanton's football career.

As they watched, the cop slammed Blanton face first into the lockers and handcuffed him before leading him away.

Blanton had been charged with possession of more than an ounce of cocaine, enough to add intent to distribute to the charge. He had been expelled and finished school while in jail because his father refused to pay his bail. Alabama had acted as if they'd never met him. His scholarship was withdrawn, along with his dream of being in the NFL Hall of Fame one day.

That had been ten years ago when he was eighteen. He'd spent a long time while serving his sentence planning revenge. After his release, he found out Davis had moved to Richmond, so he'd followed him there.

Blanton had inherited a lot of money from his grandparents in a trust he received on his twenty-first birthday, so he didn't have to work, though that was a technicality. His work was now planning the perfect murder. While he served his time, his father had tried to prevent him from inheriting what his grandparents had left him long before Davis had planted the drugs. Blanton no longer spoke to his father or anyone else in his family. He was alone in the world now. Alone with his thoughts and his plans.

He would get away with the murder of Grant Davis just as surely as he had gotten away with the B & E's. After killing Davis, he would leave the U.S. for some tropical island, perhaps Nassau in the Grand Bahamas, and live on his trust fund, which amounted to well over four million dollars.

Money had never been the issue. He never intended to play in the NFL for the money.

The fame was the issue.

Now, he would never be famous, only another unknown—a person who managed to plan and execute the perfect murder. The shame of it was that nobody would ever know the full extent of how perfect his plan to kill Davis was because they would never know what, exactly, he had done to get away with it.

But then, that was the way such plans needed to be. He smiled as he climbed out of his car and approached the house where Davis lived. Using tools for such a job, he removed a back-door window pane held in place by rubber strips and reached in to unlock the door. Then he carefully replaced the pane, securing the plastic strips once again. When he was finished with that, nobody would be able to look at the door's window and see that it had been removed and replaced.

His smile didn't falter for the rest of the day.

SEVEN

By the time Monday morning rolled around, Pantera looked forward to going work. Being able to return to the day shift had him more excited about work than he'd been in a long time.

He arrived just as Harry was parking his car, and he waited to walk in with his friend and frequent partner for working cases.

"Enjoy your vacation?" Harry said.

"Some vacation. Maybe you should piss off Childers and get the same detail."

After arriving in the squad room and getting coffee, they discussed the rash of burglaries they had worked on. Pantera had interviewed the victims of the B & E's in the hopes something would rattle a memory loose to at least give them some direction, but when he'd spoken to each one, they still knew nothing. It was as if ghosts had entered their homes.

The oddest part of the investigation were the footprints. Of the five break-ins, four had been on nights when only dew had fallen in the early morning hours, but the second of them had occurred after a day of off-and-on showers. They had expected to find footprints from the person or people who had broken into the house. Usually on such nights, muddy footprints were everywhere. However, that had not been the case this time.

Instead, they had found what looked like small, square indentions, not much bigger than the average foot. A number of these imprints ran from the street to the back patio where entry had been gained, leading

Pantera and Harry Overmeyer to think it had been a gang. That in itself was odd for burglaries. They were almost always done by one person. The items taken could have been carried by one person as well, so the reasons for so many was also a puzzle.

They also had no idea what had caused the square footprints, though it was obvious something had been glued to the soles of the shoes the burglars wore. They must have removed their altered shoes before stepping onto the patio and entering the house. It was the only way to explain the lack of mud.

When their shift ended, Pantera invited Harry to join him for a drink at The Watering Hole.

"Can I get a rain check? Ashley's sister is coming down from Washington, and we're going out to dinner." Ashley was Harry's wife, a pleasant woman who adored her husband. Pantera envied him.

"Sure. Say hello to Ashley for me."

"Will do."

Pantera drove home, showered and changed clothes before driving to The Watering Hole. It was the first time he'd been there since the robbery. As he entered, he expected Pete not to be there, but he was seated in his usual spot, his right arm in a sling.

"Pete!" Pantera nearly shouted. "Damn if you aren't here after all. I expected you to be laid up for a bit."

"Hey, Pantera!" Pete said in return. "Naw. I gotta be here in case some other bastard comes in to rob the place. Gotta take those bullets for Dean-o!" He laughed hard enough to make him cough. "Damn lungs," he said when he'd regained his breath.

Dean had been in his office and came out. Pantera said, "Dean, ya ol' bastard! What's cookin'?!"

Dean laughed. "My nuts on these hot summer days!" He stepped behind the bar. "Regular?"

"Yeah."

Dean prepared the Writers Tears and Coke and placed it in front of Pantera.

Pete said, "So I heard you caught the bastard that winged me, eh?"

"Yep. Dean here managed to shoot the kid in the leg. I found him at VCU's emergency room."

Dean said, "You mean he was dumb enough to go to the emergency room? He couldn't get the slug out himself?"

"First, according to the doctor there, it's not as easy as they make it out to be on TV. Second, he's a young kid who doesn't know shit about how things operate. He's not that bright in the first place to be making his living holding up bars and bodegas."

"He's the kid who held up the bodega?" Dean asked.

"Yep. Same one. The cashier there identified him from a photo lineup."

"Son-of-a-bitch," Pete said. "You'd think he'd not visit the same neighborhood where he robbed one place."

"As I said, not too bright," Pantera said.

Pantera stayed for over an hour, talking with his friends. He was about to leave when he heard a familiar voice shout, "Hey, Dean-o, you ol' bastard! What's cookin'?"

"My n—" Dean began, about to reply with his usual off-color retort before stopping himself. "Not much," he said instead.

Pantera recognized the voice and turned to see Harry standing there with Ashley and another woman, obviously Ashley's sister. The presence of the ladies explained Dean's altered response.

Harry walked over to Pantera. "I was hoping you'd

still be here. I told Ashley and Lisa about your invitation, and we decided we would all take you up on it." Turning to Ashley, he said, "Ashley, this is Dean, the proprietor, and Pete, his barfly." They said their hellos and Harry turned to indicate his sister-in-law, Lisa.

"And this is Ashley's sister, Lisa Dennis." Lisa greeted the men and Harry invited Pantera to join them in a booth.

Harry and Ashley sat on one side of the booth. Lisa scooted over as she sat to make room for Pantera.

Dean called out from behind the bar, "So what're y'all having?"

Harry said, "I'll have a Bud. My wife will have a sauvignon blanc." He looked at Lisa. "You?"

"Sauvignon blanc is fine for me."

"Make that two sauvignon blancs."

"Comin' right up!"

"So, Tony," Harry began. "Have you had dinner yet?"

It suddenly dawned on Pantera that he was being set up for a blind double date. He glanced at Lisa, who was smiling. The smile did not indicate whether she was hoping for a yes or a no, but the fact they had come here at all when Harry knew he'd be there said she was at least okay with the idea of having him as her dinner date.

"Not yet," Pantera said, looking back at Harry. "Why? Am I being invited to join you?"

"As a matter of fact, you are."

"Then I accept."

By the end of the evening, Pantera had found out that Lisa was two years divorced, had twin daughters Beth's age, and worked for the Library of Congress. He was surprised at how well they had hit it off. By the time he was dropped back at his car in the lot near The Watering Hole, they were so busy talking to each other

42

they were ignoring the conversation between Harry and Ashley in the front seats.

Pantera began to wonder if she would be around for more than just tonight. "So, when do you go back to Washington?"

"Wednesday. I just took a four-day weekend to come for a short visit to get away from Washington. The girls are with their father. School, you know."

"Yeah." He'd told her about Andrea and Beth, leaving out the more personal information about Andrea. "I know all about school. I'm looking forward to being with my daughters for a week at the beach this summer."

"Yes. My husband is taking the girls to London for two weeks."

"London? As in England?"

"Yes. He's from Scotland, actually. Grew up in Glasgow."

He chuckled. "Let me guess. You were mesmerized by his accent."

She laughed in return. "Well, yes. I have to admit it was one of the initial attractions. He sounds like Sean Connery."

"Well, then. I might want to meet him," Pantera joked.

She laughed. "He's taken, I'm afraid. He married the woman he left me for."

That she could laugh about such outcomes was refreshing to Pantera. He'd avoided talking about Nancy because his own feelings about her leaving were decidedly less accepting and he didn't want to sound bitter, though the bitterness had subsided significantly over time. Still, enough had lingered that he sometimes felt a twinge of jealous anger.

When he arrived home, he had a message from Andrea. Her girlfriend, Dani, would be able to come with them to the beach that summer if the schedule worked out. Andrea was anxious now to set dates so she could finalize their plans with Dani. Pantera looked at his calendar and did his best to determine when he could get away from work. Then he realized that was how he always approached his time with his daughters. Work first, then the girls.

He would put in for a vacation the next day. The hell with whatever cases he might be working at the time. Harry could pick up the slack. Once the dates were approved, he would let Andrea know.

He looked at the time and saw it was only a little after 9:30. He knew Andrea would still be up. He called her, and she picked up after the first ring.

"Hey, Daddy!"

"Hi. I got your message. I think it's great Dani will be able to come with us."

"When are we going?"

"I don't know yet, but I'm going to put in for the last week in June tomorrow. If that's not good, be sure to let me know. I can change the dates to make sure Dani can come."

"Really?! You'd do that?"

"Yes, really. The dates aren't important to me, and I know having your girlfriend with you is important to you, so I will do whatever we need to do so she can join you."

"Thank you, Daddy! You're great! I don't care what Beth says."

"What?"

She laughed. "It's just a joke, Dad. Believe me, Beth would never say anything against you. She'd defend you to the death. Take my word for it."

"You've heard her defend me?"

"Duh!"

"When?" He was curious. He'd broken her heart numerous times and his ego needed to hear this.

"Well…"

He heard the reluctance. "It's okay. If you think she wouldn't want me to know, you don't have to tell me."

"No, it's not that at all, it's just—"

"What?"

"It involves me. I was the one who sort of attacked you."

He paused and took a moment to realize this didn't surprise him. "Actually, I'm not as surprised as you think I would be."

"You think I hate you?"

"No, but of the two of you, you're definitely the one more likely to express your anger about my shortcomings, which I admit are anything but rare."

"I wouldn't go that far."

"Okay."

"It's just I said something one time about how you're not there for us." She stopped a second. "Not that that hasn't changed! You're doing a lot better at it!"

"I understand. So, you said that and Beth defended me?"

"Yeah. She got, like, really angry and said you were trying. That's actually when I stopped to realize you really were."

"Well, if it makes you feel any better, I know I've not always been there for you two. It's a major fault, and your sister's right. I am trying."

"I know." She paused. "I love you, Daddy."

"I love you, too."

After he hung up, he called Beth.

"Hey, Daddy!"

"I just wanted to call and tell you I love you. That's all, really."

45

He could hear the grin. "I love you, too!"

"Okay. Good night."

"Good night!"

He went to bed and slept as well as he had in months.

EIGHT

That night, Blanton drove back to Grant Davis's house. Earlier that day while Davis was working, he had entered the house to get a look around. Once inside, he had searched for an extra house key to make his entries easier. He'd found it in a bedside drawer beneath a stack of porn DVD's.

Checking to make sure it was the key to the house, he pocketed it, certain that Davis wouldn't look for it since he had the same key on a key ring. Still, he chose to make a copy and replace the key, following his edict that being too careful was impossible. It wouldn't do for Davis to discover the missing key by accident and replace the locks. Blanton would still be able to get in, but that was no reason to endanger his ease of access.

Blanton was surprised that Davis had no alarm system, but then the house was very modest, obviously devoid of any real valuables, so Davis had probably chosen to save the cost of installing and monitoring any kind of alarm. That would have been a wise move had it not been for the fact Blanton planned to murder him.

The only security was a motion sensitive light at the front door. Blanton had discovered this that afternoon when he'd visited. Approaching it would turn the light on. The back door had no such motion detector that he could tell, so he would use that entrance on his visits.

Now, it was 2:37 A.M. to be exact, and Blanton wanted to find out if Davis was a deep enough sleeper not to notice the tell-tale sounds of a quiet intruder. Not only that, but he also needed to return the key. But those were mostly excuses, and he knew it. He had entered the house because he could. The thrill of being able to do that at will was wonderful and bestowed its own power.

Blanton had come prepared in case he had to kill him that night. His unlicensed Beretta APX Carry, a small 9 mm, sat in its holster. Of course, he also wore his special shoes, the ones with a thin wood veneer glued securely to the soles. It prevented leaving identifiable footprints behind, no matter the type of soil he encountered—loamy, wet, or dry; hard or soft. Only squares were left behind. They wouldn't even be able to identify his shoe size from those prints. Again, too careful was impossible.

He'd read newspaper articles about the break-ins, and information about the strange footprints had not been released to the public. Blanton suspected that was something held back to prevent false confessions.

He also wore surgical gloves to prevent leaving fingerprints and a swimmer's cap to prevent leaving any hair follicles behind. He'd thought of everything. There were only two secrets to getting away with murder: Leave neither clues nor witnesses. He even used the surgical gloves when handling the bullets.

Arriving at Davis's house, he parked down the street and walked to the back of the house. Taking out the key he'd had made at a local hardware store, he opened the back door, removed his shoes, and stepped inside.

The house was cool. He could feel a small draft created by the heat pump and stood there enjoying the feel of the air as it slid down the back of his neck.

Then stepping into the kitchen, he made small sounds so he could check later to see if the bugs picked them up. He'd invested in electronics that were a step above his usual choices. For this job, he wanted all the cards stacked in his favor. Committing a burglary was one thing. If they managed to find him for those, he would get some time in prison, but probably not that much since his only crime for which he'd been caught had been the one he was framed for back in high school. That wouldn't count for much now.

But murder was a different situation. It would be obvious the murder was premeditated, especially once they figured out his history with the victim. Life in prison without parole was a definite possibility if they caught him. He considered it a certainty.

Going into the living room, he found the remains of Davis's dinner on a TV tray. He gave the leftovers a look of disgust and wondered how anyone could leave dirty plates and what was essentially garbage out like this. He shuddered and moved on.

Coming to the bedroom where he knew Davis slept, he eased the door open. Soundless. It was the one thing he'd done that might have garnered some attention that afternoon. He didn't want the door to make any noise at all when he opened it, and it had a very slight, almost inaudible, creak when he'd opened it that afternoon. He had used some WD40 that he'd found in Davis's garage, giving the hinge a short blast of the lubricant and catching any drips with a paper towel that he took with him when he left.

He doubted Davis would notice the loss of a creaky door, but if he did, he would probably chalk it up to something in the hinge shifting. If he wondered if someone had been inside his house and had lubricated the hinge, he would look around and notice nothing was amiss otherwise and decide it was nothing. Davis had left nearly a hundred dollars on his dresser, and Blanton had left it untouched. After all, if someone had broken in, would they really oil the door hinge and leave cash

49

that sat in plain view? What kind of lunatic would do such a thing? Blanton smiled. His kind of lunatic, he thought. One with a bigger plan than robbery.

As his eyes adjusted to the darker room, Blanton saw Davis lying naked on top of the covers. He stepped over to the dresser with the cash and found it still undisturbed.

Stepping to the bed, he realized he could kill him now, but he wasn't prepared to do that unless Davis woke. He wanted everything to go the way he'd been planning for a decade. He had the entire script of what he wanted to say and every meticulous detail of the deadly confrontation in his head.

He wanted it to be evening, around nine o'clock. He would enter the house quietly and watch Davis going about his routines with no inkling that his death was minutes away. Blanton wanted time to talk to Davis, to let him know who was killing him and why, should he have forgotten Blanton over the course of ten years. Besides, waking Davis in the middle of the night might draw a more violent response from him, one that was more instinct than plan. Blanton didn't want that. He simply wanted to step into the living room with his gun drawn and watch the horror dawn on Davis.

For these reasons, killing him now would only happen if he woke and found Blanton there.

He eased the drawer open where the key had been kept. Gently lifting the DVD stack, he placed the key beneath them and silently closed the drawer. Davis remained asleep.

Soon, he thought as he looked down at Mr. Grant Davis—former math teacher, current assistant principal, and full-time asshole.

Very soon.

NINE

On Thursday of that week, Grant Davis climbed from his bed, prepared for work, ate breakfast, and left, unaware he had been visited in the night. He was unaware of most things these days. Mostly, he was aware of the number of years he had until he could retire from education and collect his pension and social security. Those had been about all his ex-wife had been unable to lay her hands on in the divorce five years before.

His son, Frank, had more or less taken his mother's side in everything. Frank had joined the army and was stationed at Ft. Bragg near Fayetteville, North Carolina. Grant had communicated off and on with him over the years, but their relationship was mostly dead. His daughter, Marie, hadn't spoken to him since the divorce, having barely spoken to him for years before that. Now, he existed each day with the single thought of when he could retire from this agonizing job.

He kept his most valuable possessions in a safe deposit box in one of the older banks in town. His most valuable possessions consisted of a coin collection worth maybe a few thousand dollars, his will, and a few items of minor value left to him by his own parents.

He'd become an administrator because it paid more, which would lead to a larger pension. He needed to finish this year and work one more to be able to pay his bills and enjoy himself a little.

His career as a teacher and school administrator had led him to a life of bitterness. He'd initially wanted to make a difference in the lives of his students, but when he realized they didn't want him to do anything except give them a passing grade they rarely earned, he grew to hate each day, as well as the students. When he taught, he saw his students as ingrates, and nothing had changed with the new position.

Arriving for another day of misery, he went to his office to sit at his desk and do as little as possible until lunch, when he had cafeteria duty. Then he would do as little as possible until the end of the day. He would have students come to him for disciplinary reasons, and he would dole out the most punishment he could, but beyond that, his day was spent waiting to go home, where the waiting to retire would continue. The next day, of course, would be identical to all the others.

Around ten o'clock, he was sent a student who had mouthed off to his English teacher. Blaine Carmody slouched in the chair across from Grant, looking as bored as Grant himself felt.

"You bored?" Grant asked him.

"Huh?"

"I said, are you bored? Because you sure look like you want to shoot yourself you're so bored."

"This whole school is boring."

"Well, that's the way it is. Life is boring. Get used to it."

"You givin' me ISS, or what?" Blaine asked, referring to in-school suspension.

"I think this time I'm gonna grant your wish. I'm sending you to ISS for a week."

"For talkin' back to Ms. Ellis?" Blaine was actually upset that the punishment was for an entire week, as if his life would improve if given only two days. That amount of time in ISS was the typical consequence for disrespect, even for a multiple-offender like Blaine.

"It's the third time this quarter, Blaine."

"I haven't said nothin' to Ms. Ellis before. That was for expressing myself to Mr. Nelson and Ms. Leonard."

"Doesn't matter. It's like committing a crime. When you've been caught breaking the law several times, your time in jail goes up."

"That's not fair, man!"

"I don't give a shit! And I'm not your man!" Grant said, not caring if he got called on the carpet for using profanity with a student. He always thought that was ridiculous, given how much they cussed. He'd heard Blaine cuss at his own mother before. She hadn't done anything as a consequence when he called her a bitch, which explained a lot.

Grant's profanity obviously surprised Blaine. "You use that language with all the kids?"

Grant stared at him. "What's it to you?"

"Nothin'. It's just if I said that to you, I'd get days added to my ISS."

"Well, I'm an adult, and you're not."

"Don't matter. You shouldn't talk like that to students. It makes you look—I don't know—weak or somethin'. Ms. Ellis says profanity's a product of a bad vocabulary."

"I'm glad you learned something in her class, though I'd say you demonstrate your own bad vocabulary nearly every minute of the day."

He had Blaine sign the disciplinary report before Grant wrote "Five days ISS" in the area marked for the consequence.

Handing Blaine his copy, Grant said, "Nice doing business with you. Come back soon."

Blaine snatched the paper from Grant's hand and stormed out of the office. Grant went back to his Sudoku puzzle.

The day finally ended and Grant drove home. He prepared his dinner, a frozen pizza, and sat in his living room, eating what tasted like spiced cardboard and watching Fox News.

While Grant Davis settled himself in for the night, Blanton edged his way around Davis's house and quietly let himself in through the back door, removing the wood-soled shoes to prevent any sounds on the cheap linoleum. The lights in the kitchen were off, which Blanton considered a bonus.

Crossing to the door of the living room, he peered in. Sitting in front of the TV, Grant Davis was immersed in the ranting taking place on the screen as two men argued back and forth. Blanton wondered if Davis would see him if he stepped out into the living room, his Beretta in one hand and a bouquet of flowers in the other.

It was time, Blanton thought. The moment he'd waited for, planned with utter precision, even setting up what he considered to be the world's best alibi, had finally arrived.

He stepped into the living room, and for a moment, Blanton was right. Grant Davis continued staring at the TV, mesmerized by the silly argument.

"Grant," Blanton said, refusing to refer to him as Mister Davis.

Grant turned to see a man standing in the door to his kitchen. He didn't notice the gun at first. He was mostly confused because the man had spoken his name, and he wondered where they had met. He wore a swimmer's cap over his head, but the man's facial features were familiar.

"Beware the fury of a patient man," the man said.

With that statement, Grant noticed the gun pointed at him and looked back at the man's face, studying it and searching his mind for recognition. Then, combined with the familiar sound of the man's voice and their history, it hit him.

"Blanton," he said.

"Yes. It's good to know you've not forgotten me."

"Well, I had, but I hadn't. To be honest, I thought I would see you sooner. I always wondered if you would come take revenge on me, despite the fact I never set you up."

"Of course, you did."

"On my salary?"

"For all I know, you found it in another locker or something."

"Nope."

"You can stop with the denials. They won't do you any good now. I've planned my revenge for ten years. I doubt God himself could stop me."

"It's not nice to blaspheme."

Blanton ignored the comment. "You're awfully calm considering you only have a few more minutes to live."

Grant looked around. "This is all I have to live for," he said, indicating the room as if it held his entire life. "Not much, is it?"

"No."

"Do you have anything worth living for, Blanton?"

"Yes."

"And what's that?"

"Killing you."

Grant smiled, but it was a sad smile at best. "At least, I'm serving some good."

Blanton nodded. "I've planned this so well, nobody will ever arrest me for murdering you."

"There's no such thing as the perfect crime."

"There is now. I have the perfect setup."

"What is it?"

When Blanton had explained how he was going to get away with murder, Grant said, "I'm impressed. Maybe I was wrong. Maybe you will get away with it."

"Sometimes, you called me 'Mr. Genius' in class, but it was always sarcastic. Now, I'm showing you that oddly, you were right all along."

"Well, I must admit your plan is one I'd not thought of before. I don't know that anyone has."

"That's why it's so good." Blanton pointed the muzzle of the 9 mm at Davis's head. "Have you ever wondered what your last word would be?"

"Can't say that I have."

"Well, how lucky for you that you get to choose it. So, how about it? What do you have to say?"

"Why give you the satisfaction of—" The muffled shot made a thudding sound as the bullet traveled through the silencer and stopped Grant Davis from finishing his sentence. The bullet had entered directly over the bridge of the nose and exited the back of Davis's skull, splattering blood and brain tissue on the chair, floor, and wall behind him.

Blanton grinned.

"Sorry to stop you mid-sentence, but I'd heard enough. Besides, *satisfaction* is what I feel now, so it's the perfect last word from you."

Holstering the gun, Blanton went through the house, gathering the eavesdropping equipment he'd placed a few days before. He'd wanted to monitor the man's habits and visitors. His habits were identical every night, and he never had visitors. It was a perfect situation for Blanton. If not for Davis's job, he might not be discovered for weeks, Blanton thought.

After gathering the bugs, Blanton stepped over to the body, leaned down, and rummaged for Davis's wallet. Taking the money more to throw off the investigation than anything else, he counted the seventeen dollars before slipping a business card into the wallet, leaving it sticking out a bit so the name on the card would be the first thing anyone saw as they looked at the wallet on the floor.

After completing this essential task, he left through the back door, putting his special shoes back on to avoid footprints in the dirt that could identify his brand of shoes. He removed the swimmer's cap and, once he was standing on the deserted street, he exchanged his wood-bottomed shoes for a pair of slip-on sneakers. After placing these items in a backpack he wore, he hurried the several blocks to his car. It was the most vulnerable he had been in the commission of any of the crimes. Still, he'd noticed that Davis's neighbors almost never came out at night. He'd sat and watched for hours at least a half dozen times, so he felt relatively safe.

Besides, he wouldn't hesitate to shoot anyone who came out while he made his way to the car and freedom.

As he climbed in, Blanton felt his adrenalin flowing with the thrill the murder had given him. Maybe he wouldn't stop here. Maybe he would continue with a killing spree. Take out others just for fun.

After all, even Davis had admitted his plan was a good one—a great one even. He'd agreed that Blanton would likely get away with the murder. It wasn't something Blanton would have expected from someone who was about to be murdered. He'd expected fear, pleading, and assurances that he would never get away with it. Davis should have attempted to instill a fear in him that his plan was useless in the hopes of making him change his mind.

But he had done none of that. The man's acceptance of his fate had surprised Blanton, even taken him aback a bit. But now the deed was done. He could go home and sleep in the comfort of being assured he'd left no clues behind and his alibi was fail-safe.

TEN

When Grant Davis didn't show up for work the next morning, Harriet Ward, the school's lead secretary, stepped to the principal's office. She found Mr. Holyfield bent over some papers on his desk.

"Mr. Holyfield? I thought I would let you know that Mr. Davis hasn't come in. He's not called, and he doesn't answer his phone. That's totally unlike him."

"Maybe he decided to quit without giving notice," Mr. Holyfield said. "He's threatened it for years."

"Maybe, but you and I both know he's not serious. Do you think we should call the police to go check on him?"

Mr. Holyfield sat back and stretched. "He usually calls in if he's not going to be here, right?"

"Yes, sir."

"He's over a half-hour late. I guess you should call the police to check. Then find someone to fill in for him on his duties just in case he isn't coming in."

"Yes, sir," she said and went to place the call.

Officer Tyler Hendricks pulled into the driveway of the home of Grant Davis. He noticed the car in the driveway, inspected it briefly, and went to ring the doorbell.

When there was no answer, he stepped to the large window behind some bushes that looked into the house's living room. Seeing the dead body slumped in the chair and the splattered blood, he tried the doorknob and found it unlocked. He drew his weapon and entered, calling out that he was with the police.

Making his way to the living room, he could see dried blood on some surfaces. An unfinished dinner sat on a tray table near the body.

Looking around, he saw no weapon and concluded it had been a murder and not suicide.

Looking at the floor, he noticed a wallet, its contents appearing disturbed. Without touching the wallet, he bent over, noticing a business card sticking out of it to the point he could read the name.

DETECTIVE TONY PANTERA
RICHMOND POLICE DEPARTMENT

He called in the murder, including what he'd found in the deceased's wallet that had been lying on the floor. Then he stepped outside and waited for the detectives to show up.

By the time Pantera arrived at the scene, he had already been told the victim's name and occupation— Grant Davis, an administrator at Dunleavy High School—and that he had one of Pantera's business cards. Pantera would give them to people he interviewed regarding a crime in case they remembered something and needed to get in touch, but almost nobody else. He wondered what case the victim had been interviewed for as he drove.

Flashing his badge at the officer guarding the door, he entered and joined the forensics team in the living room. The team had just begun the meticulous process of gathering materials that could be evidence. The flash of a camera lit the room in quick bursts as photos were taken of the body and its surroundings.

Pantera recognized Paul Steinberg, one of the newer

techs and stepped over to him. Paul was busy dusting the wallet for prints.

"Anything interesting?" Pantera asked, bending over to watch Paul work.

Paul gestured at the corpse with a tilt of his head. "Other than a dead body? Nothing yet." Then he said, "Oh, wait. We found those weird square footprints again approaching the back door."

Pantera stepped out through the back door and saw the footprints leading up to where he stood. Three-dimensional photos were being taken of the prints that matched those from the recent string of burglaries.

Returning to Paul, Pantera could see his business card sticking out of the wallet. It appeared to be arranged so that his card would be noticed.

Paul asked, "You recognize him?"

Pantera stared at the man's face.

"Nope."

"Well, he's met you before, apparently."

"That could have been years ago."

"So, what do we have here?" asked a voice from behind. Pantera turned and found Harry Overmeyer bending over behind him, staring at the wallet as well. "You rubbing out all the people you've interviewed over the years now, Tony?"

"Yeah," Pantera said. "It's something I came up with while working nights."

"Well, if you didn't do it, whoever did either has a lot of luck or hellacious aim. Hit him right in the center of the forehead."

Pantera glanced at Davis's face and the entry wound. The lack of gunpowder burns or visible residue suggested the shot had been fired from at least several feet away. The crime scene techs would swab for residue, which could result if fired from less than five feet. "Yeah, I guess." His attention went back to the wallet, wondering where Mr. Davis had gotten the card and why it was sticking out of the wallet's card holders.

"We may get lucky," Pantera said. "That card's in the card holder section. Our perp may have taken a credit card and will use it to buy something from Amazon to be delivered."

When Paul had gathered what prints were on the wallet, Pantera asked, "You done with it?"

Paul looked over his shoulder at him. "Yeah."

"And you got pictures of it?"

Paul looked at the woman who was taking pictures of the crime scene. "You get this already, Diane?" he asked, indicating the wallet.

"Yeah."

"It's all yours, Detective," Paul said and stood to continue his work, his knees popping.

Pantera reached down and picked up the wallet, handling it gingerly, despite having donned the thin, latex gloves used when they entered a crime scene. He tried to push the card back into the slim pocket, but it resisted. However, when he tugged on it to remove it, it slid easily from its pocket, suggesting it had been replaced after being removed. Pantera figured the killer had dug around for credit cards, but he wondered why he—or she, he thought—had tried to put his card back in. What was the reason for that? Wouldn't the person just pull all the cards out, take the credit cards, and toss the others on the floor? Blood was everywhere, so why try to be tidy now?

Another odd thing was that his card had no prints on it. Paul had dusted the part of the card that was sticking out of the wallet, at least two-thirds of it, but the dusting had come away clean—no prints or anything else, not even his own. That bothered him and would until he had an explanation. Other than the fingerprint dust, the card was pristine, as if never really handled before.

Of course, that was nearly impossible. If he'd given the card to Mr. Davis, his own prints, along with Grant Davis's, would be on the card. If somehow Grant Davis had managed to get one of his cards from someone else for some weird reason, at least his prints would be on it, not to mention the prints of the person who'd given him the card.

Pantera turned to Harry, who was inspecting the exit wound on the back of Mr. Davis's head.

"Hey, Harry?"

"Yeah?" Harry answered without looking at him.

"This is the craziest thing I've ever seen."

Harry looked at Pantera and noticed he was holding the business card from the victim's wallet.

"What? Your business card? What's the matter? It doesn't have 'World's Greatest Detective' on it?"

As explanation, Pantera held the card up so Harry could see the unblemished print powder. He waited for Harry to figure it out.

Harry looked for a second, trying to figure out what was so odd. Then Pantera could see the reality hit him.

"What the—? No prints? How?"

"No idea. I was hoping the other world's greatest detective would be able to figure it out."

"I mean, even if they'd been wiped, there would be something—a smudge, a blemish. This looks like it's never been touched by human hands."

"Bingo," Pantera said. Then turning to Diane, he said, "Could you get a picture of this card?"

"Sure." She stepped over and snapped a photo of the card as Pantera held it out. Then he flipped the card over, and Diane took another picture."

"No prints?" she asked. "Isn't that kinda weird for a business card?"

"Yeah," Pantera said. "Very."

Diane stepped away and continued photographing the scene.

Pantera gave the wallet and its contents to a tech to be bagged. He stood there, trying to focus his attention on the rest of the investigation. He'd been called to the scene for two reasons. One, he was on duty at the precinct nearest the scene, and two, his card had been found in the victim's wallet. He had asked if Harry could be his backup because of the card. He didn't want anyone suggesting later that he had something to do with this case and had done something to the card. That was highly unlikely, even if he did know the victim from a prior case—impossible, really. But a card with no fingerprints in a man's wallet was just as impossible, yet there it was. If he'd not seen it himself, he wouldn't have believed it.

The explanation of the man having one of his cards was as simple as figuring out two-plus-two.

The explanation of a business card without prints was going to bug Pantera for days—weeks maybe.

Pantera called Dunleavy High School. Speaking with Mr. Holyfield, the school's principal, he informed him what they'd found and let him know he'd be stopping by later that day or tomorrow. Holyfield sounded sad that Davis was dead, but not upset, making Pantera wonder.

After getting the name and number for Davis's ex-wife, who was listed as next-of-kin at the school, Pantera called her. The call went to voicemail, and he wondered if she screened her calls. He left a message asking her to call him back as soon as possible.

When he and Harry had wrapped up the crime

scene investigation, they returned to the precinct. Pantera immediately logged into his computer. He searched the name Grant Davis to see what case he'd been involved in. When NO MATCH FOUND showed up on his screen, he sat back, staring at the words and feeling they were as impossible as the pristine business card.

"Hey, Harry," he said.

"Yeah?" Harry looked up from his work.

"Come here."

Harry walked over to Pantera's desk, and Pantera pointed at the screen.

"So? I get that all the time."

"I did a search of my case files to find out what case Davis had been interviewed about. That's what I got."

Harry looked back at the screen.

"And you're wondering how he got your card."

"Wow, you are a good detective," Pantera said.

"Maybe someone else gave it to him. Maybe he was asking about something he needed a detective for."

"Yeah, it was given to him by someone who didn't have fingerprints. What are we talking about? A space alien? This makes that card even weirder. How in the hell did it get in the guy's wallet?"

"Maybe everyone involved was wearing gloves."

"One problem with that."

"What?" Harry asked.

"I carry my cards in my wallet. I can't get one out without taking off my gloves. No gripping factor."

"Huh?"

"You know, nothing to create enough traction for me to pull the card out. It's like trying to pull a tooth with a child's plastic toy. No grip sufficient to do the extraction."

"Then maybe someone else had your card. Maybe they had gloves on but had it in their pocket instead of their wallet," Harry said.

"That's a lot of 'maybes' there, buddy. It's possible, but how did that person get the card? It's definitely one of mine," he said, reaching into his drawer and pulling one out to show Harry.

Harry suddenly looked as if he'd been slapped.

"What?" Pantera asked.

"That card."

"What about it?"

Harry looked at Pantera as if the mystery was solved. "Do you think it has any fingerprints on it?"

Pantera looked from Harry to the card and back. "I don't know. I doubt it, except for mine, of course, from where I grabbed it."

"What if someone came in and took one of your cards, careful not to touch anything but the edges. Maybe someone has it in for you and wanted to get you involved in this murder somehow."

"Again, that's a lot of maybes."

"Yeah, but it would explain it." Harry looked at Pantera's desk. "Hell, they wouldn't even have to go into your drawer." He reached down and plucked one of Pantera's business cards from the middle of a stack, where they leaned against the back of a desktop card holder. His fingers held the card by the edges.

Harry stared at Pantera. "I bet this one doesn't have a print on it."

"But why take one in the first place? Just to put it in Grant Davis's wallet to be found?"

"Maybe."

"There you go again with the maybes."

"Yeah, but somewhere along the line, one of those maybes will be a certainty instead. Isn't that how we solve crimes? Asking what might have happened and going from there?"

"Yes, but I try to stick to what really could have happened. Taking one of my cards to put in a victim's wallet sounds—I don't know—a little farfetched."

"It's the easiest way to explain how a business card with no fingerprints got in the guy's wallet."

"You're right there, I guess."

"Of course I am. As you said yourself, I'm one of the world's greatest detectives."

"Maybe," Pantera said. "And if you take that and a dollar, you can buy a buck's worth of gas."

Harry handed the card to Pantera. "Shall we dust one of your untouched cards for prints?"

"Maybe," Pantera answered, "but I don't think we have to."

"And you say I use 'maybe' too much."

Pantera thought for a moment. "Harry, who would have access to my desk when I'm not here?"

"Any of the people who work in here for starters. Or there are a lot of others who have access. Cleaning crew, for instance. Really, anyone who has walked through the door. How many people have you interviewed that you left alone?"

"I don't recall."

"Well," Harry said, "it wasn't me. That's all I can be sure of. Beyond that? Coulda been anyone."

Pantera nodded and placed the cards in the holder on his desk before putting the holder in the top drawer. Taking out his keys, he locked that drawer and checked to make sure the other drawers were locked with it. He'd not been this careful before, but he'd have to start being more careful from now on. The idea someone had taken one of his cards to plant it on a murder victim made him feel violated in some way.

On the one hand, he knew he shouldn't get this worked up about it. It was only a card, not the murder weapon. Still, it nagged at him that someone had done this, making sure prints were not left on the card, which suggested whoever had taken it knew it was to leave it at a crime scene. Why the perp had done that, he had no idea, and he suspected he never would know unless he found the killer and got him to talk.

"I think I'll go to the school and interview his co-workers. Maybe we can find out if he had any enemies or had been threatened," Pantera said.

"Knock yourself out. I'm going to see if there's an angle we haven't considered on the burglaries."

Pantera left the station and headed to Dunleavy. As he drove, he recalled the last time a case involved going to a school to interview the people involved. He'd been investigating the kidnapping of a young girl who was a student at the private school. He thought of that case every time he drove past Stuart Secondary where that had happened, thankful the madman had been stopped.

Arriving at Dunleavy High, he parked in the visitor's parking area and buzzed the intercom on the door to be allowed in.

As he waited for the buzz to be answered, he felt a heaviness that such security measures now needed to be included at every school. He was all for responsible people being allowed to own guns for protection and hunting, though he wasn't sure why people needed an assault rifle to hunt deer or even bear. The others, however—the ones likely to use a gun to kill another person—just made his job harder.

Once he was buzzed in, Ms. Ward, the secretary, called Mr. Holyfield, and told him Pantera needed to speak with him. Moments later, Mr. Holyfield strode into the office.

He was tall, well over six feet with a basketball player's build. His bald head revealed a scar along the top of his scalp. He extended his hand as he approached.

"How can I help you, Detective?" he asked.

Shaking Holyfield's hand, he said, "I need to find out what I can about Grant Davis."

"Sure. Come back to my office."

After he was seated in Holyfield's office, Pantera said, "What can you tell me about him?"

"To be honest, I don't know much. He was the most private person I've ever known. His ex-wife told me he wanted to be cremated. I didn't even know that."

"You spoke to his ex-wife?"

"Yes, shortly before you arrived. I thought she'd already heard from you, but apparently, you'd not been able to get in contact yet."

"I left her a message to call. I've not heard back."

"I'm sure she will call eventually. After my call, she knows what your call is about, making any urgency moot."

"Yes, but I still need to talk to her. Should you hear back from her, ask her to please return my call." He paused before asking, "Tell me, how did she react to the news her husband had been murdered?"

Holyfield thought for a moment. "As you'd probably expect an ex-wife to react. She was sad, but not heartbroken. I have the feeling the divorce was not a smooth one."

"Did she say anything that led you to that conclusion?"

"No, not exactly. It was more her attitude about his death, as if she really didn't care beyond hearing that someone she once knew but had lost touch with had died. It was as if I'd told her someone she'd known in high school had died. Sort of an 'oh, dear, that's terrible' kind of response."

Pantera nodded and jotted down a few notes.

"You don't think she had something to do with this, do you?" Holyfield asked.

"No, no. I just want to find out why they were so— distant from each other emotionally. Did they have any children together?"

"Yes, a son and a daughter. I only know that because she mentioned she would get in touch with them when I called, as if to let me know I needn't bother."

"Did she say anything else?"

"Actually, we spoke for quite a while. She asked me if I would say a few words at his memorial service, which won't be until next month. I have no idea what I'm going to say. I barely knew him."

"Do you know why the memorial won't be until next month?"

"She told me their son is in the military," Holyfield said as if that explained it.

"Don't they allow bereavement leave when a soldier's parent dies?"

"Yes, I'm sure they do, but she said they would hold off on the ceremony because he was out of the country and wouldn't want to return, as she put it, 'just for his father's funeral.' Frankly, Detective, I found that odd."

Pantera squinted. "So do I." He wondered what kind of relationship Davis had with his son. It didn't sound like much of one.

"Did he ever talk about his family?"

"Never."

"Was Mr. Davis friends with anyone here?"

"I don't think so. Doubt it, in fact. People would sometimes complain to me how he never said a word to anyone except what had to be said. It was as if he hated everyone here. I can't state that as a fact, but it certainly seemed that way." He thought for a moment. "Well, maybe hate is too strong a word. Indifference may be more accurate. Apathy, even."

Pantera sighed and repeated something one of his high school teachers had once said, "Hate isn't the opposite of love. Apathy is."

"What?"

"Nothing. Just something someone told me once."

Pantera returned to the subject. "So there's nobody here who might be able to tell me something about him? Who his enemies were? That sort of thing?"

"I'd say his enemies were the students."

"The students?"

"Yes. He hated dealing with them. The feelings were mutual."

"But wasn't that his job?"

"Yes, but he definitely hated it."

"Couldn't you fire him for that kind of approach to the job?"

"Detective, unless he hit a kid or molested one, I can't do much. He's free to feel how he wants about them. Do I wish he'd worked somewhere else? Sure. But that's not my call."

"Did he teach here before becoming an administrator?"

"No, not here. He worked somewhere in northern Virginia," he said. "I can find that out for you from his personnel folder."

"If you don't mind."

"Is there anything else I can help with?"

"Were there any students who seemed to hate him more than others?"

"Not that I know of. It was more of a general feeling about him. Similar to how the faculty and staff felt about him. He was just a guy who did his job because he had to. Or at least that's how it seemed."

"What about meetings with the assistant principals. Didn't he ever interact in a way that might tell you more about him?"

"He rarely spoke in those meetings. One administrator told me it was like having a ghost sit in on our meetings."

"What about recent encounters with students? Did he have to deal with any particular student just before his death?"

"Several, I'm sure. I can get a list of them for you."

"If you would."

"Would you need to speak to them?"

"Yes, if that's possible."

"I can arrange that, but the parents will have to be notified." Mr. Holyfield called Ms. Ward and said, "Could you find out which students Mr. Davis disciplined in the days prior to his death and call them to the office one at a time for Detective Pantera?" Listening for a moment, he said, "Thank you" and hung up.

Turning back to Pantera, he said, "Ms. Ward will let each student call a parent before you interview them. I'd suggest you speak to each parent to explain. When you're done with one, let Ms. Ward know. She'll call another student to the office."

Pantera asked, "How many students do you think there will be?"

"Maybe a half dozen. Maybe more. Can't say."

Pantera checked his watch. "So can you think of any faculty or staff that might be able to tell me something about Mr. Davis?"

Mr. Holyfield shook his head slowly as he thought. "I'm sorry. I really doubt it. You can interview some of the office staff, but I'm not sure what they could tell you that I haven't. He pretty well kept to himself."

"That would be good if you'll let them know. I can

be here all day if needed, but I'd like to finish this up today if possible."

Holyfield led Pantera to Mr. Davis's office. By the end of the day, Pantera had interviewed all the office staff and the students who had received discipline from Davis. None of the interviews had done more than make Pantera realize that while the man was not liked much, he was mostly a non-entity at the school. He could understand the administrator's comparison to a ghost. Nobody knew much about him. Ms. Ward had shared the most, and that had been little more than what Mr. Holyfield had said. The students obviously didn't like him, but they considered him just another administrator who seemed hell-bent on making their lives miserable. Pantera had learned nothing from anyone that would suggest a reason for his murder. None of the students struck him as hating Davis so much that killing him crossed their minds. Pantera was at least thankful that none of the parents objected to their son or daughter being interviewed to find out anything about Mr. Davis.

He knew this could just be a random killing, but he doubted that seriously. The burglaries seemed to be setting up this murder in some way. The information about the square footprint patterns had never been released to the press. The likelihood of someone using the same M.O. was similar to the odds of winning the lottery.

People who rarely interacted with others were never victims of a planned killing unless something from their pasts had caused someone to murder them. It was possible that this was a burglary gone wrong, but he also doubted that. Davis had been awake and watching TV when he was killed. The officer who'd found the body had said the TV was blaring, as if Davis might be a little deaf. The perp had never entered the burgled homes while the residents were awake and certainly not while they were watching TV. In those cases, confrontation had been avoided. Now, however, it had been part of the plan, which was why the burglaries seemed like preliminary jobs, as if the perp had been rehearsing for the real thing.

Pantera had just enough time to head to the precinct and complete the paperwork on the interviews. Harry was out on another investigation when he arrived, but he showed up before Pantera went home.

"So, Tony, how did the school interviews go?"

"Fruitless. Waste of time, in fact."

"In the famous words of Detective Tony Pantera, there are no bad interviews because even those that discover nothing eliminate something."

"True, I guess. It wasn't any of his co-workers. None of them knew him well enough to want him dead."

"How long has he worked at Dunleavy?"

"Five years."

"And no one knew him? That's odd. Even the most introverted people will make at least one friend at work."

"Not this guy."

"So what's next on the agenda?"

"Talk to the ex-wife and their kids. The son is in the army and held up the memorial because it wasn't a good time for him. There's also a daughter. I'll get their contact info from their mother when she finally returns my call. Then I'll contact his old school in Alexandria. Find out from them whatever I can, though I'm starting to think it won't be much."

"Wow. Sad, isn't it? This guy doesn't have even a slightly decent relationship with anyone. Talk about your loners. The son might be the only one at the memorial."

"If that," Pantera said. "Who knows? Maybe the killer will be there, too."

"Yeah," Harry said, "and maybe someone's going to walk through the door tomorrow and confess."

Pantera chuckled. "Hey, that maybe's a certainty. Crazy Carl will read about this one and won't be able to help himself."

"I meant someone legit."

"I know what you meant," Pantera said. He shook his head at the lunacy of it all. A poor wretch like Grant Davis is murdered for whatever reason in his own home, and a dearth of evidence might mean whoever did it will get away with it, possibly because of Davis's own self-exile from society.

Harry stood up, rinsed his coffee cup, and said, "Well, I'll see you tomorrow. Just a hint, though. It might help to know why your pristine business card was sticking out of Davis's wallet."

"Yeah, that's another one that may remain a mystery forever."

"Later," Harry said as he left the squad room.

"Yeah, later."

When Harry left, Pantera sat staring at the spot where the business cards had once sat for the taking. Whoever had done this had likely sat in the chair opposite his and pilfered a card—perhaps more than one—without being seen. It bothered him that a killer had sat across from him and he'd not known it.

He stopped by The Watering Hole on his way home. It wasn't on his usual route home, but he needed a drink and the improved mood Dean and Pete always supplied.

After two drinks—his personal limit when he was driving without having eaten—he said his goodbyes and left. He'd felt better in the company of the two friends, but the sour mood returned on the drive home.

ELEVEN

The next day, Pantera received a preliminary report on the evidence collected at the scene of Grant Davis's murder. He had not been able to proceed on anything because they basically had nothing until hearing from forensics. When Harry came in, Pantera shared the news from the report with him.

"I have good news and I have bad news," Pantera began.

"Give me the good news first."

"I stopped by The Watering Hole last night and Dean and Pete said to tell you hello."

"I take it the bad news is not as mundane."

"Correct assumption." He lifted the evidence report to read from it. "The evidence report on the Davis murder says, 'No discernible evidence was found at the scene. The only prints found at the scene were from the victim. Footprints found approaching the residence's back door and patio matched the square patterns found at recent burglaries. What hair fibers that were found matched the victim's hair. No shell casings were found. Products from which DNA could be extracted were absent from the scene. There were no signs of forced entry. The alarm system had been disabled.' Apparently, Davis never even had someone come visit him, not even family."

"The footprints are the same as the square ones we found at the burglaries?" Harry asked.

"Yep. And there's only one track leading to and from the house. If we could find someone with square-soled shoes, we'd have our killer."

Harry sat in Pantera's visitors' chair. "We're dealing with one smart criminal here, Tony."

"Tell me about it."

"So, this burglar or burglars break into homes and steal shit. They don't harm anyone, just go about their business and get out with the loot, some of which is mostly not worth the trouble. Then one day, one of the burglars shows up at Davis's house and kills him, apparently for no reason."

"That's how it looks, but I'm betting we're missing something."

"Yeah, a motive."

"And I don't think it's more than one burglar anymore. I'm pretty sure it's only one person, the same one who killed Grant Davis."

"You might be right. Probably are. Someone this smart wouldn't want to trust others with the knowledge. But that brings up another question. Why so many tracks back and forth between the street and the back of the burgled houses? The loot could have been easily carried out in a sack or something."

"Good question." Pantera thought of the pristine card. "Maybe this guy is doing stuff to throw us off. Purposely leaving false clues."

"Other than the footprints, what else has he left?"

"That card. It was sticking out of Davis's wallet in such a way that it looked like he wanted it to be found."

"Why?"

"That's another good question, and I don't have an answer." He thought for a second and added, "Yet."

Harry's phone dinged, signaling a text. Looking at the screen, he raised his eyebrows.

"What is it?" Pantera asked.

"Looks like you have an admirer."

"Oh?" He reached for Harry's phone. "Let me see."

"You don't need to see. I'll tell you. My sister-in-law, Lisa, wants me to ask you if she can have your number. She says you didn't ask for hers, so she's taking the initiative."

"Really?"

"Yeah. Imagine that. Someone out there wants to get to know you better. Will miracles never cease?"

Pantera pondered the road that would be traveled if he said she could have his number and decided he might enjoy that ride. "Give it to her. Who knows? She might just be wanting to ask for my meatloaf recipe."

Harry's fingers whizzed along his phone's keyboard. Seconds later, Pantera received a text.

"That was fast," Pantera said.

"She's a woman who knows what she wants and goes for it. You better be careful, Tony."

Pantera read the screen.

"What does she say?" Harry asked.

"What do you think? She wants my meatloaf recipe," Pantera said.

"Seriously, what did she say?"

"She says the girls will be with their father tomorrow evening. She'll be in town and wondered if I might like to meet up somewhere. She suggested The Watering Hole."

"That dive?"

"It's not a bad place."

"Maybe not for the likes of you and me, but for a date with Lisa?"

"Hey, you brought her there for drinks."

"Yeah, but I'm her brother-in-law. Besides, we went there to meet you at the dive where you hang out."

Pantera considered this. "Does she know where Shagbark is?" he asked, referring to an upscale restaurant in Richmond.

"Probably not, but she has GPS."

Pantera typed a message and sent it. A reply came moments later: *I accept your invitation to enjoy some drinks and dinner*. "Wow, she does move fast, doesn't she?" Pantera said to Harry.

"Like I said, you might want to watch out."

"We need to get back to work," Pantera replied and returned to looking at the lab report with no information.

"Spoil sport."

Pantera had not heard back from Joanna Davis, Grant Davis's ex-wife, so he called her number again. He was connected to her voicemail, and he left a message. "Ms. Davis, this is Detective Pantera with the Richmond Police. It is very important that you give me a call as soon as you can. I have a few questions I need to ask you about your ex-husband." He provided his phone number and hung up.

He turned to his work, hoping to hear from her before that afternoon and was surprised when she called back less than a minute later.

"Detective? This is Joanna Davis. Sorry for not getting back to you before, but that sort of got lost in the list of things I needed to do."

"Yes, ma'am, I was wondering if we could talk for a bit. I'm having trouble learning much about your husband."

"He's my ex-husband, Detective." The ice in her tone left no doubts about how she felt about her ex.

"Yes, ma'am. I apologize. I knew that but misspoke."

"So, what do you want to know?"

"Could you tell me what kind of man he was? Did he frequent bars? Was he a womanizer? Did he gamble? That sort of thing. I'm looking for anything that might lead to understanding why he was murdered."

79

"Well, let's just say it's a good thing I have an alibi, 'cause I wanted the bastard dead."

He was shocked at the venom in her voice. "Since you mention it, what, exactly, would your alibi be?"

"I was visiting my daughter in Knoxville the entire week. She's a sophomore at Tennessee."

"Okay, that sounds like a pretty good alibi," Pantera said. "What about your ex-husband, then? I take it your parting was not amicable."

"It sucked."

"I have found that in cases where the separation, as you put it, sucked, there was a very specific reason for that, usually that he was abusive in some way."

"Not really. He was just an asshole and I got tired of his shit."

"Was he abusive?"

She paused, and Pantera waited for the half-truth. "No. He was just—I don't know—an awful person. He was lazy. Oh, he had a job, but he never did anything around the house to help out. Wouldn't even do the dishes or help with the yard work. He'd come home and do zilch. He'd even give the keys to his tests and stuff to our son and have him grade his papers. He was just a lazy bum."

"Did he have any enemies?"

"Besides our kids and me? Nah. Nobody that I know of. His students didn't like him, but that was too long ago to matter now. He's been in Richmond for five years. His former students have probably all forgotten him by now. He was very forgettable."

"Did he ever talk about any one student or perhaps a colleague who had threatened him?"

"No colleagues, but he complained about his students all the time. He hated them. I always wondered why he became a teacher, hating kids the way he did. I

80

don't even know for sure if he loved our kids. He almost never saw them after he left and only interacted with them before that when it suited him."

"I see," Pantera said, prompting her to continue.

"I always told him he coulda done something else. He'd have made more money if he had. Teaching doesn't pay worth shit."

"So you're not aware that he gambled or was fooling around with another man's wife, or anything?"

"Nah. That's not him. He wasn't gay or anything. He just wasn't the type to have an affair. And he was too much of a penny-pincher to gamble. He'd get mad at me for buying just one lottery ticket. I do it for the fun of it. I don't expect to win anything. But when we were married, he'd hit the roof. Over five bucks! What a cheapskate."

"Are you sure there's nothing else that you're not telling me?"

Another pause. "Whatcha mean?"

"People usually know someone is lazy before they marry them. The hatred you have for your ex suggests there's more to it."

She took a deep breath. "I'd just rather not say, okay? Maybe—" She paused again before continuing. "Maybe someone else will shed some light on it, but it's not for me to say, okay?"

"You won't tell me?"

"Like I said, it's not for me to say. I don't have to answer any of your questions, right?"

"No, but doing so could help find his killer."

"Why would I care about that? I think whoever killed him did the world a favor."

Realizing he would get nothing helpful from this call, Pantera said, "Thank you for returning my call, Ms. Davis. I was wondering if you could give me the contact information on your children. Perhaps they will tell me something that could provide a lead."

"Sure, but I doubt they will tell you anything."

"You never know," Pantera said, his pen poised to jot down the information.

She gave him their phone numbers, and asked that he not call the daughter until that evening so as not to interrupt her classes.

"Thank you, I will make sure I do that."

"You might not be able to get my son to answer. He's kinda busy with the army these days and isn't even in the country right now. Won't be back for a few weeks."

"I understand," Pantera said and ended the call.

He tried the son's phone number in case Ms. Davis hadn't been telling the truth about his being out of the country, but the call went immediately to voicemail. He left a message similar to what he'd left Ms. Davis, figuring it might be a while before he heard back.

He would keep his word and not bother the daughter until that evening. He doubted she would be any help, anyway. If she was as angry at her father as her mother was, he was certain she wouldn't be helpful. Still, it was a loose-end that he would need to tie up. He knew the daughter wouldn't have been able to kill him, given her mother was there with her all week and she'd had classes to attend, which provided her an alibi. As a student, she would lack the funds necessary to hire anyone, so he only hoped she could provide something that could qualify as a lead. He wasn't sure about Ms. Davis's financials. If she became more of a suspect, he'd try to get a subpoena for her bank and phone records.

That evening before he left work for the day to meet Lisa, he phoned Grant Davis's daughter, Marie. On the second ring, she answered.

"This is Marie," she answered.

"Good evening, Miss Davis. My name is Detective Tony Pantera. I'm working the case of your father's murder. Do you have a few minutes to talk to me? I have just a couple of questions."

There was a pause on the other end. "I'm on my way to join some friends for a study group."

"This will only take a few minutes. Are you driving?"

"I'm walking. It's not far."

"What can you tell me about your father?" he asked, ignoring her hint she would rather not talk now.

She sighed. "Other than I'm glad he's dead, and I'd give a medal to the person who killed him if I could?"

Pantera was rather surprised at the response. Grant Davis was apparently not a good person. Pantera had his own problems with his daughters, but he couldn't imagine they would ever say such a thing about him.

"Do you mind if I ask why you feel that way? If his own daughter hates him that much, then it's a near certainty that others did as well."

"He wouldn't have done to them what he did to me, so I doubt anyone hates him as much as I do. But I didn't do it. I was in classes, and I was with my mom when I wasn't."

"Well, unless you can be in two places at once or somehow had the money to hire someone to do the job, someone else hated him enough to murder him. It's my job to find that person. Are you willing to help me?"

"Listen, Detective. It's not your fault that my dad was an asshole of the first degree. Believe me, I wish the circumstances were different. You think I wanted a father like that? I couldn't stand the sight of him."

"Can I ask what he did to you that he didn't do to others?" Pantera suspected what the answer was, but he had to ask anyway despite wishing he didn't have to.

"You said this would only take a few minutes. That answer would take an hour at least. Hell, I've been working on that answer for years, so I guess it would take a lot longer than an hour."

"Miss Davis, I'm not a psychologist, nor do I wish to get into your personal life, but I'm just trying to do my job and solve this case. If your father had any, shall we say, predilections that could have caused someone to hate him enough to kill him, it would be helpful to know that."

"Well, your response tells me you already know what I'm going to say. Yeah, he raped me. A lot. Since I was five until my mom caught him with me and told him to move out. I think he probably had sex with me more than he did my mom. He was an asshole. A piece of shit. The only reason I'm coming to the memorial is to make sure he's really dead. Is it possible he raped some young girl and her father blew him away? Yeah. Is it possible someone from his past ran into him and decided it was time that piece of human filth was taken off this earth? Yes. Now, do you have any more questions? I've reached my study group, and I'd prefer not to have to continue our conversation in front of my friends."

Pantera felt a knot in his stomach grow tighter.

"One more," he said, mostly because he was curious and wanted to know the answer. "Why didn't you tell your mother he was doing that to you?"

She was crying now. "He threatened that he'd kill all of us if I did."

He could think of nothing to say. She was certainly justified in feeling the way she did about her father, who hadn't been a father at all but a rapist. Finally, he said, "I'm sorry that happened to you, Miss Davis. I hope you find peace."

Through her sniffles she said, "I'm sorry. I shouldn't have snapped at you like that. It's just you dredged up a lot of memories."

"I understand. I wish I hadn't needed to do that. So, there's nothing you can tell me about your father and his relationships with other people?"

"No." It was nearly a whisper. "Why would I want to know anything about him?" With that, she disconnected the call.

Hanging up, Pantera could still feel the knot in his stomach. He suspected it would be there for a while. At least now he had the answer to why Davis's ex hated him as much as she did.

Looking at the clock, he realized he needed to leave to meet Lisa at Shagbark. He suddenly felt excited to meet her there while also wishing he could go home and get drunk to try to forget the pain he'd caused Marie Davis with his call.

He knew, though, that meeting Lisa was the better choice, so he gathered his things and left.

Twenty minutes later, he arrived at Shagbark. Parking in the lot behind the row of businesses where the restaurant was located, he walked around the corner of buildings and strolled up to the restaurant. He took a peek inside to make sure she wasn't at the bar, and as he did, he heard her voice behind him.

"Hi, stranger."

He turned to find her smiling at him.

"Looking for someone?" she asked.

"As a matter of fact, I was," he answered. "Shall we have a drink while we wait for our table? I made the reservation for fifteen minutes later than when I told you to be here so we could enjoy something to drink first."

"Sure. I could use a glass of wine."

Holding the door open, he said, "After you" and

gave her his best smile as he felt the knot in his gut ease.

As she passed, he noticed her perfume but didn't recognize it. "What perfume are you wearing?"

"Gucci Guilty," she said, "though I'm not guilty of anything all that bad." She chuckled a bit and turned to enter the restaurant.

Pantera stopped to inform the maître d' of their arrival for and that they would be at the bar.

Once at the bar, Lisa ordered a Chardonnay and he asked for a shot of Johnny Walker Black since they didn't carry Writers Tears Irish whiskey.

They sipped their drinks as they chatted.

"Glad to see you're not a gulper," she said.

"Gulper?"

"Yes, you know. Someone who downs a shot in one gulp. I like that you sip it and enjoy the flavor."

"Well, to be honest, I have gulped in my time, but that's always the cheaper stuff that is just meant to calm my nerves."

She laughed softly. "It's also good to see your nerves don't need calming."

He shrugged. "Not so sure about that. I have a case that's driving me insane."

"Can you tell me about it, or is it some sort of dark secret that needs to be kept from the press?"

"No, it's no secret, though certain aspects are withheld to be sure Crazy Carl doesn't know enough to confess and be tried for it."

"Crazy Carl?"

"Yeah. He's this guy who comes into the precinct every once in a while and confesses to some crime that he didn't commit. Guy's crazy as can be. But with the cutbacks in mental health assistance, I guess he can't get the meds or other help he needs."

She frowned, genuinely disturbed. "That's sad."

"Yeah. Some enjoy life; some muddle through it; and people like Carl don't know up from down."

"So what's so disturbing about this case that you can tell me—since I might be a plant by the Washington Post." She laughed again, sounding in the crowded bar like a soft violin beneath the noise of the rest of the orchestra.

"Well, whoever killed our victim is good at what he does, and by 'at what he does,' I mean leaving behind no clues. None. Not even a stray hair fiber or footprints, even on a rainy night."

"Wow. I didn't know that was possible. What does he do? Float through the air?" She took a sip of her wine while waiting for his answer.

"Oh, no. He walks, but the prints can't be used to help us, other than be part of what we think of as his signature."

"His signature?"

"Yeah. Part of what lets us know he's our culprit in a crime. They started as small burglaries. Then he graduated straight from that to murder. The burglaries netted some items of value, but nothing extraordinary. Then suddenly, boom! We find the victim dead in his chair, a hollow-point having been fired directly into his forehead."

"Oh, my God. Do you think someone may have put a 'hit' out on the guy?"

"Could have. Let's just say he wasn't exactly a model citizen."

"So, he was part of the underworld of crime himself?"

"No, not exactly. In fact, he was an assistant principal at a local high school."

"Then how was he not a model citizen?"

Pantera looked into her eyes, gauging whether or

not to tell her the truth about Grant Davis. He knew it could be a lie his daughter told, but Marie Davis's anger and obvious shame over what had been done to her was all too real. Either that, or she needed to go to Hollywood.

"I don't know that this is appropriate for a first date," Pantera answered.

"I'm a big girl. I can handle it. I asked, so what's the harm in answering my question? I can't blame you if I don't like the answer."

Pantera sighed and said, "Let's just say he wasn't a good person and leave it at that."

Lisa's expression changed to disappointment, but he stuck to his decision.

"I know you'd like to talk about it," he said, "but I really can't."

"Well, anyway, good luck with your investigation," she said.

He changed the subject to her daughters, and she was soon chatting about them.

The maître d' came over and told them their table was ready. They enjoyed a delicious meal of duck breast.

"I love duck when it's properly prepared. You can always count on it to be tender and flavorful," she said.

After the meal, they walked around the area a bit before heading to where she had parked. He opened her door for her, but instead of climbing in, she stepped closer to him.

"I had a lovely evening," she said.

The smell of her perfume wafted to him as she leaned closer. He kissed her, and as he did, she wrapped her arms around his neck and made the kiss last longer than he'd intended.

"Harry thinks the world of you," she said when they'd parted from their first kiss. "I do, too."

He was surprised at her candor. He was used to women who were more like him—reserved and moving slowly where romance was involved.

"I like you, too."

"I have a confession," she said.

"I'm a cop. I'm used to listening to them if you want to get it off your chest."

When he smiled at his joke, she returned the smile.

"I didn't really have to be in Richmond tonight. I made that part up to get you to take me out." She paused. "I'm glad I did."

"I'm glad you did, too."

"I felt like if I waited for you to ask me out, I'd be waiting for a while. You aren't one of those fast movers with women. I like that."

"Good. A lot of women don't. They want to be swept off their feet, as if Prince Charming were real."

"I stopped believing in him when I was sixteen."

"Oh?"

"Yeah. Long story. Lots of heartbreak and teenage angst."

"I'm sorry."

"Oh, don't be. I learned a valuable lesson—that everyone has flaws, and life is about finding the one with the flaws you can abide."

"I have a lot of flaws myself."

"We all do." She looked around as if tired of their surroundings. "For instance, I need a bed to sleep in tonight. Would you know of one?"

Pantera could only describe the look in her eyes as smoldering, as cliché as that was.

Unsure if he wanted this to happen, he went with his instincts that the night would be unforgettable. "It just so happens there's half a queen-size bed I know about as long as you don't mind sharing the other half."

She smiled at him. "I take it I would be sharing that other half with you?"

"Provided that suits you."

She smiled and leaned in for another kiss. "That suits me just fine."

"What about your work tomorrow? It's a long commute to D.C."

"I had the foresight to arrange for the day off."

That night after she fell asleep, Pantera lay in bed beside her, marveling at how the night had transpired. The sex had been perhaps the best in his life. She was an enthusiastic lover, as well as a vocal one, unafraid to express what she wanted.

What he wasn't sure about was if Lisa looked at this as a one-night stand to scratch an itch or if she saw this as a more permanent situation, one where she might arrange to stay the night occasionally. Or was she interested in having this possibly develop beyond just the occasional night of very satisfying sex? He wasn't sure, and when he thought about it, he didn't care whether it was a one-night-stand or an occasional night. What he didn't want right now was something bordering permanent. He definitely liked her for more than the sex, but he wasn't sure if falling in love was where he wanted any relationship to go. He was aware of the torch he still carried for his ex-wife, Nancy, as hopeless as that situation was.

Of course, neither he nor Lisa were in love. But he did like her, and she obviously liked him.

Finally, he decided it was too early in whatever the relationship was becoming to worry about such things. He'd been honest when he'd told her he was a worrier, and this late-night sojourn into soul-searching about their possible futures was ample evidence of that. He knew from experience that he would have to turn the mental conversation with himself off if he expected to get any sleep tonight.

He turned on his side and felt her move up to him, spooning with him like a lover of a dozen years instead of one night.

He heard her sigh and wasn't sure if it was a sigh of contentment or regret. And did she think in her sleep that she was spooning with him or someone else?

He decided he'd never know the answers to these questions and finally dropped off to sleep.

TWELVE

Melinda Jackson sat in her home the following morning with her old-fashioned desktop phone in her lap. She didn't own a cell phone—never would since she was forty-two and had lived her life without one—and as she sat thinking about what she needed to do, she continued to do her best to talk herself out of doing it.

Her house was across the street from a man who had been murdered. An officer had stopped by when they were investigating the crime scene. He'd wanted to know if she'd seen or heard anything the night before.

She'd denied seeing or hearing anything, but it was a lie. Her parents had always advised her that talking to the police could end up causing trouble, sometimes big trouble. The kind of trouble that could lead to her death.

The truth was she had seen something. It had been an odd thing to see, and at the time, she'd thought nothing of it other than how odd it was for a man to wear such odd shoes and a cap like that.

She'd been watching TV and had pushed her substantial girth up from her chair to go to the bathroom when she had noticed movement across the street through a window. It had appeared a man there was removing a strange pair of shoes. The soles appeared to be large squares. Light from a streetlamp just down the street lit up the shoes, but not the man's face, so she hand't seen that. The only thing she had noticed at first besides the shoes was the man's build, which seemed fairly muscular.

The man had then removed what looked like a

close-fitting cap of some sort, and placed both the shoes and cap inside a bag he'd been carrying. He had then started moving down the street in what could best be described as a fast walk, as if he needed to be somewhere. He'd passed beneath the street light, but all she'd been able to see was his build and tousled hair

She'd thought no more about it until the police arrived at the house the next day.

Now she worried because she had lied to the police when she'd said she'd seen nothing the night the man was killed. Would they arrest her if she called and confessed that she hadn't been truthful? What about the man she'd seen? Would he find out she'd talked about him and come for revenge?

She had already called 4-1-1 and had the number to the police department. It was written on a pad beside her. Lifting the receiver from its cradle, she dialed the first five numbers before hanging up. She was so frightened her heart seemed ready to burst from her chest.

No, she thought to herself, maybe calling wasn't a good idea after all. Her parents had never lied to her as far as she knew, so why think calling the police was a good thing now? What could she tell them if she did call? That the man wore a snug cap and weird shoes?

Okay, she could add that the man had sandy hair, what she always thought of as "surfer's hair" because it was shaggy and the same light color of hair worn by the boys who hung out at the beach where she'd grown up in Santa Monica in California. She had always liked the surfers, and they had liked her when she had her figure and the willingness to do whatever it took for them to notice and spend time with her. Their hair had been sun-bleached, and this man's looked the same.

Melinda wondered how much the information she had would help the police in catching the man. Probably none, she thought. Certainly not enough to risk her life or her freedom for.

Lifting the phone from her lap, she placed it back on the table and pushed herself out of the chair. She would have some cake and watch TV while trying to forget the idea of calling the police. She hoped that would be enough to end the constant nagging her conscience had been engaged in the past few days.

As she ate her cake, she noticed it was time for her favorite game show. It was an old one from decades ago, but she liked it. It was always funny how the contestants would come up with ridiculous answers to the trivia questions that even she knew the answers to.

The thought of calling the police faded with her enjoyment of the show.

THIRTEEN

B lanton sat with the morning edition of the Richmond Times-Dispatch. There was only a short article about the killing of Grant Davis. Blanton figured the brevity could be blamed on the lack of any information for the press to use. Most of the article dealt with Davis's job as a local high school administrator. It contained little in the way of information about the death, other than he'd been shot while watching TV. The report claimed the killing might have been the result of a botched burglary but that the police had no official leads to that effect.

They have no leads at all, thought Blanton as he turned to the sports page. He would wait to implement the next step in his plan for getting away with murder.

The only thing he thought about now was how much he wanted to kill again. He'd had what he considered a good reason for killing Davis. Now, he longed to kill for the sake of taking a life. He could kill anyone who pissed him off. Women who rejected him came to mind. The sense of nearly god-like power overwhelmed him like a drug he had to have. Revenge had been a driving force in his life. Now, he could continue exacting that revenge on others who had wronged him.

The entire process of killing Davis had been amazingly simple, and now that he knew what he could do to escape detection, he could break into any house and kill anyone he found there. He could do anything he wanted, in fact. This knowledge made him feel—he

95

searched for the word—exhilarated.

He'd received an almost sexual thrill from the killing. When he considered killing a woman, his first thought was of Roxanne. He'd gone out with her a couple of times before she ended it. She'd not given a satisfactory reason for not wanting to see him again when he'd pressed her, so basically it meant she didn't like him. That's how it had often been. His looks got him a date or two, but the girl would decide they weren't "right" for each other, whatever that meant.

Taking out his phone, he found Roxanne Beard in his list of contacts. That was one great thing about the cell phone world. People almost never changed their numbers now, no matter where they lived. Roxanne certainly would not expect a call from him. She might see the incoming call identified only by the words "Private Number." She'd had his number in her phone at one time but might have deleted him after ending their short-lived relationship. It would be just like her, he thought.

Figuring he had nothing to lose, he pressed the button to call her.

Roxanne Beard felt her phone vibrate. She was at work and didn't have time to take a call and glanced at the caller ID to know who was calling, at least. When she saw the name Blanton, she cringed. She'd not heard from him in nearly nine months, ever since she realized what a perv he was and that she didn't want to see him again. She wondered why the hell he was calling her now as well as why she hadn't deleted him from her contacts list. Now, though, she was happy she hadn't.

One thing that bothered her about him was how he used his last name with everyone, even people who were supposed to be his friends, not even telling anyone his first name. It seemed as if he thought using his first name was being too familiar or something.

Also, he'd been making crude sexual jokes and asking personal questions after only two dates. She knew a lot of people jumped in the sack after one date, but she wasn't that kind of girl, and second, she wouldn't answer some of his questions even if she had screwed him. What kind of guy asked a girl how often she masturbated after only two dates? She guessed it would be one thing if they'd had sex and she'd done it for him, but she considered that very private, and his question made her want to get away from the creep as fast as she could.

And now he was calling her again?

Roxanne pressed "ignore" on her phone and turned her attention to ringing up the next shopper at the Food Lion where she worked, hoping he would just end the call and forget her. The idea he'd called made her want to change her number, but that was too much of a hassle since she'd then have to notify everyone to change the number they had for her.

When her phone dinged that she had a voicemail, she wanted to scream. She knew she could just delete it and ignore him, but she also knew she was incapable of not at least listening to the message. Her curiosity was too great to even consider ignoring the message, no matter how weird or creepy it might be. The message might at least shed some light on why he'd called her after she'd made it clear she never wanted to see or hear from him again.

When she went on break, she listened to the message and shuddered.

Hey, Roxanne. What's up? This is Blanton. I'm sure you remember me. I jerked off last night thinking of you and thought I'd call to see if you wanted to get together.

I'll wait for your call or call you back if I don't hear from you.

The message sounded more like an ominous threat than anything else and frightened her. She deleted the message and then cleared her deleted message box to make sure it was gone for good.

What a creep! she thought. When her break ended, she returned to her job, doing her best to forget about the call and the disturbing message.

That afternoon as Roxanne arrived home, she didn't notice Blanton in his car down the street from her small house, waiting for her to arrive. He'd not had enough time that day to complete the necessary work, but he was patient. If she worked tomorrow, he could do it then. He might be patient, but he was also anxious to install the surveillance equipment. He could be here in the morning to see if she left in her work uniform, but he knew a better way to find out if and when she worked.

Watching people as they went about their lives while unaware they were being observed was one of the worst things a person could do to another, so Blanton embraced the desire to do it. Stealing a person's privacy was worse than stealing their money. Money could be replaced, but privacy was gone forever. It was the evil nature of stealing people's privacy that drew him. He knew that what those he watched did when they thought they were alone defined exactly who they were and what they were about.

He could use the knowledge in many ways and had considered blackmailing the people he watched and recorded, but that was too risky. Blackmail always made exposure necessary. It was always when the blackmailer went to retrieve whatever he'd demanded that he was caught.

After Blanton drove past Roxanne's house, he called the Food Lion where she worked.

"Hey, can I speak to Roxanne?" he asked, as if he called her there all the time.

"She just left a little while ago," the guy who answered said.

"Is this the manager?"

"I'm an assistant manager. What can I do for you?"

"Will she be there tomorrow? I'll be in town then and maybe I can stop by. I owe her some money—like a couple hundred bucks—and need to just give it to her."

"Let me check," the man said. A moment later, he was back on the line. "She works ten to six tomorrow."

"Great, I'll drop by. It'll only take a second."

"Shall I tell her you called?" Blanton knew the next question would be for his name.

"No, that won't be necessary. I can just drop in tomorrow and pay her back. It'll be a good surprise for her. She probably thinks I've forgotten I owe her the money, so I can't wait to see the look on her face, but thanks." He disconnected the call before the assistant manager could reply.

Six hours, he thought. That would be plenty of time to install his surveillance gear.

FOURTEEN

When Pantera's alarm sounded at 6:30 the next morning, Lisa was already up and drinking a cup of coffee. He put on his robe and went out to the kitchen, finding her seated at the breakfast bar.

"Hey," she said. "I hope you don't mind that I helped myself to some coffee."

"Of course not," Pantera said. "I'd be upset if you wanted some and didn't make yourself a cup."

"I'll be leaving when I finish this. I have an appointment in D.C. later this morning, not to mention I don't want to be in your way as you get ready for work."

"I thought you said you were off today."

"I am. It's a dentist appointment. Time for a cleaning."

"Oh, okay." Pantera considered this news and realized he wasn't the reason she had arranged for the day off. Her dentist was.

"Maybe you could come see me soon. I can give you a grand tour of the Library of Congress," Lisa said.

"That doesn't sound like a bad idea at all, but to be honest, I'd want to bring my daughters. Beth would especially enjoy that."

"That would be great. She could meet Denise and Emma," Lisa said, referring to her twin daughters that were Beth's age.

"I'll let you know when."

After Lisa had left, he tidied up a bit before heading for work.

Harry greeted him as he entered with, "So, how was

the date?" Two other detectives, Morris and Unger, whom everyone called Felix after the character Felix Unger in *The Odd Couple*, were seated at their desks and looked up.

"Pantera had a date?" Felix asked.

"So when did pigs sprout wings?!" Morris said.

"It went fine," Pantera answered, "assuming it's anyone else's business."

"My wife called me this morning," Harry said. "Said Lisa had called on her way back home to express her thanks for introducing you two to each other."

"Wait," Morris said. "She stayed the night? Pigs have started flying!"

"She told you she stayed the night?" Pantera asked.

"Well, no, she didn't. She told her sister, who happens to be my wife, that she stayed the night. Ashley tells me everything."

"Great. Now my life is a caged animal in the zoo, there for the entertainment of everyone with a few minutes to stop and look."

Harry said, "Hey, she didn't give any details, only that she had a great time and ended up staying the night. She's a sexy woman, Tony, and very—shall we say— open-minded. I pretty well figured she would spend the night when she made the date."

Pantera began looking at his times with Lisa differently. This had only been their second encounter, the first being a hastily arranged blind date of sorts.

Pantera looked at Harry and jerked his head in a "come with me" gesture, and Harry followed him into the hall, which was deserted for the moment.

"What do you mean, 'open-minded'? Should I worry about her cheating on me if it becomes serious?"

"What? No. Nothing like that. It's just Lisa doesn't hide the fact she loves sex."

"I love sex, too. Does that qualify me as 'open-minded'?" Pantera's voice hissed with anger.

"Calm down, man. I was mostly just yankin' your chain."

"Yeah, well, I have a problem with how people view men and women differently. A man's expected to like sex. They're often seen as willing to do it anywhere with anyone. Then women who enjoy sex are somehow seen as sluts, or they have some kind of 'tag' put on them as being 'open-minded,' or the milder version, 'fun-loving.' The vast majority of women love sex, Harry, and it's wrong to give them labels because of it."

"Hey, sorry, man."

Pantera took a deep breath, calming himself. He hated that his personal life was now the topic of discussion in the squad room, but there was more. "Sorry. I know I overreacted, but there's more to this all-too-frequent view of women that bothers me now. You see, my daughter has come out as a lesbian. She's fifteen and has a girlfriend she likely fools around with some, as teenagers frequently do. Your comment made me think of how she will have to deal with people's shit her entire life."

"Sorry. I didn't mean to yank your chain that hard. Lisa's a nice lady. I'm glad you two are getting along. And I agree with you about how women and men are viewed differently. You know I do."

"Then you need to change how you talk about them."

"I didn't know that about your daughter, though. Are you and Nancy okay with it?"

"Of course, we're okay with it. She's our daughter. We've raised her to be a loving person, but it's not our place to tell her whom she should love. That's up to her and who she is."

Harry flashed a grin. "I guess I was wrong about you. You're pretty liberated yourself."

Pantera let the comment lighten the tension that had dominated the conversation. He smiled and put a hand on Harry's shoulder. "I only wish everyone was—at least in the way of letting others live their lives. It would be a happier world to live in. Now, let's get to work."

As he turned, he saw Crazy Carl approaching them as he shuffled down the hallway. "Oh, great. That's all we need."

"Equality goes for the mentally ill as well, Tony," Harry said.

"Good. I'm glad you feel that way. You can take whatever confession he has for us today. Just be sure to call him Lenny and not Carl."

"No problem," Harry said and stepped toward Carl/Lenny, who was still several yards away. "Hey, Lenny. What brings you to our fine establishment today?"

Pantera stepped into the squad room, followed by Crazy Carl and Harry. As he entered, Carl/Lenny said, "I'm afraid I've done something bad."

"Well, they say confession is good for the soul, Lenny," Harry said and directed him to the visitor's chair beside his desk. As they sat, Harry said, "So, what did you do, Lenny? What do you need to get off your chest?"

As Lenny began his confession, Pantera's phone rang.

"Detective squad. This is Detective Pantera. How may I assist you?"

"I think I'm being stalked," a female voice said. "I called and they sent me to you."

"First, can I get your name?"

"Roxanne Beard."

"Okay, Ms. Beard, why do you think you're being stalked?"

"He called me for the first time in like eight months or so and left me a disgusting message. I thought he'd forgotten all about me, but he—well, he called and it has me kind of rattled."

"So you know who this is who called?"

"Yes, We dated a while back but I broke it off when he got, well, kinda weird. Like, he got too familiar with me."

"What do you mean by 'too familiar'?"

"Can't I talk to a woman?"

"Unfortunately, there are no women detectives here right now. I understand your reluctance, but I'm afraid right now I'm all you have. Believe me, I've heard it all before, so there's no reason to be embarrassed.

"Oh," she said. Pantera waited for her to answer his question. When she didn't, he repeated it. "So, what do you mean by 'too familiar'?"

She answered with evident reluctance. "He asked me questions about my sexual habits."

Pantera jotted down notes to enter into a report later if it became necessary.

"What's the guy's name?"

"Blanton."

"What's his first name?"

"I don't know. He only goes by his last name. It's something else that's weird about him. He doesn't even tell people his first name. I asked, and he said he never uses it."

Pantera jotted down the last name and asked, "Why do you say he's stalking you now?"

"His message said he had—" she paused. "Well the term he used was that he 'jerked off' the night before thinking of me."

"Do you still have the message?"

"No, I deleted it then deleted it from my trash."

"If he calls again and leaves another message like the one you deleted, don't delete it this time. You can use it as evidence if he denies leaving the message."

"Oh. I never thought of that. I just wanted to get rid of it."

"I understand. Did the two of you have a sexual relationship when you dated?"

"No. I only went out with him twice. Then he got—I don't know—creepy."

"When you say he got 'creepy,' was he making comments like the ones in the message he left you, or did he do something?"

"Do something?"

"You know. Touch you where you didn't want to be touched. That sort of thing."

"Oh. No, he didn't do that. He just, well, asked me a weird question."

"What question?"

"Do I have to go into that with you?"

"If you want to file a stalking report, I need to know the full details so we can determine a course of action. The truth is that some women call in about a stalker, but it turns out not to qualify as such. Stalking involves repeated instances of harassment. Has he done more than ask you a question months ago that you thought was creepy and then call to leave that message?"

"His message said he would see me again later. Detective, I don't want to see him again. Do you think it's appropriate he would call and say stuff like that?"

"What I think is appropriate doesn't matter, Ms. Beard. It's about whether his actions qualify him as a stalker. What was the question that made you upset during your second date?"

She paused a second before asking, "Maybe I could call back later and talk to a woman detective? This is really kind of personal."

"As I said, I'd hand your call off to a woman, but the only detectives on duty right now that are in the squad room are men. Believe me, I agree with you that this guy is a creep, but in all honesty, I need more information before I can do anything more. My hands are, unfortunately, tied because of the rules we have to go by here."

Roxanne heaved a sigh on the other end, obviously indecisive about what to do.

"Relax, Ms. Beard. Believe me, I've heard every personal question in the book. What you tell me won't shock me at all."

"Well, it kinda shocked me."

"I understand."

She sighed again. "Okay. He asked me how often I masturbate."

"Alright. Now, I have to ask this, so please don't think I'm trying to blame you. I'm not, but it's something that a defense counsel will ask, and you need to be prepared for it if the question comes up later. Were the two of you getting involved in any form of sex when he asked you this? For instance, had you been getting into any passionate kissing or petting? That kind of thing? Right or wrong, that would change how your situation is perceived by a jury."

"No. He was driving me home from a movie."

"What movie?" Pantera wanted to make sure it wasn't something X-rated or close to it. This wasn't because seeing such a movie would necessarily give this guy Blanton the right to ask such a question, but Blanton could use it as evidence Roxanne Beard would be open to such a question.

106

"*Single White Female*."

"That's not exactly a new movie."

"It was part of a theme feature we went to. Something about the best Hitchcock that wasn't from Hitchcock, or something like that. I forget."

"Were the two of you discussing the movie when he asked this question?"

"What would that have to do with it?"

"Well, Ms. Beard, I've seen that movie, and there is a female masturbation scene in it, though only a brief moment of it."

"Why are you giving me a hard time with this?" Pantera could tell the young woman was near tears.

"I'm sorry, Ms. Beard. This is a serious allegation, and if we arrest this man on a stalking charge, I can guarantee you his attorney will be asking these questions when you're on the stand, perhaps even more personal ones."

"Okay! We were talking about the damn movie!"

"Were you discussing that particular scene?"

"Only because he brought it up."

"Did you tell him you didn't want to discuss that scene?"

"I did when he asked me that question!"

"What had you said about that scene before he asked you that question?"

"Nothing. He asked me what I thought of it. That scene. I told him I didn't think anything about it. That's when he asked me that question."

"And now he has called you back and left the message you spoke of?"

"Yes. Can we do anything?"

"I would suggest going to the courthouse and filing for a restraining order on him."

"Is that all?"

"It's the best we can do right now. I understand your anger and embarrassment over this. I understand you're in fear of this guy, but this isn't enough to have him arrested for stalking. One creepy question months ago and one creepy phone call don't cross that bar, I'm afraid. Now, if you get a restraining order and he continues to harass you, then we have a case against him."

"Restraining orders only work if the guy abides by it. You don't understand! I'm scared!"

"I know you are frightened, and you should do whatever possible to stay away from him." He thought about his daughters and decided to at least do a little more than what regulations allowed.

"Tell you what. First, if you take out a restraining order and he violates it, then you have a case of stalking that can be pursued. At this point, my hands are tied. If we arrested every creep out there, we'd be doing nothing else. I know that's not what you want to hear, but that's the reality. I don't like it anymore than you do.

"If he calls you again, save the message and call me here. My name is Detective Tony Pantera. Ask for me.. If he ever approaches you, hurry to the nearest public area if you're not already in one. A restaurant, any place of business, really, will do. Just get to where there are other people around. In the meantime, if you'll give me your address, I will see if I can get a patrol car to cruise by over the next few days at least."

"Thanks. I know you're trying, at least." she said.

"I'm sorry if my questions and handling of this call were, well, rather unsympathetic, but it's how we're trained to handle these calls since the vast majority of them turn out to be nothing."

"But mine isn't just nothing. I'm really scared of this guy."

"I know. Do you promise to take out the restraining order?"

"Yes. And thank you for trying," she said and disconnected the call.

Pantera glanced over at Harry, who was still interviewing Lenny about whatever crime he'd seen in the papers or on the news that he felt compelled to confess to.

Shaking his head, he tore off the sheet where he'd been taking notes on the call from Roxanne Beard and tossed it in the wastebasket. At this point, her call was just another call, and he didn't need to file a report of any kind since there was nothing that could be done beyond what he'd already done for her--provide her some advice and his personal number to call. He felt bad for Ms. Beard and hated that he couldn't do more for her.

FIFTEEN

B lanton waited until 10:30 to enter Roxanne's house. He'd been busy early that morning arranging an alibi of sorts in case he needed one for the night Davis had been killed, but he had reserved the rest of the day to do what he had to do at Roxanne's. Thankful for the privacy fence that surrounded the back yard, which he thought of as an invitation to burglars, he used his tools to jimmy the cheap lock on the back door. Unlike the front door, it had no deadbolt. He wasn't sure who decided the front door needed more protection than the back door, but he was thankful people could be that ignorant. After all, the front door was open to public view. The back door was the one hidden from passers-by, especially with that privacy fence.

He had studied locks for years and could have unlocked the deadbolt as well. It just would have taken longer. This way, he need not worry about losing the extra time needed to break into the house if there'd been a deadbolt on the back door.

Lifting the suitcase carrying his surveillance equipment, he walked through the door as if he owned the place. After all, for the next several hours, he did.

He found the extra house keys more easily than he had found Davis's. They were on a hook in the kitchen. He tried the keys and unlocked the deadbolt and doorknob lock on the front door as well as the cheap backdoor lock. He would get duplicates made and return these keys to the hook before Roxanne arrived home.

Again, his aim was to make his visit undetectable. He didn't want Roxanne to vary her daily patterns of

110

life, so not allowing her to know anyone had been inside her home was important. Besides, she would likely call the cops and have him arrested.

He wasn't worried about the call he'd made to her before, though. They could trace such calls, but that wouldn't get them anything. He'd made the call from a burner, and he'd even been smart enough not to make the call from his home. He'd actually read of a case where Detective Pantera found a kidnapper because the kidnapper was stupid enough to make a call to the mother of his victim from his home on the victim's phone. It was amazing how usually intelligent people could make stupid mistakes.

Blanton smiled at the memory of how thoroughly he had researched Pantera. He felt it an obligation to find out everything possible about an adversary. Knowledge was indeed power, and he could feel the power he had over Pantera. He had researched every news article mentioning him that could be found on the internet. He'd learned how he had solved the kidnapping case as well as finding a serial killer, all in the past year. He had discovered the public notice of his divorce and had read the divorce decree that was available in the public records section of the courthouse. That's where Blanton had learned of Pantera's two daughters.

He'd found pictures of Pantera's ex as well as his daughters in a news article about how the older girl had won some high school golf tournament. The whole family had posed for a photo, which had been posted on the Richmond Times-Dispatch website's archives.

The younger daughter was too young for his tastes. But the older one? He'd call her ripe for plucking. She was fifteen or sixteen. Mentally a girl, but physically a woman.

Blanton went about installing his equipment,

making sure everything was hidden from sight. He placed two cameras in the air ducts in the bedroom and bathroom, as well as in the living room so he could watch Roxanne watching TV and listen in on her side of a conversation if she called someone from the room where most people spent most of their waking hours.

He was about to gather his things to leave when he heard the front door's deadbolt clicking open and someone entered the home. He glanced at his watch. It was 2:54, much too early for Roxanne to return from work.

He hid in a closet and waited. Whoever it was went about whatever tasks they had with a sense of familiarity with the house and its layout.

When the intruder entered Roxanne's bedroom, he could see her through the slit of the slightly open closet door. A young woman around Roxanne's age entered the room and began to undress. She went to a dresser and removed clean panties and a bra from a drawer and placed them on the bed.

This had to be a roommate. He mentally kicked himself for not checking this out. He'd assumed Roxanne lived alone. The young woman finished disrobing and stepped into the bathroom.

He heard her stop there. The movement was sudden. She'd seen his suitcase filled with his spying equipment, which he'd left on the bathroom floor. He'd not had time to retrieve the bag, and it wouldn't have done any good if he had. His equipment was scattered about the small room, and he'd not had time to clean up the mess caused from stripping wires.

The fact that the roommate shared the bedroom with Roxanne told him they might be more than just roommates, which in his mind explained why she hadn't been so interested in him.

Stepping from the closet, he moved up behind the naked young woman. Suddenly wrapping his arm around her neck, he held her there as she struggled in vain to extricate herself. His muscular right arm held her there while his left hand clamped over her mouth.

Her hands clawed at him but encountered only his bathing cap and other clothing, which was made from nylon, a slick material that made escaping someone's grasp easier should something like this ever happen. He prided himself on thinking of every contingency, and he was happy he'd considered this one.

Her efforts lasted only a few seconds as he twisted her neck to the side, snapping it. She was dead within seconds.

Taking her body to the bed, he laid her there. Taking her phone from the pocket of the jeans she'd worn, he wrapped the body and her discarded clothes in a sheet and replaced the clean bra and panties in their drawer. Then he hurried to finish cleaning up after himself. He would take the body of the young woman who had interrupted his routine with him. He could leave her there, but finding a dead body in the bedroom had a way of involving the police. If the police found his handiwork, the entire day's labors would be for nothing.

Moving the body would be risky, but he knew how he could accomplish it with little risk of being seen by a passer-by.

Once he'd hurriedly cleaned everything up, he took the wrapped woman and the bag with his equipment outside and placed them beside the privacy fence near a gate that led to the side street, which was little more than an alley between houses. Leaving the house, he hurried to his car down the block and drove to where the gate was. After opening his trunk, he looked around and opened the gate. Lifting the young woman's petite body

113

with ease, he dropped it into the trunk, slammed the lid, retrieved his bag, and hurried to sit behind the wheel. Smiling, he drove off.

His luck held. From what he could tell, nobody saw anything since most of the neighborhood was at work, and there were few reasons for a car to use the side street there.

He drove to the nearest hardware store and had the duplicate keys made. Returning to the house, he returned the keys to their hook before driving home. It was after four o'clock when he drove away for the last time that day, so he knew Roxanne would arrive mere minutes after that. He hoped his need to hurry didn't leave any traces of evidence, but he trusted his sense of thoroughness.

He decided he had plans for the girl's phone, so he knew he couldn't turn it off until he'd done what he wanted to do. Doing so would require knowing the passcode, and that would be nearly impossible. If the I-phone stayed on, he would only need the girl's fingerprint to open it.

Instead of going home, where the phone's location and movements could be traced, he drove to a hotel near the airport and paid for a room for the night. After checking in, he left the phone there and went home, where he retrieved his laptop to be able to monitor what happened when Roxanne arrived home.

He considered the body in his trunk and decided he would go out in the middle of the night to dump it where it would probably lie for weeks without being discovered.

That night, he sat in his hotel room eating takeout and watched as Roxanne walked through the house, calling out her roommate's name, Wendy, and obviously wondering what had happened to her. Blanton watched the screen when she phoned her the first time. Wendy's phone, which sat on the small table in the room, rang and vibrated.

Roxanne's body language suggested worry and tension. After phoning Wendy, she made another call, this one apparently to Wendy's employer. He listened as she asked when Wendy had left work. The reply she received did not help alleviate her worry.

Picking up the I-phone, he went down to his car, which he'd purposely backed into a parking space that put the trunk facing some trees and shrubs.

Opening the trunk, he took Wendy's right hand, assuming she was probably right-handed, and pressed the index finger to the button. Bingo. The phone opened.

Returning to the room, he searched her contacts and found Roxanne. Then he looked at various texts the roommate sent to get an idea of her typical wording. She used forms of "fuck" a lot, as well as "I got the boogie fever," whatever that meant. She seemed to pepper her texts with the comment, as if it were a personal mantra. She also used "cuz" for "because," among other individual wordings and spellings.

Opening the texts to Roxanne, he sent her a text, pretending to be Wendy.

hey! i figured i would let you know i got the boogie fever! for real.
where the fuck are you?
let's just say I'm not home? r u?
of course! i was worried sick! r u coming home?
nope.
then when will you be home? tomorrow?
nope. quit my job. quitting every-fucking-thing. i'm gone.
what about your clothes?

i'll come by soon to get them. just leave them in the laundry room on that table.

are you fucking kidding me? i love you!

yeah, well, that's life. i don't luv you anymore. i've found someone new. i got that boogie fever for real.

shit, girl! and you didn't quit your job either. i called. they said you left hours ago. didn't mention shit about you quitting!

they'll figure out i quit when i don't show up.

why you doin this?

cuz i can. later.

wait!

can't. gotta go. i got the boogie fever. ☐

wendy! NO!!!!

He ignored the reply.

Picking up his laptop, Blanton started the recording of what had just happened. He smiled as Roxanne tossed her phone down on the sofa table and cried after he didn't respond to her last text. He would go by in the next few days when he saw she was leaving the house dressed for work to pick up the roommate's clothes. He might even leave Wendy's house keys on the laundry room table to make it seem more realistic that the roommate had decided to vanish.

Switching to the live feed, he watched as Roxanne finally went to bed, undressing and taking a shower first. He was surprised to learn she shaved her mons. Disappointment washed over him. He'd had fantasies of pulling her pubic hair out one strand at a time while she lay bound and gagged.

The next day, he would buy a prepaid phone to use for future communication with Roxanne, claiming Wendy's new lover had bought it for her. He would no longer need Wendy's phone, so he shut it off and removed the SIM card. He would toss the phone and SIM card into separate dumpsters the next morning.

SIXTEEN

Melinda Jackson phoned her sister Cassandra that Monday. Cassandra lived in Memphis, so the phone was their only way to connect for now. They tried to get together like this at least once a week, just to gab and enjoy each other's company. They'd liked each other even as children, rarely getting into the fights and arguments other sisters did. They would even set the time and date for the next call at the end of their visits.

When Melinda made the call, Cassandra asked, "So, what's new with you?"

"You're not going to believe it."

"Try me."

"I witnessed a crime."

"You didn't!"

"I told you that you wouldn't believe me."

"What happened?"

"I was watching TV and got up to pee. When I did, I just happened to look out my front window, and this man was taking off these shoes that looked really weird and some kind of cap he wore. It looked like he had to struggle some with the cap, so it musta been tight to his head. Anyway, the next morning they found the man across the street had been shot."

"My word! Did you tell the police what you saw?"

"You know Mama and Daddy told us we shouldn't talk to the police."

"That's because Daddy sold drugs."

"Well, maybe so, but I thought about what they said, and I felt maybe I shouldn't call. It's not like I can tell them who it was or anything."

"Melinda, you gotta call them and tell them what you saw!"

"And end up in court testifying? No, thank you."

"Melinda, we're not talking about some guy who did some small vandalizing on a car or house. This is murder!"

"And if it turns out my information got him caught, then he might come murder me!"

"No! No! No! That's not right. You need to hang up this instant and call the police and tell them what you saw."

"I didn't see that much!"

"Okay, tell me what you saw."

"I saw this man removing these weird looking shoes and a tight-looking cap. Then he ran off down the street, and I saw he was blonde, like those surfer boys we knew back home."

"And what if they arrest someone and he's a brunette? They'd have the wrong man, and it would be your fault!"

Melinda hadn't thought about that. What if they did arrest the wrong man just because they didn't know he was a scraggly-haired blonde with a muscular build?

"What if they get mad because I didn't tell them when they came over that day to ask if I'd seen anything?"

"You already told them you didn't see anything?"

"Yes. They came over the day they found the body and asked me if I'd seen anything. I told them I hadn't."

"Why?"

"Because of what Mama and Daddy said about talking to the police!"

"Forget that, Melinda! You have to call."

"Will they arrest me for not saying anything?"

"They might not be happy about it, but they can't

arrest you. It's not like you were harboring a criminal."

"So I should call them and tell them?"

"Are you hearing me okay? Yes. That is exactly what you have to do, and right now."

Melinda heaved a sigh as big as her girth. "Okay, then. I will."

"Call me as soon as you finish with the police. I need to know what they said."

"I might have to call you to send bail money."

"Don't be ridiculous. Now, call!"

"Okay, okay. I'll call."

The women hung up, and Melinda dialed 4-1-1 to get the number to the police precinct.

When someone at the police station answered, she said, "Hello, I have some information about a killing that happened the other night in my neighborhood."

"May I have your name and address?" the person on the phone asked. Melinda thought she sounded impatient.

"I'd prefer not to give my name right now."

"Then your address, or at least the name of the victim. We have more than one homicide."

"Oh, of course. The man's name who was killed was a Mr. Davis. He was a school principal or something."

"Okay. Please hold while I connect you to one of the detectives working that case."

A moment later, Melinda listened as the burr of a phone ringing repeated itself for seven or eight rings. Melinda grew impatient herself.

Finally, a man answered the phone. "Detective Pantera. How may I assist you?"

Melinda began by explaining why she hadn't told the officer who had come to her door the day Davis's body was discovered.

"Thank you, ma'am, but I'm not really interested in that. Do you have something to report on the murder?"

"Yes, I do. You see, I was getting up from watching a show on TV to go, well, to go to the bathroom—when I happened to glance outside my front window. The one that faces the street. I saw a man running from Mr. Davis's back yard. His feet seemed—I don't know—encumbered, I guess you'd say. When he stopped on the street, he removed his shoes and I could see that they had these large soles. They were square and I thought how odd that was. Anyway, he pulled those weird shoes off and then he removed some kind of cap. I don't know what it was, but it seemed like he had to tug the thing to get it off. Then he ran down the street toward the corner carrying a large bag of some kind where he'd put the weird shoes and the cap. He passed under a street lamp and I could see he had what looked like shaggy blonde hair. I remember because it looked like the hair on the surfers when I was young living in L.A."

Pantera held his breath as he listened to the woman sounding as though she was ranting this as quickly as possible to get off the phone.

This explained the odd footprints, as well as why there seemed to be no hair fibers that didn't belong to Mr. Davis in the house. Most people didn't realize the rate that hair fell from the scalp, but the average number of hairs lost in a day was between fifty and a hundred.

"Thank you, Ms—" He paused, waiting for a name.

"Do I have to give my name? I don't want any trouble from the police or the young man who killed Mr. Davis."

"He was young?" Pantera asked, forgetting about the caller's name in his effort to get more details from her about what she'd seen.

"Well, I didn't see his face, but he looked like he

121

was in good shape. You know, like maybe he worked out or something. And like I said, he reminded me of the surfers when I was a teenager in California. He definitely looked like a fast runner. He was down the street in no time."

"He wasn't facing your window when he removed the shoes and cap?"

"Well, he was, but he wasn't under a street lamp then. It was dark."

"What about the bag? Did you see it clearly? Can you tell me how big it was?"

"Not that big, really. It looked like a large gym bag."

"Okay, thank you. I understand not wanting to give your name, but we can keep that information confidential to avoid having you in the paper."

"What about if he goes to trial? Won't I have to testify?"

"It's possible, but to be quite honest, ma'am, we can figure out who you are based on what you've told me because of where you live."

"Oh, I didn't think of that," she said, sounding disappointed.

"We can keep your identity out of the press. They don't need to know anything about this, and if you testify, it will help put him where he can't bother you."

"Okay," she said, though she still sounded doubtful. "I guess I should go ahead and tell you my name is Melinda Jackson. I live across the street from where Mr. Davis lives. Or lived." She gave Pantera her address.

"Thank you, Ms. Jackson. We'll be in touch."

After hanging up, he made a note to go see Ms. Jackson to follow-up on the interview. He wanted to see if, given time, she remembered anything else about that night.

Harry came into the squad room from the bathroom and saw Pantera scribbling notes.

"What's up?"

"Got a call from one of Mr. Davis's neighbors. A Melinda Jackson who lives across the street. She saw something that night that she didn't tell the officer who stopped by to question her."

"What did she see?"

Pantera explained what he'd learned from Ms. Jackson, and Harry said, "So that's what made the shoe imprints? What do you think he had on the soles?"

"Wood maybe? Cardboard? Who knows? But it's something. All we have to do is find a guy who looks like a surfer with shaggy blonde hair and big square pieces of something glued to the bottoms of his shoes."

"And who wears snug-fitting caps," Harry offered with a smile.

"I'm going to head over to Davis's home and look around some," Pantera said. "You wanna tag along?"

"We're both on this case, right?"

"You bet."

"Then let's go."

Harry knew that Pantera liked to visit a crime scene after it was processed by the scene techs. When the crime involved murder in a house, he wanted to spend an hour or more in the home, just looking around and getting what he called "a feel" for the victim who'd lived there.

When they had parked in the driveway of Davis's home, Harry walked up to the front door, but Pantera walked around to the back.

"Where you going?" Harry called after him.

"To where the killer entered and exited the house."

Harry followed and when they arrived at the back door, Pantera leaned down and inspected the door.

"Crime scene guys already determined he picked the lock," Harry said.

"Yeah, I know, but that takes time. Not to mention Davis was maybe twenty feet from the back door but heard nothing."

"Maybe he'd gone to sleep."

"Awfully fortuitous for the killer, don't you think, to have his victim happen to fall asleep watching TV the night he plans to kill him."

"What if the TV was turned up loud?"

"Again, possible, but awfully fortuitous."

"I guess you're right."

"And why this guy? Robbery wasn't a motive, just the killing. We need to find whoever had it in for this guy enough to go to such lengths to kill him. I mean, the shoes, the cap? This killer took pains not to be caught. I'm wondering if this might be a professional hit."

"Tony, how do you know robbery wasn't the motive? The wallet had no cash in it, but he might not carry cash."

"Did you see the guy's watch?"

"Yeah. Was it special?"

"It was a Montblanc. The bottom end of the sale price is around two grand. They can easily go as high as two or three hundred."

"Grand?"

"Yep."

"Who would spend that much for a watch?"

"The people who can afford them. It's a status symbol."

"How do you know so much about watches?"

"My dad owns a Montblanc. Paid over fifty grand for his."

"Damn. Your dad rich or something?"

"Or something. My parents saw the computer age

coming. They invested their life savings in Microsoft stock when it went public back in 1986."

"Wow. How much is that worth today?"

"Let's just say they don't have any money worries."

"So your family's rich? Why you breaking your back doing this?"

Pantera looked at Harry as if he'd asked why rocks were hard. "Long story. Maybe I'll tell it to you one day."

Harry could see pain behind the statement and dropped the subject.

"So where does a public school administrator get enough jack to buy such an expensive watch?"

"Beats me, but that's not what's important. What is important is that our perp didn't bother to take it. *Ergo*, robbery wasn't the motive. Murder was."

"I didn't know the watch was that expensive. Maybe our killer didn't either."

"Maybe, but you ever see anyone who would break into a house to rob it and leave what at least appeared to be a gold watch behind?"

"Nope."

"Well, then. There you go. Simple."

Walking back around to the front door, Pantera spun the numbers on a lockbox on the doorknob that held a key for entry. It was the same kind of box realtors used to hold the keys to houses for sale so they could be shown by any realtor.

Opening the door, they entered the house.

Fingerprint dust covered most of the surfaces in the kitchen and living room. There were a few places in the bathroom and bedrooms that had been dusted, but the CSI team felt their best bet was in the two rooms the killer had obviously been in, so they'd not spent a lot of time in the rest of the house searching for clues, especially fingerprints. It was maddening that they hadn't found any prints other than Grant Davis's.

Harry began looking around the living room while Pantera moved toward the back rooms of the house.

"There's not much chance he was back there, Tony."

"Getting the vibe," Pantera answered.

After fifteen minutes, Harry heard Pantera call from the back of the house, "Hey, Harry, come look at this."

As he walked toward the back, he said, "Where are you?"

"In the bedroom."

When Harry entered, Pantera was squatting down at the far side of the room near the foot of the bed.

Harry joined him and asked, "What is it?"

"That's what I'd like to know." Pantera pointed at where the carpet met the baseboard. Harry could see a very small amount of white dust there.

"What is that? Cocaine?"

"You ever hear of anyone who uses coke who's that careless with it?"

"No."

"Neither have I." Pantera licked the end of a finger and stabbed it into the dust. "It looks like chalk or something."

"How did it get here?"

Pantera looked up to see where it might have fallen from. "Maybe from there," he said, pointing at a central heat and air vent above where they stood. The vent was situated in the wall a few inches from the ceiling.

"I saw some wooden chairs in the kitchen. Would you bring me one?" Pantera asked.

Moments later, Pantera stood on the chair and peered into the vent. "We need to find out if he had some duct work done recently," Pantera said. "Get a sample of that dust. I'm willing to bet its gypsum or something used in drywall."

Harry went outside and retrieved a small evidence bag from Pantera's car and scooped some of the dust into the bag. He sealed it before labeling the details of where and when they'd found the dust, including the time, and signing along the adhesive strip.

Pantera noticed one of the screws holding the vent in place was loose. He used his fingers to unscrew it and saw a tiny amount of the powder cascade from the vent.

"What are you thinking?" Harry asked. "Surveillance camera?"

"That's exactly what I'm thinking," Pantera said. He stretched to where he could look at the room from the vantage point of the vent and saw that a camera inside could be easily aimed at the door to the bedroom. A wide-angle lens could include the far half of the bed and dresser as well.

Harry looked down where the dust had fallen when Pantera had unwound the screw a bit. "Tony, this dust fell away from the wall, though. Hardly any landed near the baseboard."

"Did any land near it?"

"Maybe. I don't know."

Pantera proceeded to remove the vent. Much more dust drifted to the floor, landing next to the baseboard and up to about four inches from it.

"Maybe the guy's dust-buster missed a spot," Harry said.

"Maybe. Or Davis vacuumed and didn't notice the powder." This was possible since the house appeared to have been kept amazingly clean.

Pantera looked around for more evidence that a camera had been placed in the vent, but found none.

"It's a start," he said.

As they left the house, Pantera glanced over at the house where Melinda Jackson lived. He noticed a woman peering out the front window at them, a look of intense curiosity on her face.

Pantera waved at her, and she pulled the curtain closed. He walked over to her front door and rang the bell. When she opened the door, he said, "Good day. You must be Ms. Jackson."

"Yes."

"I'm Detective Pantera. We spoke on the phone earlier today."

Sudden relief took over her suspicious features, as if a long-lost cousin had come to visit.

"Detective! I'm so glad it was you! I thought I might have to call you again and tell you someone was snooping around at Mr. Davis's house. You gave me a scare!"

"Sorry to frighten you, Ms. Jackson." Indicating Harry with a small wave of his hand, he added, "This is my partner, Detective Harry Overmeyer. You might see one or the other of us at the scene of the crime. If you do, just ignore us. We're just doing our jobs."

"I will," she said with enthusiasm, as if she were being invited to be a part of the investigative team.

As they drove off, Harry said, "The woman you said was reluctant now appears the opposite."

Pantera shrugged. "I guess I have a way with women."

They drove back to the precinct and logged the powder into the lab. Pantera asked for a rush job on it. "We just need to know what it is. I doubt seriously that's it's drugs."

"I can have a prelim for you tomorrow," the tech said.

"Thanks!" Pantera said.

Looking at Harry, he said, "It's quittin' time. You have time to stop at The Watering Hole for a beer? I want to check on how Pete's doing."

"Sure," Harry said. "Let me call Ashley to let her know I'll be a little late."

They left the precinct in separate cars and drove to The Watering Hole.

SEVENTEEN

B efore they entered the bar, Pantera stopped Harry and said, "When Pete was shot, I found out his last name, and I swear I've heard it before.

"What is it?"

"Pete Bray."

"Are you kidding?"

"No. That's his name."

"There was a story about ten, twelve years ago. A guy named Pete Bray saved a family from a fire."

Pantera suddenly remembered the story. "Wait, the family of four that the guy went in and pulled to safety?"

"Yeah. Do you think he's the same Pete Bray?"

"We can ask him."

"If he is, we've been drinking with a real, live hero. There was a big write-up in the news, even got picked up by the *Post*," Harry said, referring to the *Washington Post*. "He was a neighbor from a few houses down the block.

"As I recall, there was one member of the family that didn't survive."

Harry thought for a minute. "Yeah, a kid about seven. He wouldn't go with the guy because he was scared. When the guy went to pick the kid up, the ceiling fell in on them. The guy was hurt and survived, but the kid didn't make it."

They stepped in and saw Pete sitting in his usual spot at the bar. Dean was behind the bar, in what Pantera realized was his usual spot.

"Hey, Dean-o! How they hanging?" Harry said.

"Hey! It's a couple of Richmond's finest!"

"I notice you never say finest what," Pantera said, and Dean laughed.

"Catchin' many crooks?" Pete asked.

"Not as many as I would like," Pantera said, "but I think I have a question for you."

"What is it?"

"Are you the same Pete Bray that saved that family in the fire?"

Pete's smile disappeared instantly, his entire demeanor shifting. Pantera also noticed a slight change in Dean's posture.

"No," Pete said. "That wasn't me."

It was an obvious lie, and Pantera glanced at Dean, who just shook his head slightly, indicating it was a subject not to be discussed, at least not with Pete in the room, which he always was unless he went to the bathroom.

"Sorry. I was just wondering," Pantera said.

Pete exchanged a glance with Dean and returned to his beer.

As much to change the subject as anything else, Dean said, "So, what'll it be today, guys? The usual?"

Both detectives responded that would be fine and sat silently at the bar, nursing their drinks. The mood had switched from jovial to awkward in the span of a few seconds. Pantera wanted to apologize but knew he couldn't. An apology would mean he didn't believe Pete, who knew he wasn't believed, but would be determined to continue the charade.

When a couple who'd been seated in a booth paid and left, Pete said, "Sorry, Tony. You deserve better. Yeah, I'm the same guy, but I figure you know that. I just don't like to talk about it."

Pete took a swig of his beer and said, "I just keep

131

seeing that little kid, cowering in the corner, flames everywhere, smoke building up at the ceiling. I could see he wanted to come to me, but he was scared out of his mind. He has just started to take a step toward me when the roof caved in on us. I was hit by a beam and found myself on the floor. My back got burned pretty bad. I couldn't see the kid at all. He was swallowed in the flames. I knew I couldn't save him and wasn't sure the kid would want me to if I could. Burn treatments are as painful as the flames themselves. Maybe more."

"I'm so sorry, Pete. If I'd known you didn't want to talk about it, I'd have kept my mouth shut," Pantera said.

"Wasn't your fault. You don't know what I saw—what I see damn near every day since. Believe me, asking me if I'm that Pete Bray ain't the worst thing anyone said to me about it." He paused for a second. When neither Pantera nor Harry asked what that was, he told them anyway.

"A woman came up to me at this big memorial service for the kid. I didn't want to attend, but I figured it was the least I could do. Lots of politicians were there for the photo ops. Certainly not to mourn the kid or find out about the faulty heating system a big corporation was allowed to manufacture that killed a dozen more people before it was finally dealt with." He took another swig. "Anyway, this woman, who I didn't know from shit, told me, 'it was God's will and so God must have more for you to do and it must have been the kid's time to be with God.' That's what she said, verbatim. I remember it like it was ten seconds ago. Anyway, I ain't believed in God since. I want no part of a God that would take a little boy that way. If that were true—if God was ready for the boy to, as they put it, 'come home,' why not make it something less painful, less traumatic for those left behind? Why not just have the kid playing ball and drop dead suddenly from a heart attack?" He sipped. "No, I can't believe in a God that would take a child that way.'

Pantera suddenly didn't want his drink, or dinner either for that matter. He liked Pete a lot. He was a good man with a big heart, but it was a heart that had been broken many times, certainly more than Pantera knew, but that was the way it was with most people. He'd learned not that long ago that Pete had had a daughter who died of a drug overdose after becoming a prostitute. Now, there was this. It occurred to Pantera that some people were like tragedy magnets, modern-day Biblical Jobs who were visited with painful event after painful event. But Pete wasn't like Job in one way. He'd turned his back on God and religion.

When Pantera and Harry finished their drinks, they paid their tab and stood to leave. Pantera walked over to Pete, put his hand on his shoulder, and said, "Love ya, buddy." Turning, he walked out, followed by Harry.

They exchanged a look and drove off in their separate directions without saying another word.

The next morning, neither of them mentioned the stop at The Watering Hole the evening before. An email from the lab was waiting in Pantera's inbox.

The material they'd found was dihydrous calcium sulfate, otherwise known as gypsum, the light-density rock found in drywall. Pantera shared this news with Harry, who whistled. "Seems we have a clue," Harry said.

After calling over a dozen heating and air conditioning contractors in the area closest to Davis's home, he found none that had performed any work at Davis's address. He then phoned Melinda Jackson, who told him she'd not noticed any work trucks or vans at Davis's house, ever.

He then called one of the companies he'd spoken to and asked if recent duct work was detectable.

"Most likely, yeah," the man on the phone said. "It's like anything. New always looks better than old."

"Would you be willing to take a look at some ductwork and let me know if it had been worked on recently?"

"I can look at it," the man said, "but I ain't promising anything. If it hasn't been replaced but just had some minor work done, it might not show, but I can't imagine anyone calling someone like me for a little job. Too expensive and too easy to do it yourself. I don't know of anyone who'd take on a small job that didn't involve at least some replacement or something. Not worth our time."

This explained a lot to Pantera when it came to trying to find contractors willing to take on a small job. Even ones that advertised "no job too large or too small" had their limits, apparently.

Pantera arranged to meet the man at Davis's house that afternoon after the guy left work for the day. He said he would do it out of civic duty since it was a police matter.

"I can be there around 5:45. That good for you?" the man asked.

"Sounds fine," Pantera answered.

Pantera was surprised when the man was on time. He'd figured he'd have to wait for a while.

It took the man ten minutes to take a look at the vent and ductwork in the bedroom. When he was done, he looked at Pantera and said, "That ain't been worked on in a while. Some of the ductwork needs to be replaced. It's been bent where it meets the wall on the inside. Looks like someone took pliers to it."

"Thank you for your help. Are you sure you don't

want to bill the city for your time?"

"Nah," the man said. "I did find one thing that was kinda weird, though."

"What's that?"

"This." He held out a small piece of wire that had been snipped from a length of it. The piece was no more than an eighth of an inch long. About a millimeter of thin, braided copper stuck out from one end.

Pantera thought he knew what had happened now. The killer had made his way into Davis's home prior to the killing and installed cameras to watch Davis for reasons only the killer knew. He must have removed the cameras after killing Davis. He could have had the equipment in the bag he'd been carrying that Ms. Jackson had seen. Pantera figured the snippet of wire was more of an oversight when he'd installed the cameras in the first place.

Pantera knew enough about internet cameras that there had to be something to capture the digital images sent out by the camera in order to send them out to a receiver to be viewed. A wire would have to connect to the device that would send the images out into the internet.

Pantera checked the floor beneath the vent in the living room. After moving the cumbersome sofa to see the floor beneath the vent, he found a tiny amount of gypsum dust. He doubted even the crime scene techs had noticed since it was well away from where the body had been found and behind the sofa. There had been a camera there, too. He took one of the kitchen chairs and stood upon it, trying to peer into the ductwork behind the vent. It was too dark to see anything, but he did notice that one edge of the ductwork had been bent along the top of the duct. Pantera wondered if this was part of something the perp did when installing the cameras.

Finding the entrance to the attic, he managed to climb up into the chamber. There, he noticed that dust had been disturbed recently, showing a trail that led to an area next to a small vent that led to the outside of the house. Taking out his phone, he snapped pictures of the trail, using his flash to improve clarity.

Sweating from the heat in the cramped space, he crawled over to where the trail led. Next to the vent, he found small patches where the dust had been disturbed. Something had been set there recently, leaving behind small imprints in the dust that had settled on the floor of the attic over the years. He doubted there were any fingerprints there. This guy was smart enough to wear gloves.

He took more pictures of the imprints in the dust. He couldn't wait to share these with Harry to get his take on what had happened. He was certain Harry would agree with his assessment that the killer had planted cameras and a device for sending the pictures to the cloud and had watched his victim for at least several days before coming in to kill him.

This was further proof that Davis was not a random victim. Whoever had killed him had planned it meticulously, leaving behind clues he probably thought nobody would ever find. After all, who went into an attic to investigate a murder that happened in the home's living room?

Someone who finds gypsum dust below an air vent, Pantera thought and smiled.

EIGHTEEN

Blanton watched Roxanne as she prepared for work. He planned to go by and get the clothes she'd left on the table in the laundry room of the house. He didn't want any suspicions to grow from Wendy's disappearance.

He wanted to play with Roxanne's perceptions some more. Torture her emotionally. The more rattled she was, the easier prey she would be. People who had a lot on their minds were more easily manipulated, failing to think clearly through a situation.

After she left, he drove to Roxanne's and let himself in the back door with the key he'd had made. Gathering the laundry and a few other items that belonged to Wendy, he left. He planned to watch her for at least a few more days before killing her. He would have planned to rape her too, but that would leave DNA behind.

He knew she'd probably called the police about the message left on her phone. He'd whispered the message to avoid having his voice pattern available. He was equally certain she had told the police his name, but a search would reveal nothing of him. He'd leased his home under another name, using a forged driver's license as identification. His lease was under the name of Charles Whitman.

The name was famous, in a way. Charles Whitman had killed fourteen people and wounded another thirty-one at the University of Texas in 1966. He'd committed his crime from the top of the university's clock tower, where he'd had a 360-degree view of the campus. The shootings had made national news at the time, but the name, a common one, was mostly forgotten. But not by Blanton. He'd been fascinated with the former Marine since writing a report on mass killings when he was in high school.

Once he'd decided to get his revenge on Davis, he'd known he would need another identity, so he'd settled on the name of a man he'd admired so much.

He took Wendy's clothes and other belongings to the dump and went home. He kept only a pair of Wendy's panties and a locket she'd had that had been taped to a note from Roxanne. Apparently, the locket had been a gift from Roxanne to celebrate their relationship. The note expressed how much she loved Wendy and how she'd never felt that way about a man. It had concluded with a plea for Wendy to return to her.

He decided to burn the note and was about to do that when another idea struck him. He smiled at the thought of it and went to retrieve his new prepaid phone from his bedroom. With prepaids, there was no contract, and this number would be registered to another of his aliases with an address that didn't even exist.

Setting the phone to record, he took a long-nozzled lighter and, ensuring his hand couldn't be seen in the picture, started his phone video. With the note set so she could see it was the one she left with the locket, he lit the paper and recorded it as it burned.

When he had finished, he watched the video to make sure nothing in the video could lead back to him and sent it to her in a message with the caption, "My note to you, from Wendy."

He watched Roxanne at home on his computer as she opened the file and saw the love letter being burned. If he'd been capable of pity, he would have felt it for her then. She was certainly pitiable. She'd poured her heart out to her female lover and was forced to watch the utter rejection.

"How does it feel to be rejected, Roxanne?" Blanton said to the image on the computer screen.

Blanton continued watching as she prepared for bed. When she turned off the light, he sat back, figuring he would need to kill Roxanne soon. She might decide to do the job for him, and that would steal the pleasure of seeing her eyes when she discovered he was the cruel one all along, not Wendy.

Leaning forward again, he switched the feed to watch Pantera at home. After a few minutes of watching him mostly wandering around his house before sitting down to the piano to play, he shut the computer down. Still, he admired Pantera's musical ability. It wasn't good enough to record, but it wasn't bad.

Roxanne lay in bed, staring up into the dark room. Her misery was suffocating her, making even breathing difficult.

She did her best to discover what had gone wrong between her and Wendy. They'd been fine the last time they'd seen each other. Wendy had not shown any indication she was about to leave her. She wasn't the type of person who made rash decisions either. In fact, Roxanne would kid her because she would overthink problems and have difficulty reaching a decision on how to handle them.

This just wasn't like her, and no matter how hard she thought about the days leading up to Wendy's disappearance, she could not make those memories mesh with Wendy's behavior now.

Not only that, but Wendy would also never leave a job without informing her boss she was quitting.

It seemed as if Wendy's personality had completely

changed, as if she'd become a different person in the course of a single day. It made no sense.

As she lay there, thinking about the video she'd watched, something kept nagging at her about it. It wasn't anything she could pinpoint exactly, but something was wrong with the video. There was—she didn't know—a mistake or something. An image that didn't make sense. It was as if—.

Sitting up, she switched on her bedside light. Taking out her phone, she ran the video once more, watching it this time to see if she could tell what didn't make sense. At first, she noticed that the hands of whoever was burning the letter were never in the picture. It almost seemed on purpose. As the video played, she concentrated on the surrounding images.

When she saw it, she froze. As with Wendy's sudden decision to leave, this made no sense either.

A number of beer cans were on a table in the background, perhaps a dozen in all. She wasn't sure, but they looked like Budweiser cans. Wendy hated alcoholic beverages of any kind. Her parents were, as she had put it, hopeless drunks. Her father would often become abusive when he was drinking. The slightest incident could send him into a rage. She had hinted he'd done other things while drunk as well that she didn't want to talk about, and Roxanne suspected the worst. Wendy swore she would never date anyone, male or female, who drank. She avoided drinkers as if they had a terrible disease that could be spread with casual contact. She could be wild, but that wild person was more of a character she played. Wendy might have changed, but she hadn't changed that much.

Adding it all up—the lack of hands in the video, the behaviors that just did not fit Wendy's personality, the many beer cans on the table—it became obvious to

Roxanne that this wasn't Wendy at all. With that came the thought that if it wasn't Wendy, who was it? And why was this video sent from another number and not Wendy's? The other texts she'd received the night Wendy disappeared were from her phone. This message was from someone else's. None of this made sense.

Her heart began slamming into her ribcage. With all the other inconsistencies, she wondered if the worst had happened. Had Wendy been kidnapped? Killed? Was someone now playing cruel games with her? Who? The more she considered everything together, the more convinced she was that Wendy had been kidnapped.

But why use Wendy to torment her? Who would do such a—

With sudden realization, she knew the answer to her questions. Blanton had somehow kidnapped Wendy. The timing of his calls and Wendy's disappearance were too coincidental. It was the only way any of this made sense, though it was a crazy sort of sense.

She couldn't let him know that she knew, however. That might send him further over the edge and serve to change his stalking to an outright physical attack. He might even kidnap her, too.

As tears sprang to her eyes, she began praying that Wendy was alive.

Her hands trembling, she opened her contacts and pressed the button to call Wendy. She wondered why she hadn't done this sooner.

Her call went to directly to voicemail. Roxanne wondered if Wendy would ever get a message from her, but she left one anyway as if she did not suspect Wendy had been taken.

"Wendy, call me. Please?! At least talk to me, okay?" She disconnected the call and lay back, staring again into the dark room.

NINETEEN

R oxanne checked the notes she'd made on her phone after talking to the detective and found his name and number, but the name seemed off from what she remembered. Her screen read, "Pandora," and she knew that wasn't right. Autocorrect had made the change, but she hoped it was close enough to the detective's name that the person who answered would be able to connect her to him.

When the call was answered, she said, "I need to speak to a detective there that I spoke to the other day. His name is something like Pandora."

"Detective Pantera?" the woman asked.

"Yes, that's it. Can I speak to him?"

"He's off duty right now. Would you like to speak to another detective?"

Roxanne considered this and decided one was as good as another.

"Sure."

After a moment, a man was on the line.

"Detective Crosswell."

"Hi, my name's Roxanne Beard. I called the other day and spoke to a Detective Pantera about a guy who's stalking me." She didn't mention how the detective had told her Blanton's actions didn't rise to the level of stalking.

"Yes?" The detective asked to prompt more information.

"Well, I think he may have kidnapped my roommate."

"You think he has, or you know he has?"

"Well, I sorta know he has, but it's not like there's been some kind of ransom note or anything. I just know."

"What's this guy's name?"

"Blanton."

"Is that his first or last name?"

"His last. When we met, he told me nobody ever uses his first name."

"What's your roommate's name?"

"Wendy. Wendy Atwater."

Crosswell jotted this in his notes.

"How long has your roommate been gone?"

"Since Saturday."

"That's three days."

"I know," she said. To Roxanne, he sounded like disappearing for three days was a common thing, like everyone did that at least once a month.

"You're sure she hasn't gone off to shack up with some guy?"

"Even if she did, she wouldn't have shacked up with this guy. He drinks."

"And that's supposed to be a deterrent?"

"For Wendy it is. She doesn't like to be around people who drink."

"Maybe she changed her mind."

"She'd rip off a leg first."

"You sound rather sure of yourself."

"I am." She waited a second while the detective said nothing, then said, "Her parents were major alkies. She hated being around anyone who drank. And besides, she's not interested in guys."

"Okay, maybe she ran off with another woman." When this was met with silence, he asked, "So, what makes you think this guy Blanton is the one who

143

allegedly kidnapped your roommate?"

She told the detective about the video of the letter being burned, as well as the texts Wendy had sent.

"So you and your roommate are—shall we say—more than just roommates?"

She could hear the disdain. "Yes, but that shouldn't make any difference."

"Well, ma'am, I'm afraid it might. You see, we get a number of calls like yours when one person is jealous of a relationship their prior lover has with someone else. Maybe your roommate decided she prefers men after all. Maybe she just got tired of being with you. It's sad, I know, but it happens all the time. Of course, kidnapping is a bit of a harsh accusation in these matters, but people have made those accusations before. I'm sorry, but without more to go on, there's really nothing we can do. People leave their lovers every day. It's often hard to accept. Until you have more proof that something bad has happened to your roommate, we can't spend valuable manpower looking into this."

"But I know there's something wrong!"

"Was this guy a frequent visitor to your home?"

"No. He's never been inside before."

"You say your roommate texted you to tell you she was leaving. She knew enough about where you live to tell you exactly where to leave her stuff to be picked up, something her alleged kidnapper probably wouldn't know since he'd never been there."

"But—"

"I tell you what. Do you have the text she sent you telling you she'd left?"

"Yes."

"Would you read it to me?"

"Why?"

"Just want to check something."

She opened the text and read it to him.

"That sounds very particular. Does she use words like 'I got the boogie fever' often?"

"Yes."

"Well, then, there you go. How well did this guy who you say might have kidnapped her know your roommate?"

"I don't know that they'd ever met.," she said, knowing her complaint would go nowhere.

"Yet, he knew idiosyncratic phrases she used?"

"But—"

"Look. If someone gets a ransom demand, let us know. In the meantime, we can't do anything about this, okay? Now, you have a nice night," Detective Crosswell said and hung up.

Roxanne sat in the dark, steaming about the conversation. She had to admit that the detective's explanations were logical and even likely to him because he didn't know Wendy the way she did. The police would apparently need a dead body before doing anything.

She considered calling again when the detective she'd talked to before was there but realized he had only told her to get a restraining order, as if those really worked with people like Blanton, not to mention she didn't know his first name, which would be a problem in a restraining order. Pantera wouldn't be any different from the detective she'd just spoken to, so why bother?

She sat in the dark of the bedroom, sobbing tears of rage and immense sadness.

The next morning when Pantera arrived, Detective Crosswell stopped by his desk.

"I had a call last night from someone who talked to you about a stalker. She's a bit of a kook."

"Why did she call this time?"

"Same thing, I guess. Says she thinks this guy she told you about kidnapped her roommate, who was someone she was also sleeping with."

"And?"

"And nothin'. She's just convinced this guy kidnapped her lover because of a video where the allegedly kidnapped girl burned a love letter your kook had given her."

"That's it? Just a letter being burned?" Pantera could see where Crosswell was going with this. Sometimes overly suspicious people could be as time-consuming as people like Crazy Carl and their confessions to every crime in the city.

"Yeah, she says her roommate would never date a drinker, and she saw lots of beer cans on a table."

"She sounds rather desperate."

"Yeah," Crosswell said. "And for the life of me, I'll never understand how someone could have sex with someone of the same gender. It's creepy."

"Why do you think that?" Pantera asked, his hackles rising.

"It's just not right. God meant for men and women to have sex, not men and men or women and women. It's disgusting."

Looking at Crosswell, Pantera considered how this was the hatred his daughter would face all her life.

"People can't help whom they love, Crosswell. It's not like men and women who shouldn't be together don't fall in love. It's an emotion."

"It's about sex, Pantera. Nothin' but sex."

"You're wrong there."

"What? You decide you're gay?"

"People don't 'decide' they're gay. It's emotional, not just physical."

146

"Yeah, right. You sayin' they aren't having sex?"

"No, but you and your wife have sex, yet it's more than that, right?"

He snorted. "Sometimes, but it ain't the same."

"Again, that's where you're wrong. Gays and lesbians love their partners the same way heterosexuals love theirs."

"Why you so defensive about these pervs if you're not one of them?"

"I have my reasons for how I feel. That's all I'll say. To say more would betray a trust."

"You know someone like that?"

"Yes. And she's a wonderful human being who wouldn't hurt a soul. She's more righteous than a lot of the so-called 'righteous' people walking the streets every day."

"Not if she's a muff-muncher."

His anger boiled over, and Pantera punched Crosswell in the face. The two men rolled to the floor, doing their best to land punches. Other detectives had to separate them. Crosswell's nose was bleeding and bent, and Pantera figured he'd broken it. Pantera's cheek was swelling, and he knew he'd have a black eye later. Pantera was as surprised at his response as anyone.

Suddenly, Lt. Gariepy was storming out of his office. "What the hell's going on? You two got a beef?"

"Crosswell just said something that pissed me off," Pantera said, as if that explanation was enough.

"Both of you—in my office! Now!"

Pantera sauntered into Gariepy's office with Crosswell behind.

They sat in chairs facing Gariepy as the lieutenant sat with a huff. "Now, what's this all about?"

"I don't know," Crosswell said, his nose sounding plugged. "I just said something about gays and lesbians

147

that pissed Pantera off because he apparently knows one." He glared at Pantera and added, "Or is one."

Ignoring Crosswell's final remark, Gariepy looked at Pantera. "What do you have to say?"

"That he's right, at least until he said I might be gay."

"So you punched him?" Gariepy asked.

"Yes. And I'll do it again if he says something like he did."

"I feel like I'm a teacher breaking up a fight between third-graders," Gariepy said. "You both know better."

"Yeah, well," Pantera said. "He needs to keep his bigotry to himself."

"What exactly did you say?" Gariepy asked Crosswell.

"Pantera said something about how someone he knows who is a lesbian is righteous. I said she wasn't if she was a muff-muncher. That's when he sucker punched me."

Pantera listened while Crosswell talked, taking some satisfaction in the muffled sound coming from the man, as if he had a bad cold.

"Why would something like that get you that riled, Pantera? You've never been like that before."

Pantera figured he had to tell more, but not in front of Crosswell, who would have the news all over the squad room before five minutes had gone by. "I'd like to speak to you in private," Pantera said to Gariepy.

"Why?" Crosswell asked. "I'm the guy you hit, so I should be part of any discussions."

"Because I'm not revealing the identity of the person I know who's a lesbian in front of you. It's none of your damn business, but I think Lt. Gariepy needs to know. He'd understand more if he knew."

Gariepy looked at Crosswell. "You're dismissed," he said. Crosswell rose with a jerk and slammed the door as he left the room.

"Okay, what is it?" Gariepy asked.

"My daughter came out as a lesbian earlier this year," Pantera said.

"Really?"

"Yeah, really."

"It's not just a phase? Kids go through confusion sometimes, especially when it comes to sex."

"I don't think so. She's in love with a girl now. She says she's never been attracted to guys. She told her mother that even her earliest romantic thoughts about famous people were about women. To me, that says it's not a phase or just about sex. She says when she was seven, she had her first crush on a female singer. I forget who. So, it's not about sex. At seven, what does a kid know about sex if she's never been molested?"

"Well, I understand your anger, but it doesn't give you the right to go punching out your co-workers."

"I apologize for losing my temper."

"Apologize to Crosswell, not me."

"I will. But later, not now."

"Whatever. Just work it out between you, but no fists."

"Got it."

"And there will have to be consequences—beyond paying any medical costs he might have."

"Yeah. I know."

"I'll think about it and get back to you."

"Yeah, sure." Pantera stood, understanding this was the end of their talk. "Thanks for at least listening."

"No problem. How are you and Nancy handling it?"

"Well enough. She's our daughter. Mostly, I'm concerned with how she'll handle cretins like Crosswell

149

who use the Bible to justify hating an entire segment of the population."

"Yeah, well, steer clear of him and those like him. I don't need to have to bail you out of jail for a bar fight."

"Okay. I guess I have to learn how to deal with the cretins myself."

"Well said. Now, get to work."

Pantera left the room and felt the stares from the detectives in the squad room, including from Harry. He went over to his friend and said, "Can we go investigate something?"

"Sure. What?" Harry asked.

"Anything. I just need to get out of here."

They left the squad room and climbed into Harry's car. Pantera had wanted to drive his, but Harry refused. "Nope. You're too upset. I've seen you drive when you're like this, and your mind just isn't on what you're doing. Now, where to?"

"I could use some more coffee."

"Me too," Harry said and drove to a nearby diner.

When they were seated, Harry said, "So what was that all about?"

"He was saying some nasty stuff about lesbians."

Harry grinned. "And you're a lesbian? I hate to break it to you, Tony, but men who like women are called straight, not lesbians."

Pantera frowned at Harry, and Harry said, "Sorry. Go on."

"I shouldn't have to. Have you forgotten that I told you my older daughter, Andrea, came out to her mom and me a few months ago?"

"Oh, yeah, I forgot. It's not like I think about it the way you do. Now I understand the anger." The coffee arrived, and Harry said, "I'm sorry."

"Yeah. I don't care that she's a lesbian. I just worry

about guys like Crosswell and their evil twins, women like him, who can be a lot worse."

"You can't fight everyone, Tony. It's not as if you'll change their minds."

"I know, but it just pissed me off. I felt like he was calling my daughter a 'muff-muncher.' He's a shit."

"So, what do we do today?"

"We go back to some of the houses this creep robbed before dialing in on Davis."

"What for?"

"To check for gypsum dust along the baseboards."

"You think he might have set up his cameras in their places?"

"It's possible."

"And if he did, what will that tell us? We already have pretty good evidence it's the same guy."

"It'll mostly just add to what we know of his M.O. Plus, it will give us something to do without having to go back to the precinct right now."

"Okay. When do we get started?"

"As soon as I finish this cup and order another to go."

"Make that two to go," Harry said and downed what remained of his coffee.

That morning after Pantera left for work, Blanton entered the detective's house and removed the surveillance equipment from where he'd placed it behind several of the vents. He had enough now, so the cameras and such were no longer needed. Before replacing the vents, he left small gifts where his cameras had been, knowing that Pantera would eventually find them if he was observant enough. He also left behind some of the listening devices. He didn't need video anymore, but eavesdropping was always beneficial.

TWENTY

While Harry drove, Pantera used Harry's laptop to get the phone numbers to call the owners of the homes that had been burglarized. He was able to make an appointment to get inside each of the homes, but only one house was available before that afternoon, one owned by a well-to-do family with a housekeeper.

After being given the address, Harry said, "You realize this is likely a wild goose chase. It's been a while since the homes were broken into, and any gypsum dust has likely been vacuumed up."

"I get that, but since we have nothing else to go on right now, I think we at least need to give it a try. How would you feel if he left behind this tiny clue and it turned out he left his equipment there?"

"Like it wasn't a waste of time, but honestly, I think it will turn out to be just that."

"Anytime you can cross off something from the possibilities, it's not a waste of time."

"I agree we should look. I just don't think it will pan out."

When they arrived, they were greeted by a housekeeper that they had met when they first investigated the break-in. Her name was Ms. Elias, a short, stocky woman in her fifties. She had been working for the owners for a little over seven years.

"Hello, Detectives!" she said, apparently happy they had stopped by. "Mr. Lovelace called and said you'd be stopping by. What can I do for you?"

"We'd just like to look around one more time. It's

possible there could be evidence we missed before."

"Oh? Like what?"

"We believe the person who burgled this house is involved in another case. He left behind some telltale clues, hard to notice, and we hoped we might be able to look around to see if there are any similar clues here."

"What kind of clues?"

"We'd rather not say," Pantera said.

"Heavens! I wouldn't tell anyone."

"I know, Ms. Elias, but it's still investigative policy not to share such information until it becomes necessary."

"Well, okay." She looked at Harry as if seeing him for the first time.

"I'm sorry. I've forgotten your name," she said, frowning.

"I'm Detective Harry Overmeyer."

"Oh, yes, of course." She said to Pantera, "Will you need me to help you look?"

"That won't be necessary, ma'am," Pantera answered. "You just go about your work, and we'll let you know when we're finished. It shouldn't take long, maybe ten or fifteen minutes."

"Okay, but if you need anything, I'll be in the kitchen." She paused. "Unless you don't want me in there in case I destroy some evidence without realizing it."

Pantera chuckled. "No, ma'am. Wherever you need to be is fine."

She left them and Harry said, "Okay, there's a housekeeper here. It's a good thing you didn't tell her we were looking for gypsum dust on the floors. She might have become upset, claiming you were accusing her of doing a shoddy job."

"Nonsense."

153

"It also raises the odds that we won't find anything. She looks pretty thorough to me."

"I agree. This place is spotless," Pantera said before adding, "but a lot of people ignore the area right next to a wall, especially if it's behind a piece of furniture."

"Where do you want to start?"

"You take the downstairs, and I'll take the up."

"Okay. See you in a few," Harry said, and started off for the back of the house, planning to go room to room, checking the baseboards beneath the vents.

Pantera did likewise upstairs. Twenty minutes later, the two detectives met in the living room.

"No dust upstairs," Pantera said.

"Ditto for downstairs."

Pantera stepped into the kitchen, where Ms. Elias had just begun mopping the floor.

"Excuse, me. Ms. Elias?"

She stopped and turned to him. "Yes?"

"Do you do all the cleaning of the house?"

"Yes. Why?"

"Have you vacuumed all the floors since the break-in?"

"Of course. Do you think I would let such an important job go?" Her face showed that to her, doing such a thing was tantamount to purposely walking through the house with mud caked on her shoes.

"No, ma'am. I was just wondering. Do you recall seeing any white dust along the baseboards?"

"White dust? Like drugs?"

"No, ma'am. More like a chalky dust used in construction."

She thought for a moment before saying, "No. I think I would have noticed that."

Pantera smiled. "Yes, ma'am, I do believe you would have."

154

"Is there anything else?"

"No, ma'am. We can let ourselves out."

"It was nice to see you both again," she said.

By the end of the day, they'd found no gypsum dust in any of the homes. As they strode into the squad room, Harry said, "Told you we wouldn't find anything."

"Okay," Pantera said. "Let's assume we didn't search the houses. Once I mentioned that we needed to do that, would it have gnawed at you if we hadn't?"

Harry considered. "Yeah, I guess it would."

"Then we managed to give ourselves peace of mind."

"Point taken," Harry said. "So, what next?"

"I guess we wait until something else occurs to us that we missed."

"Lucky us," Harry said. As he started out of the room, he received a text. Glancing at it, he said, "You want to come for dinner Friday? Lisa's coming into town."

Pantera thought about it and said, "I'll have to let you know."

"Tony, Ashley's not the one who asked you to be there. Me either."

Pantera paused for a moment before saying, "Lisa did?"

Harry nodded. "You turn down the invite, it's like saying 'thanks for the fun, but I'm not interested.' Not good."

"What makes you think I am interested?"

"Maybe it's the gleam in your eye when I told you just now that Lisa asked us to invite you."

Pantera glanced around the room as if to verify nobody was listening to their conversation and sighed. "Look, Harry. Yeah, she's a wonderful lady. The interest is definitely there, but I'm not sure if it's just lust or a

Charles Tabb

real caring. Besides, frankly, I'm still carrying a bit of a torch for my ex."

"Nancy?"

"Yeah."

Harry pursed his lips and blew air out in exasperation. "You mean the one that's happily married to the guy in Charlottesville?"

Pantera sighed again. "Yeah. That one. Do I have another ex-wife?"

"Not that I know of." Harry sat in the chair beside Pantera's desk and leaned forward. "Tony, you gotta move on, man. That ship has sailed. Hell, it's half way around the world by now."

"Yeah, I know."

"And the best way to move on is to find someone else. Weren't you dating Detective Hamilton at one time?" Harry asked, referring to Olivia Hamilton, whom Pantera had gone out with twice before realizing he wasn't ready to date yet.

"We went out twice, Harry. I'd not call that 'dating.' I'd call it sticking my toes in the water."

"Can I ask you a personal question?"

"You can ask whatever you want, but I don't have to answer."

"Fair enough. Did you two have sex?"

"No."

"But you slept with Lisa, right?"

"Yeah. You know that already."

"Then maybe you are ready to move on, but you're afraid to."

Pantera's jaw set. "I'm not afraid of anything."

"Except acknowledging that Nancy has moved on but you haven't."

They stared at each other, neither blinking. Pantera was thinking about Harry's accusation and knew he was

156

right, but he wasn't ready to admit it yet, at least not to Harry.

Harry was waiting for a response.

"Tell Ashley you didn't get the text until you left. I'll give you my answer tomorrow," Pantera said.

Harry leaned back. "Fair enough, but I'm not going to lie to her. I'll tell her you need to wait until tomorrow to let me know. I just won't tell her why. She'll just think you might have other plans but aren't sure."

"Fair enough," Pantera said.

After Harry left, Pantera sat back and thought about his relationships. Harry was right. He needed to move on from Nancy. She was married and happy. He could see the love she had for Phil, her husband, in the way she looked at him. It was much like the way she looked at Pantera when she was still in love with him. Phil was a good stepfather to his daughters, and though they weren't friends, Pantera liked the man.

He pictured the conversation if he decided to call Nancy to tell her how he felt. He wondered if she would laugh at first, as if he might be joking. Then he considered how embarrassing the rest of the conversation would be for both of them. She didn't love him anymore, and he needed to move on. Harry was right. The best way to do that was to see if he could become interested in another woman. That's why illicit affairs often turned into divorce even if the affair was never discovered. Love for one person replaced the love for another.

Pantera wondered if love was really that simple, like a game of five-card draw where unwanted cards were replaced with others. Sometimes those cards were better than the first ones; sometimes they weren't.

He sighed as he stood to go home, figuring life was a gamble in any number of ways.

He drove by The Watering Hole and had a drink before going home. After all, when a guy was troubled and didn't want a therapist, who better to spill his guts to than his bartender?

When he arrived, he was more than a little shocked that Pete wasn't there. He'd never stopped by to find Pete was absent. Pete's favorite line regarding whether or not he was at the bar was, "I'm breathin', ain't I?"

"Where's Pete?" Pantera asked.

"You're not gonna believe this," said Dean. "He's on a date."

Pantera's jaw dropped. "You're right. I don't believe it."

"Yep. There's a neighbor of his, a widow. She asked him over for dinner, and after months of hemming and hawing, he accepted."

"Months?"

"Yeah. She's been needling him to come over, but he was, shall we say, reluctant."

"Why?"

"Scared of a change, I guess. She's a nice lady. I've met her."

"Why would he be afraid? If she's a nice lady, he should—" He froze in mid-sentence.

Dean looked at Pantera. "Tony? You okay?"

Pantera smiled. "Yeah. I just figured out something."

"What?"

"That I'm stupid."

"Come on. You're not stupid. You're one of the smartest guys I know."

"Stupid comes in categories. Take math for instance. Do you know anything about calculus?"

"No. Math was never my best subject in school."

"Mine either. So when it comes to calculus, we're

158

both stupid. That doesn't make us stupid about everything. We're just ignorant about calculus and other higher math."

Dean thought about it. "I guess you're right."

"And in some other things, I can be as stupid as they come. As stupid as Pete over the past few months while trying to decide whether to accept the invitation."

"Are you talking about you're stupid when it comes to love?"

"Yeah. That's exactly what I'm talking about."

Dean laughed. "Join the club, Tony. We're men, aren't we? That's sort of part of the deal. It's like God said, 'Okay, you get to stand up and pee, but when it comes to loving someone, you'll be as stupid as they come.' It's life as a man."

Pantera lifted his glass in salute. "Yeah, but that doesn't mean we can't learn."

After two drinks and more conversation, Pantera said goodbye and left. Climbing into his car, he pulled out his cell phone and texted Harry. *Tell Ashley—and Lisa—I'll be there Friday for dinner*.

A few minutes later, he received a reply with an irony Harry knew nothing about. *Smart man*.

TWENTY-ONE

By Friday morning, Roxanne had made a decision. If the police wouldn't do anything about this, she would. She was off work that day and spent the morning composing the text she intended to send to the number that had sent the video. She hoped at least to get Blanton, who she had convinced herself was behind this, to call her.

She took fifteen minutes composing the message, wanting to scare the person who had taken Wendy.

I know this isn't Wendy. She would have called me by now, and she doesn't date anyone who drinks. You see, I noticed the beer cans everywhere in that video you sent me. I've told the police she was kidnapped and who I think did it. So you might as well let her go and leave town—Blanton.

She hoped the fact she'd named him would do the trick. She knew it was possible Wendy really had left her, but she didn't think so. Wendy was the kind of person who would sit down and talk first, not just disappear.

She read the message a few more times and, her heart beating a strong rhythm against her ribs, she pressed send and burst into tears.

Eight miles away in his apartment, Blanton had his computer on. He was watching Roxanne. She was spending a long time composing a message on her phone. When she finished by sending the message and dissolving into the tears he was getting bored with, he knew she'd messaged Wendy or the prepaid.

When the text appeared, he felt his anger rise as he

read it. He knew he would have to take her soon. If she had really contacted the police, they would not be able to find him since he was known by various other names in Richmond, so he wasn't worried about that. Nobody there knew where he'd come from, regardless of which name they called him. He was a ghost.

Still, it was time to end this. He would enter her home that night and kill her. Then he would remove her body and dump Roxanne next to where he'd left her roommate and lover.

He had watched her every night since installing the surveillance camera and eavesdropping equipment. He had seen all he wanted to see. Now it was time.

Sitting at his dining table, he planned how he would end her life.

Pantera was off that Friday, a one-day suspension without pay for punching Crosswell. Crosswell had received only a warning since he'd not thrown the first punch. Pantera figured breaking the guy's nose was worth the day's pay and the co-pay on Crosswell's insurance. Hell, he'd have paid more to punch the asshole, so the loss of money didn't bother him.

That afternoon he went to a local clothing store and bought new slacks and a shirt for that evening. He figured if Lisa wanted him to be there, he should at least do his best to look nice.

He polished his shoes and showered, shaving for the second time that day before heading out. On the way, he stopped and bought a mid-priced bottle of pinot noir, arriving at the Overmeyers' house promptly at seven.

When he rang the doorbell, muffled conversation drifted from inside. The door opened, and Lisa stood there, smiling as she stood back to allow him to enter. For a moment, Pantera stood there, staring at her.

"Well, are you coming in, or should we come out?"

"I think I'll come in," he said.

"Hey, Tony!" Harry said. "You take your steak medium rare, right?"

"Of course."

Ashley stepped into the room from the kitchen. "You brought wine?" she asked.

"Yes. A pinot noir."

"Great. Should go well with the steak."

"Where are the boys?" Pantera asked. The Overmeyers had two sons in high school.

"Staying with friends," Harry said. "Have a seat. We'll eat soon. I just have to grill the steaks, and that won't take but about ten minutes."

They sat for a while, drinking some of the wine Lisa had brought, a cabernet sauvignon imported from Italy.

Conversation was brisk and animated, and dinner was delicious. Around midnight, Pantera stood and said, "Well, it's time I should be going."

"Leaving so soon?" Lisa asked.

Pantera smiled. "I don't want to overstay my welcome."

"Nonsense," Lisa said.

"No, really. I'm picking up my daughters tomorrow at their house in Charlottesville. I should be going."

"Mind if I walk you to your car?" Lisa asked.

"Not at all."

They strolled outside, and she leaned against his door, which prevented him from getting in along with keeping them close to each other. "I hope you enjoyed the evening and you're not rushing off because it was a bore," she said.

"No, I completely enjoyed myself. I really do have to pick up my daughters in the morning."

"Are they staying for the weekend?"

"Yes."

"Hmm. Seems I picked a bad time to come down from D.C. I was hoping you'd invite me to dinner at your place tomorrow night."

"I'd love to, but you understand why I can't."

"Yes. I do."

He leaned in and kissed her goodnight. The kiss lingered as their passion rose, but he leaned back before things went too far.

"I'll see you again?" he asked.

"Count on it."

Roxanne pulled herself from her car, feeling her legs wanting to cramp from standing all day at her register. Taking out her key, she opened the front door. Walking past the sofa table, she dropped her purse on it and walked toward her bedroom, switching on lights as she went. When she flicked the switch that lit her bedroom, she gasped.

Blanton stood only inches in front of her, holding one of her scarves. before she could scream, he wrapped the scarf around her throat and began pulling the ends, cutting off her ability to breathe.

Struggling against him, her hand went to her neck, trying in vain to pry her fingers beneath the material. He pulled tighter and she felt the material seeming to fold itself into her flesh. She wondered if he would end up crushing her windpipe. The sound of his breathing against her ear was all she could hear beyond her own pulse. As she lost consciousness, she did her best to scream at him, but no sound came as she crumpled to the floor.

Blanton stood over her for a moment before leaning down to check her pulse. She was still alive.

163

He had been removing the hidden equipment as he waited for her to arrive home. Some of the equipment lay on the bed, and he removed it before lifting her onto the mattress and using the scarf to tie one hand to the bedpost. Going to a drawer, he gathered other scarves and in minutes, he had her tightly cinched to the bed.

Several minutes later she woke and pulled against her restraints as the memory of how she came to be there flooded back.

He'd taped her mouth closed with duct tape, so she could only grunt at him as he stood over her.

Taking a sharp knife, he began cutting her clothes from her. He wore his swimmer's cap and other clothing to prevent particles from his body being found later and analyzed for DNA, and he intended to keep his outfit on. He would have his fun, though.

As he cut the clothing, he talked to her.

"I'm really sorry about your roommate. Wendy, right? Yeah. She had the bad fortune of coming home when I didn't expect her to. In fact, I had no idea you even had a roommate until she walked in and caught me installing the equipment that I've been using to watch you since that day. Sad, though, isn't it? If she'd been thirty minutes later, she'd be alive." He looked down at her. "And maybe you'd still be alive come morning."

He could see the panic rising in her, which pleased him. "Yes, she's dead. I'm the one who sent you those texts and burned your letter. But why did you have to notice the fucking beer cans? Or why did she have to be such a prude about people who drink?"

He watched her panic for a moment before continuing. "I guess it's good that you're the only person in the area who knows my real last name. It's funny, because if you knew any of the names I use here, I might have just fled instead of coming here to kill you. But you see, they'll never find me by knowing the name Blanton. How fortunate for me that I chose at the last second to use my real name with you to avoid having you find me if I decided I didn't want to see you again."

He had finished cutting away her clothes and saw her blush. "Oh, you don't need to be embarrassed. I've seen you naked plenty of times now. When you'd shower. When you'd get ready for bed. When you'd— well, you know what you've done when you were alone."

He loaded the remaining surveillance equipment into a box. "I'll be right back," he said, and carried the box out of the room. Ten minutes later, he returned.

"I pulled my car around to the side street. Nobody's stirring. It's practically an alley."

He opened a drawer in the bedside table and pulled out Roxanne's vibrator. "I'm sure you remember this," he said, smiling. "Too bad you'll never know how much better I am than this piece of plastic."

When he'd finished with her, he stepped into the bathroom and masturbated, flushing his semen when he was done.

Coming back into the room, he advanced on her, another scarf in his hands. Her panic rose again and she tried to squirm away, but he sat on her, ending her struggles.

Wrapping the scarf around her throat, he pulled with all his considerable strength. She struggled, but he knew it was fruitless. After a few minutes, he checked her pulse. She was dead.

He wrapped her and the torn clothes in the sheets and blanket that had covered the bed and carried her out the same way he'd done with Wendy, loading her into the trunk and driving away. It was late now, and he wasn't afraid of being seen.

He would take her straight to what he considered his personal dumping site and leave her there. Then he would drive home, shower, and wait for his next move to materialize.

I could get used to this, he thought.

TWENTY-TWO

When Roxanne did not show up for work that Monday, her first workday since Friday night, Bob Gilchrist, her manager for that shift, thought she might have forgotten her schedule. She'd forgotten before and he was ready to fire her when Sara Dodd, the head cashier, stepped into his office.

"Where's Roxanne?" she asked, having noticed she was a cashier short.

"Forgot again, I suppose."

Sara stood there, frowning. "She knew Friday evening when she left that she was scheduled."

"Oh?"

"Yes. She told me, 'See you Monday' when she left. It wouldn't be like her at all to know she was supposed to be here and not show up or call."

"So, what do you want me to do about it?"

Sara, who didn't care for Bob since he'd squeezed her ass one day before swearing it had been a joke, said, "What you usually do. Nothing."

She pulled out her phone, found Roxanne in her contacts, and pressed the button to call her. The call went straight to voicemail.

"That's weird."

"Maybe she's quitting and doesn't want to talk to you right now," Bob said.

"Maybe," she answered, but she was bothered by something. "Did you know she has a stalker?"

"Really? No."

"Yeah. She said she reported it to the police."

167

"What did they do?"

"Nothing. She told me they said it didn't rise to the level of stalking, though from what she told me, this guy's a real creep."

"Every woman knows a creep," he said. He was bent over a report and didn't notice as she glanced in his direction.

"You can say that again," she said. "Still, I think I'll have the police check on her."

"Don't be ridiculous. Next thing you know, they'll be here asking questions, and she probably decided to just leave town without telling anyone. Customers don't like to see the cops here asking questions. It unsettles them."

Roxanne's no-show was bothering her more than normal. She knew Roxanne had been depressed lately after her girlfriend had left her. She considered her idea about having the police check on her and decided it would at least let Roxanne know people cared about her, something a depressed person needed. Sara hadn't considered Roxanne suicidal, but then she wasn't a psychiatrist and couldn't be sure.

"I'm calling the police to check on her."

"Sara?! Shit!" he said as she left his office, ignoring him.

Twenty minutes later, she received a call that Roxanne wasn't answering the door.

"Is there a car in the driveway?" she asked.

"Yes. A blue Toyota Camry," the officer said.

"That's her car. Is there a way for you to enter the house? She's been depressed lately and I'm afraid for her."

"Let me go around and peek inside where I can. I'll call you back, ma'am."

When the officer found the back door standing

open, his suspicion grew. Entering, he called out, "Ms. Beard? Police. Can you hear me?"

No answer.

He pulled his service revolver and held it aimed upwards as he walked through the house. When he reached the bedroom, he found a bare bed, scarves of various colors dangling from the bedposts.

He was a young officer, but he recognized that this was a potential crime scene. The combination of the open back door, the scarves apparently used to tie someone to the bed, and the missing woman's car still in the driveway, its engine cold, was enough to call in detectives.

After calling the precinct to report a possible kidnapping, he phoned Ms. Dodd back.

"Ms. Dodd?" he said when she'd answered. "This is Officer Wagner again. How well do you know Ms. Beard?"

"She's an employee here at the Food Lion where I work."

"She isn't here, and there are a few suspicious things about the condition of her home. Has she mentioned anything that might help?"

"What kind of suspicious things?"

"No blood or anything, if that's what you're thinking. Her back door was wide open, and there are other things that make me wonder that I'd rather not go into. Again, has she said anything to you that might indicate why she's not here?"

"She told me she'd reported a stalker."

Officer Wagner felt a chill run down his spine.

"Did she mention a name?"

"No, but she talked to a detective about it. I don't know the detective's name. Actually, there were two different ones she spoke to. I remember because she was frustrated they wouldn't do anything, especially after the second call. They said it didn't rise to the level of stalking, though I can tell you Roxanne was scared."

Officer Wagner ended the call and waited for a detective to arrive. The scene gave him the creeps. He'd be happy to pass this to someone else.

Pantera had enjoyed the weekend with his daughters. Among other places they'd enjoyed, he had taken them to Lewis Ginter Botanical Gardens. The girls loved what they called the butterfly house. Beth always wanted a picture taken with butterflies perched on her. That Saturday, a butterfly had perched on her nose, making for a wonderful photo of her with her eyes crossed.

Andrea was looking forward to the beach trip they would take soon. Pantera could tell this enthusiasm grew from the fact she would be able to spend the entire week with her girlfriend.

He'd received a minor bruise on his cheek in the scuffle with Crosswell, and his daughters had asked about it.

"Well, I got in a bit of a fight. Not a big one, just, you know, a little altercation."

"During an arrest?" Beth asked.

"No," Pantera answered. He wished this conversation would end. He'd always preached against violence and didn't want his daughters knowing about the fight. "I'm a little embarrassed to say this, but it was with another detective."

"What?!" Beth was shocked. Andrea seemed speechless.

"Yeah. We had a—well—a disagreement."

"What about?" Andrea asked.

"This other detective said something about gays and

170

lesbians that I didn't like." He watched Andrea for her reaction. Her mouth dropped open and she blinked several times.

"What did he say?" she asked.

"It's kind of ugly. I'd prefer not to say. Just know it wasn't nice, and it made me think of all the hatred you'll be facing in your life just because of who you are."

Andrea smiled and her eyes sparkled in a way that made him realize how beautiful she was. "Daddy, you can't go around punching out everyone who says something stupid about LGBTQ's. It would be a full-time job."

"I know."

Beth asked, "Did you tell him Andrea's a lesbian?"

"I don't have permission to do that," Pantera said. "I don't tell anyone unless Andrea says I can." He remembered telling Harry and blushed. "Well, I told my partner, Detective Overmeyer, and I sort of had to tell Lieutenant Gariepy, but afterwards I figured it wasn't mine to share."

Andrea said, "You can tell people, Daddy. Like you said, it's who I am." She giggled. "But don't make it the first thing you say to someone!" She lowered her voice to imitate her father. "Hi, glad to meet you. My daughter's a lesbian." She continued laughing at her joke, and Pantera and Beth joined in.

Sunday night he took them home with promises to see them soon. After their stay, he sat considering how far they'd come. Because he'd shown interest in their lives, their relationship had begun to blossom. He felt closer to them than he had in years.

Now Monday had arrived, and his day became worse almost immediately.

He took the call about a missing female and a scene

171

that suggested possible foul play. Harry was off that day, so he drove to the house on his own. As he stepped toward the front door, Officer Wagner met him.

"Detective?"

"Yes. Tell me what you found."

"I was called out here on a welfare check by the young woman's work supervisor." He looked at his notes. "A Sara Dodd, with Food Lion. The missing woman hadn't shown up for work, and because the missing girl had reported a stalking, Ms. Dodd was worried.

"Upon arriving, I knocked and rang the doorbell, which doesn't work. Calling out, I received no response and notified Ms. Dodd. She asked if a car was in the driveway." Wagner indicated the blue Camry. "I described that car, and Ms. Dodd told me it belonged to the missing woman. She asked me to check further.

"When I went around to the back of the house, letting myself in through the gate of a privacy fence, I noticed the back door was standing open. I investigated and found a bed without covers or anything on it, but scarves appeared to have been tied to the bedposts to allow someone to be tied up there."

"A lot of people like to be tied up for sex," Pantera said, already doubting that had been the case.

"Yes, sir, but with the car there and the missing sheets and blankets, it didn't feel right, especially since the missing woman had reported a stalking."

Pantera would find out which officer had taken the call later from call records. He could get the notes from whoever took the call to get a name for the stalker.

"What is the missing woman's name?"

Officer Wagner checked his notes again. "A Roxanne Beard, age twenty-six. She works at the Food Lion over on Cherry Street."

Pantera felt his heart lurch, along with his stomach. He recognized her name. She was the young woman who'd spoken to him about being stalked, and he'd not had enough to launch an investigation since the alleged stalker had only contacted her once. From all appearances, she had been able to handle the situation.

"Shit," Pantera uttered. "I took her call. It wasn't enough to qualify as stalking."

"Oh." Pantera could see in the officer's eyes that he thought Pantera might end up wishing he'd looked into it. He agreed, but his hands were tied on the call. He could get reamed out for investigating something that didn't qualify as a crime or even a misdemeanor as a waste of taxpayer dollars.

"Let's take a look at the back door," Pantera said.

Officer Wagner led the way to the fence and stepped through it with Pantera following. Pantera noticed how isolated the narrow side street had been where the gate was. Entry through that gate would likely not be seen by any neighbors. No houses actually faced the street that ran along the side of Roxanne Beard's house. It was less of a street and more of an alley between the backs of houses. It appeared to exist more as a convenient way to get to busier streets. Being on the northeast corner of the tiny intersection and facing the west toward the busier residential street, the south side of Roxanne Beard's house, not the back, faced the narrow alley. The lot on the southeast corner was empty.

They entered the house through the open back door. "Did you touch the door?" Pantera asked.

"No. Just walked in, calling for Ms. Beard."

They walked through to the bedroom where Wagner had found the stripped bed.

"What about in here? You touch anything?"

"No, sir."

"Good. To make sure you don't now, put your hands in your pockets." Wagner did so, and Pantera walked around the room, keeping his own hands in his pockets.

He saw the gypsum dust before he was standing beside where it had drifted down to the floor. He looked up. A vent stared down at the room. The realization that this may involve the same person who'd murdered Grant Davis, as well as burglarizing several homes, made a shiver run up his spine. He'd dealt with a serial killer just a few months ago and prayed this wasn't another.

She had mentioned the name of the guy she said was stalking her, but he couldn't remember it now. It would be in his notes.

Then he remembered. He had thrown the notes out because they hadn't amounted to anything. No crime, no notes.

He only hoped Crosswell had kept his. He was going to have to ask for them, and he wasn't looking forward to that.

When Pantera walked through the small living room, he noticed more gypsum dust below a vent that offered a perfect view of the sofa where Roxanne probably sat much of the time she was in the room. The only other furniture was a sofa table stretched along the length of the couch, a wooden chair that looked too uncomfortable for anyone to sit in for long, and a TV. The room was small enough that there didn't seem to be room for much else. Pantera thought the perp probably didn't worry about leaving the dust behind after taking out the equipment, which also meant they would find no fingerprints and probably no fiber evidence. The day was shaping up to be a nightmare.

He found a stepstool in a floor-to-ceiling cupboard in the kitchen and took it into the living room. Setting it up beneath the vent, he climbed up to look through into the ductwork. He could see nothing there, but he didn't really expect to.

"What are you looking for?" Wagner asked.

"Something I didn't expect to find, but I had to look anyway." He pointed at the small amount of gypsum dust. "See that?"

"What is it?"

"Gypsum dust." Pantera pointed up at the vent. "I've seen this before. Recently. The perp sets up cameras and other equipment to spy on his victims before killing them."

"You mean there's more than one?"

Pantera looked around the room, shaking his head. "I don't know, but maybe." He took a breath. "Probably. It depends on what happened to Ms. Beard."

He found pay vouchers for each girl in a drawer. He knew Roxanne worked at a local Food Lion. Wendy, it turned out, worked at a local restaurant, probably waiting tables.

He would call their employers for information on how to locate next of kin.

The crime scene techs arrived and went to work. Soon, the house was dusted for fingerprints that Pantera could have told them they wouldn't find. Despite this, he had them also dust the vent edges, as well as the area just inside the ductwork. As with everything else, they found no prints other than those that were probably from the two women who'd lived there.

That afternoon, Pantera arrived back at the precinct to do the paperwork on the Beard case. He was there when Crosswell arrived for the night shift.

"Hey, Crosswell," he said "Just the man I need to see."

The detective strode over to Pantera's desk.

"Yeah?" His nose was still bandaged with a metal brace taped over it. He still sounded stuffed up.

"First off, I'm sorry I slugged you the other day. I was out of line. You just—well, you sort of hit a nerve with me. You see, my daughter recently came out as a lesbian. I know the kind of hatred she'll face, and your comments sort of brought that up to me."

"Your daughter? Really?"

"Yeah."

"How old is she?"

"She'll be sixteen in a few weeks."

"Wow, that's kinda young to make decisions like that, isn't it?"

"I don't know, really. She says she's always known she isn't interested in guys. That's how I know it's not a choice. She wouldn't choose this. Who would? She'll face disgust and possibly even violence all her life."

Crosswell nodded. "Yeah, I was out of line, too. I didn't know that about your daughter. I was just trying to be funny. I can sort of see where my comments might piss you off." He paused. "You're not trying to get out of paying my share of the medical bills, are you? 'Cause that ain't happening."

"No, I'll pay them. No problem there."

"Okay."

"I also wanted to talk to you about something else."

"What?"

"You have the notes on that call that started all this?"

"Yeah, why?"

Pantera took a deep breath and let it out slowly. "Because she's missing, and I think she's either been kidnapped or killed."

"Oh?" Crosswell sat in the chair beside the desk.

"Yeah. There's evidence he was watching her—had

surveillance equipment set up behind the vents in two of the rooms, living room and bedroom."

"Holy shit. Then she was being stalked."

"And the rules we're forced to follow prevented us from doing anything about it. The weird thing is, the M.O. matches the guy who killed the assistant principal, Grant Davis."

"Son of a bitch."

"Yeah."

"You and Overmeyer are working that case, aren't you?"

"Yeah."

"Does he know about this new one?"

"Not yet. He's off today. I figure I'll let him get some sleep tonight since I likely won't be getting any. I can fill him in when he gets in tomorrow."

"You want those notes?"

"Yeah."

Crosswell stood and went to his desk. He pulled a file and came back. "Here's what little I have. Where are your notes on the call?"

"Threw them out."

"What?!"

"Yeah. I figured she was just overreacting to a guy's lack of manners. It really sounded like nothing."

"Yeah, but you shouldn't throw out notes on any call. You know better than that."

"It seemed like such a waste of time."

"It wasn't, though, was it?"

"Nope." He thought about the gypsum dust. "Not at all."

TWENTY-THREE

Pantera opened the file with only the single sheet of paper inside. He had to hand it to Crosswell. He was meticulous. Pantera wondered where his own attention to detail had gone. He used to be as detail-oriented as Crosswell. Now, he could be haphazard when he felt it was a waste of time to do more. "You've become lazy," he told himself.

He searched for the name of the man who Roxanne Beard said was stalking her. He remembered it started with a *B*, but little else. He also recalled that she did not know his first name. He had thought it was odd that she would go out with a guy twice without knowing that.

Scanning the document, he found the name— Blanton. His smile widened as he turned to his computer and typed a few commands. Three Blantons were listed in the online phone directory they had. He copied and pasted their last known addresses into a document and printed it. One of the possible suspects listed was on Pantera's way home, and he decided to stop there when he left work to see if he could either eliminate that person from his suspect list or move him into the further investigation needed category. He knew enough about the perp's physical appearance to know he was fairly young and fit, based on the description Grant Davis's neighbor had given them.

First, however, he had some follow up to do regarding the missing ladies' next of kin.

He phoned Food Lion and spoke to Sara Dodd.

After the introductions were out of the way, Pantera

178

told her that Roxanne was officially listed as missing. He asked for Roxanne's emergency contact information.

"Well, the first name on the list is her roommate, Wendy."

"She's not been seen for a few days herself," Pantera told her.

"Yes, I know. Roxanne told me she'd left."

"What about her parents?" he asked.

"They live in Culpepper," Ms. Dodd said, and read him their address and phone number.

"Thank you," he said, and hung up.

Next, he phoned Wendy Atwater's employer, a small diner downtown.

After he'd introduced himself, he asked for Wendy's emergency contact information.

"Is she dead?" Gloria Tinsdale, the woman on the other end of the call asked.

"I don't know, but she's missing."

"She's not been to work in days. Trevor took her off the schedule after her roommate said she'd left town. That girl was pretty torn up about it, too. I think they might have been more than just roomies, if you know what I mean."

Pantera assumed Trevor was either the owner or manager of the diner, and he didn't want to get into any discussion of the missing women's private lives, especially given the woman's tone as she suggested they were lovers, as if homosexuality were a contagious disease and she was glad Wendy was no longer there.

Ms. Tinsdale provided him the information he needed. Pantera said, "Yes, well, thank you for this information. If we find her, we'll make sure she calls you."

"Don't bother. After this long, she's pretty well fired anyway," the woman said and hung up.

He called the police in Culpepper to ask them to find out if Roxanne Beard's parents had heard from their daughter and let the police there know she was missing under suspicious circumstances. He left his number if the parents wanted to speak to him.

Meanwhile, instead of doing the same regarding Wendy Atwater, Pantera drove to Wendy's mother's home, which was in Chesterfield, just south of Richmond. When Ms. Atwater answered the door, she was wearing a thin cotton robe and looked as though she might have the flu. Either that, or she was terribly hung over.

"Yeah?"

"I apologize for bothering you, Ms. Atwater," Pantera began. "I'm Detective Tony Pantera with the Richmond Police."

"You don't have jurisdiction here," she protested, as if he were there to arrest her.

"No, ma'am. I wanted to ask if you've seen your daughter Wendy lately? She's been missing for the last several days."

The woman frowned, as if the act of answering was a bother. "That girl don't come around here no more. Told me if I ever came looking for her, she'd shoot me. Can you arrest her for saying that? It was a threat. And that little bitch would do it, too."

Pantera ignored her question. "So you've not seen or heard from her?"

"No, and I don't want to." With that, she closed the door in his face.

He stood there a moment before going to his car, wondering how it was that a mother and daughter could drift so far apart and hate each other so much. How bad had Wendy's home life been that she would threaten to shoot her mother if she ever tried to find her? That may have been a lie, but would any mother lie to paint her relationship with her daughter as being that broken?

As he drove back to Richmond, his phone rang. He didn't recognize the number, but it was a 540 area code, so he assumed it might be either Roxanne Beard's parents or the Culpepper police. It turned out to be the parents.

"Detective Pantera," he answered.

"Detective?" The voice on the other end sounded frantic. "This is Louise Beard, Roxanne Beard's mother. I just got off the phone with the Culpepper Police and they gave me your number. Roxanne's missing?!"

"Yes, ma'am. She didn't show up for work, and one of her managers called for us to check on her."

"Oh, dear God! We told her to be careful! We warned her that some people would hurt her if she wasn't careful who she got to know."

"Yes, ma'am. But right now, we have nothing definite. She might have just decided to leave town for a while. She was apparently rather broken up that her roommate moved out." He didn't mention their relationship to her, not wanting to possibly upset her further.

"She's not like that, Detective." He heard gentle sobs on the other end of the call. "Oh, dear. This is going to turn out badly. I just know it."

"If we hear anything, you will be contacted," Pantera said, wanting to end the call. "If you hear from her, will you let me know?"

"Certainly. Thank you, Detective—" her tone told him she had forgotten his name.

"Pantera."

"Yes, thank you, Detective Pantera." With that, she said goodbye and ended the call.

He stopped at the precinct and took care of making

notes about his visit with Ms. Atwater and his phone call with Ms. Beard. Then he left work to drive to the home of the first person named Blanton he wanted to see.

He pulled into Jason Blanton's driveway. As he approached, he was met with the sound of loud barking from the other side of the front door. He rang the bell, which served to make the barking increase in volume.

"Quiet, Igor!" he heard a woman say. He heard a chain lock slide into place before she opened the door.

"Yes?" she said over the barking from behind her. Pantera could see a large, mixed-breed dog behind her, his hackles raised. The woman was perhaps in her sixties.

"I'm sorry to bother you, ma'am. My name is Detective Tony Pantera with Richmond PD. I have a few questions for you if you don't mind."

"A detective?" she asked. "Have I done something wrong?"

"No, ma'am. It's just a routine questioning kind of thing."

"Do you have identification? You can't be too careful these days."

"Certainly," he said, taking out his badge and holding it out for her to read. "I'm sorry for not showing it when you opened the door. I was thinking more about your dog."

"Yes, he can be rather protective." Her tone suggested she was warning him to watch his step in case he wasn't who he said he was.

"Yes, ma'am." Igor's barking continued until she turned to him and said, "I said, hush, Igor! I'm talking to the man. Now, sit!"

The dog did as he was told but was still antsy about the unexpected visitor, occasionally huffing a bark under his breath in case Pantera forgot he was there.

182

"Ma'am, I was wondering if you have a son who lives with you here?"

"No, why?"

"We're investigating a crime and we have reason to believe his last name is Blanton. Is that your name?"

"Yes, my name is Charlotte Blanton. I live here with my husband. We have two daughters, but they don't live here."

Pantera asked, "Is your husband able to come to the door?"

Charlotte Blanton glanced back at Igor before saying, "He's not home right now. He still works." Then she added hastily, "But he'll be home soon if you don't mind waiting in your car."

"That won't be necessary." He thanked her for her time and started to leave before turning back to her. "I don't suppose your husband is in his late twenties to early thirties with an athletic build, is he?"

She chuckled. "Sorry. No such luck. He's my age and hasn't had an athletic build since, well, since forever."

He thanked her again and left, hearing her tell the dog how good he was as she closed the door.

As he drove home, he hoped the remaining two Blantons would be more helpful. Jason Blanton could be crossed off the list.

When he arrived home, he had two messages. One was from his ex-wife, Nancy. He could tell from the tone of her first word that it wasn't good news.

"Hey, Tony. Phil's father had a stroke. Phil's flying out this afternoon, and I'm joining him Monday. Would it be possible for me to drop the girls off with you for a few days? I know this is short notice, but I don't want them staying alone. I trust them, but I don't trust all their friends. You know how it is. Word gets out that parents

183

are out-of-town, and suddenly, it's 'we've got a party pad' whether or not the kids who live there plan it. Today is the last day of school, which is fortunate, so they'll be on break anyway. I know you're planning the beach trip for a few weeks from now, but I really could use the help. Call me back when you get this so I'll know if I have to make other arrangements."

It hurt him to know she thought he might refuse. Yes, when they were still married, he was often an absent father, but he had been trying his best to change that. She knew this but seemed to insist that he'd not changed or that he was at least not making the effort to do so. It made him understand how ex-cons could feel.

He listened to the next message before calling her back. It was from Lisa.

"Hey, sexy. I'm just calling to ask if you could make it up here Tuesday night. I have this function that just came up, and I was hoping you could be my date. You could even stay over if that works for you. You rise early anyway, and the drive south from DC is much easier in the morning since ninety percent of the traffic is coming north on I-95 into the city. You could be back in Richmond in ninety minutes, so you could leave around 6:30 and make it to work by 8:00. I know it's a lot to ask, but I assure you we'll have fun."

He sighed. If the girls weren't coming to stay, he'd have gladly accepted the invitation. He knew he could probably ask the girls to stay that one night alone, but he also knew that was what he would have done before trying to change his parenting habits.

He called Nancy first and told her he'd gladly take the girls, assuring her that she didn't even need to ask. He even told her about the call from Lisa and how he wouldn't be joining her, adding, "I'm doing my best to become a better father."

"I know you are, Tony, but old habits die hard."

"Well, I'm a trained cop. I know how to kill something, even habits."

She laughed softly at his joke, making him happy that it had lightened the mood.

"I'm sorry to hear about Phil's dad. I hope he's okay."

"It seems to have been a minor stroke, but he's lost some feeling in his right side. We'll see what happens."

They disconnected, and he called Lisa back.

"Hey, sexy, yourself," he said when she answered.

"Hi there! So, can you come up?"

"I'm afraid I can't," he said, and explained about his daughters.

"That's fine," she said.

"It's not as if I wouldn't be there if this hadn't happened. I would have loved it."

"I know, and thanks."

"So, what's the occasion? I hope I'm not missing some award ceremony for you."

"No. It's actually a political thing. There's this dinner with a number of people in the House and Senate, and they want me to hobnob and push for additional funding for the library."

"Hey, it's their library—the Library of Congress—so they should have no trouble pushing a few more million your way."

"If it were only that easy. Let's just say one side is more prone to funding things like a library than the other."

"I won't ask which side is which," he said. "Maybe we could get together sometime soon when I'm not keeping my girls."

"That sounds like a good idea." She changed the subject. "How's your case coming?"

"The murder of the assistant principal?"

"Yes."

"Actually, things happened that might help solve it, but I can't tell you right now."

"I understand. But it's going well?"

"As well as can be expected." He paused. "Mostly, I'm worried about a young woman who might have become involved but didn't want to."

"Oh? What happened?"

"Again, can't say, but she might be in danger."

"I'll be praying she's okay."

"Thanks," he said. "She could be just fine, though. Hopefully, she will turn up safe." As they hung up, he realized that may not be the case at all. That bed with its scarves obviously used to tie someone's feet and wrists to the bedposts was an ominous sign that all was not well. In fact, he hoped she was still alive, but he knew the odds of that were slim based on what they'd found, including the gypsum dust.

TWENTY-FOUR

Early the next morning, Nancy dropped off two very sleepy and grumpy teenage girls. Pantera didn't take it personally. They had been forced to get out of bed much earlier than they were used to, first to pack, then to make the hour-plus drive from Charlottesville.

"Thanks, Tony. I owe you one."

"Don't worry about it," Pantera answered. "I just hope Phil's dad is okay."

"I'll tell him you said that." She kissed the girls goodbye and hurried out the door.

Turning to his daughters, he said, "You two look like you got two hours sleep, tops."

"Two-and-a-half," Andrea said.

Beth followed with, "Maybe three."

"Well, I have to work today. Can you two fend for yourselves until I get home? Get some rest and we can go out to Renaud's."

"Will you play the piano?" Beth asked.

"If he'll let me."

"You know he will, Dad. If he didn't, the wait staff would complain," Andrea said.

Pantera frowned at Andrea. "Why would they do that?"

"Because, whenever you play, you leave a big tip."

"I do?"

"Yes," Beth said. "A big one."

"I always leave a nice tip."

Beth yawned. "Not as much as you leave when you play their piano."

187

"Well, it's a privilege to be allowed to do that."

"So, are you going to play?"

"I can play here, you know. I have a piano right over there," Pantera said, pointing to the upright piano that sat against one wall of his living room.

"It's not the same as watching everyone enjoy your music."

"Well, it's not my music. I play songs written by other people."

Beth joined Andrea in another yawn.

"Why don't you two set an alarm for ten and get some rest. I have to leave for work. Harry might get there before me and think I've had an accident."

They struggled to their feet and gave Pantera a kiss on the cheek before heading to their rooms. Pantera felt like a million bucks and started to leave but was stopped by Andrea calling from her room.

"Dad?"

He stepped to her door. She was looking at the floor near one wall. "What is it?"

"What's this stuff?"

He walked around the bed to see what she meant and felt his blood freeze.

Along the baseboard in her bedroom lay a thin coating of white dust.

She noticed his reaction. "Dad? Are you okay?"

Instead of answering, he looked up the wall to the vent.

"Dad? You're scaring me. You look all pale."

He glanced at Andrea. "I'm okay. It's just that we've seen this recently in our investigations."

"What is it?"

"Gypsum dust."

"Why does it have you upset?"

Beth now stood at the door, listening. "What is it?"

188

"Nothing, baby. We've got it."

She came to see what Andrea had found.

Pantera took out his phone and pressed a button to call Harry. When Harry answered, Pantera said, "Harry? He's been in my house."

"Who has?"

"Mr. Gypsum Dust."

"I'll be right there."

When Pantera had disconnected the call, Andrea said, "Dad? What's wrong? Who's Mr. Gypsum Dust?"

Pantera looked at his daughter and realized exactly what the dust meant. The creep had watched his daughter, assuming the cameras had been in place since before their last visit. He'd seen her getting ready for bed. Watched her undress to put on her robe to take a shower down the hall.

His gaze returned to the vent. "I'll tell you later," he said, hoping he could somehow avoid telling her that her privacy had been stolen from her.

He left the room, returning with a stepstool and removed the vent from the wall. The space beyond was empty except for one thing—a picture of Andrea, her back to the camera. She was naked. It looked like a video still that had been printed on paper. The pixilated image was clear enough to see it was Andrea.

He swallowed the rage that threatened to erupt into a scream. The son-of-a-bitch had known Pantera would find out he'd been inside his home and installed cameras behind the vents. Now he knew that the bastard had left the gypsum behind for a reason. He'd probably left it in Davis's and Roxanne Beard's house on purpose to let Pantera know his M.O. regarding that aspect of his crimes. It had not been a blunder on his part. It had been a way to toy with the investigators.

He crumpled the sheet of paper in his hand and

climbed down from the stool.

"Daddy? What is it? What's written on that paper?" Andrea asked. Insisted, really.

"Have a seat, baby."

He could see that her fright was palpable, and she could tell that what he'd found had made him angry beyond anything she'd seen before.

If he could have avoided telling her, he would have, but she would obviously never let him do that.

"We're dealing with a sick man who breaks into homes and installs camera equipment to spy on people."

Her eyes widened as the full meaning of his words hit her. "You mean, he spied on me when I was visiting?"

"Yes. Maybe it was the last time you were here, or perhaps the time before. I don't know. The equipment has been removed."

"He watched me…in here?"

"Yes."

She glanced quickly to the bed and then at the vent, gauging the camera's line of sight, Pantera supposed.

"Oh, God!" she began to cry.

"It's okay, baby. We're going to catch him and make him pay."

"What if he puts stuff out there on the internet? Everyone will be able to see me—" She paused. "Well…*see* me!"

"I know, baby. We're going to do everything we can to prevent that from happening."

She looked at the crumpled paper. "What's on that?"

"You really don't want to know, honey."

"But I have to, Dad!"

He took a deep breath and let it out before handing her the piece of paper.

"Oh, God!" she said, more tears coming now in sobs.

Beth stood over her sister, and when she saw the picture she gasped.

"I need to check the rest of the house," Pantera said and left the room.

Entering his bedroom, he saw that the vent was above a dresser with a mirror mounted to the back. He couldn't tell whether any dust was behind it without moving the dresser away from the wall. He managed to heft the dresser a few inches and peered behind it. He saw the dust where it had settled.

Going into the living room, he saw again that the TV stand was blocking the floor beneath the vent. Moving it, he saw the dust there as well.

The room he dreaded checking was the one where Beth slept when she was there. As with Andrea's room, he rarely entered it. He stepped inside the room to find Beth already there, sitting on the bed and staring at the dust beneath the vent.

Retrieving the stepstool, he climbed up and removed the vent, praying nothing like the picture he'd found in Andrea's room would be there. When he saw the piece of paper, his heartbeat quickened from a combination of fear and rage.

Praying it wasn't like Andrea's picture, he looked at the paper and sighed. At least Beth wasn't naked. She was lying on the bed in her pajamas, reading a book. While he was happy not to see his younger daughter naked in the picture, he knew that whatever devil from hell had done this had seen her undressed. For a moment, all he could think about was his desire to kill the man who had stolen his and his daughters' privacy.

The doorbell rang and Beth jumped as if shocked. Pantera climbed down from the stool and reached out for her. She stood and allowed her father to enfold her in his arms. He held her there for a moment while blinking away his own tears. He needed to be strong for them, to let them know he would hunt this animal down and see to it he was punished like the evil creature he was.

"Am I...naked in the picture?"

"No, baby. You're lying in bed, reading." He hoped she would not realize that what the picture showed didn't matter, that the man had seen her naked at some point and probably had video of her getting undressed stored on his computer.

When the doorbell sounded a second time, he stepped back from Beth and said, "I'll be right back. That's Harry." He was surprised how thick his voice sounded.

As he left the room, Andrea met him at Beth's door. "Daddy, do you want me to answer it?"

"No, baby. I'll get it."

Stepping to the door, he let Harry in. "How bad is it?" Harry asked.

"Bad. He left cameras that he's removed. I didn't notice the gypsum dust before because it was behind furniture except in the girls' rooms, which I almost never go into. Andrea called me to her room to ask what it was."

"Do you think the cameras had been installed before they stayed here?"

"I know they were." He held out the picture of Beth reading in bed and Harry took it.

"Son of a bitch," he said, staring at the picture. "Where did you find this?"

"Behind the vent. He left it for me to find. He's teasing me, Harry. He's practically daring me to find him." He paused for a second before saying, "There was another picture of Andrea, but if you don't mind, I won't

192

show you that one. She's—" He took a deep breath. "She's got her back to the camera, but she's naked."

Pantera could tell that Harry was angry. His jaw clenched and he squinted, something he would do when especially incensed about something.

"We're gonna get this bastard, Tony. We're gonna find him and make him pay for this."

"He's laughing at me."

"You'll get the last laugh, Tony. I promise."

Pantera suddenly stared at Harry, a suspicion dawning on him.

"What is it?" Harry asked.

"Harry, have you checked your house for gypsum dust?"

"Ashley works from home. She's home all day."

"That's right. Sorry. This has me flustered a bit." Ashley Overmeyer ran a small business making special ordered t-shirts, wall hangings, mugs, and other bric-a-brac she sold online. He looked at Pantera. "You going in today?"

"Of course. Sitting here won't catch him."

"What are you gonna do with the girls. They can't stay here."

"You're right." He thought about how he might handle this situation. Most of the people he knew worked. "Do you think Ashley would let them stay at your place for the day? They won't bother her while she works."

"I'll give her a call. I'm sure she'll be okay with it."

"Thanks. I owe you."

"Don't mention it," Harry said, and stepped outside to make the call.

Pantera found both girls in Andrea's room, talking about what had happened. "Girls, I'm afraid you can't stay here today. This guy is obviously able to get in here, and I can't leave you by yourselves. I'm taking you to spend the day at Harry's."

"We're not babies!" Andrea complained.

"No, but you're not exactly a SWAT team, either. I can't stay with you today." The girls sighed in unison. "Get your bags. They have a guest room where you can get some sleep."

He started to leave but stopped. "I promise I'll get this guy, okay? I won't stop until I do. I swear."

"I know," Andrea said.

When they walked out to the car, Pantera saw Harry disconnecting the call to Ashley and raised his eyebrows in question.

"No problem," Harry said. "She's thrilled, in fact."

Climbing into his car, he started it and rolled down the window. "See you at the precinct?"

"I'll be there," Harry said.

When he arrived at the Overmeyers', Ashley met him at the door.

"Come on in, girls! I might even knock off early, and we'll do something. I know just sitting around here all day with nothing to do will get boring."

"Thank you so much for this, Ashley. I owe you."

"Forget it, Tony. I'm more than glad to do it. Today was going to be a slow day anyway. This helps me as much as it helps you."

"Well, anyway, thank you."

"What time will you pick them up? Or do you want me to bring them to your place?"

"No, I'll stop by this evening around six to get them."

As he started to leave, Ashley said, "How many days will they be able to come over?"

Pantera wanted to kick himself for not considering more than just today. Finding that gypsum dust and the photos really had thrown him for a loop.

"Oh, yeah. If you're okay keeping them for more than just today, how about at least the next two days?"

"Looking forward to it."

Pantera left, thankful he had friends like Harry and Ashley. Given what had transpired that morning, though, it was the only consolation.

TWENTY-FIVE

On his way to work, Pantera thought about Nancy's flight time and gauged when she would be available to take a call. He didn't want to call while she was going through security, since that was irritating enough without learning your daughters had been spied on in their most private moments.

He hoped she wouldn't blame him, but he knew she would, at least partially. If he wasn't a detective, this wouldn't have happened. Besides, he more or less blamed himself, so having her do that too would be expected.

When he finally called her, he asked, "Are you at the gate?"

"Yes. We should board soon. What's up?"

"I'm afraid I have some bad news."

"What?" He could already hear irritation rising in her voice.

"When Andrea went into her room, she found gypsum dust on the floor beneath the vent. We've been working a case where the perp hides surveillance equipment behind vents and spies on his victims. The equipment was gone when I looked."

"Couldn't it be just where some of the dust fell on its own? Maybe there was a tremor or something and it just fell down there?"

"No. I found a picture behind the vent. He wanted me to find it."

"What was in the picture?" The fear in her voice told him she already knew what the picture would be but she asked anyway, perhaps hoping she was wrong.

"It's Andrea from behind. She was naked."

"Oh, my God," she said, almost a whisper. "What about Beth?"

"He watched her too, but the picture was just of her in her pajamas reading in bed."

"Still, she didn't snap her fingers and suddenly appeared in her pajamas. Tony, a man has watched our daughters getting undressed!" She suddenly lowered her voice, apparently realizing she was loud enough to be heard by other passengers at the gate. "A man you brought into our lives!" she hissed.

There it was. The accusation he could not deny. "It's not as if I invited the asshole to put cameras in my house."

"I know that." She was silent for a moment. "What are we going to do about this? Do the girls know they were watched?"

"Yes, they know. I couldn't very well keep it from them. My rage at what I'd found was too obvious. I'm going to find this bastard and make sure he pays for what he did."

"He should be castrated," she said. He had to agree with her on that. "Should I cancel my plans and pick them up? Maybe arrange for all of us to fly out? I'm not sure what we should do."

"No. I took them to stay with Ashley, Harry's wife."

"Can she watch them during the day until I get back?"

"Yes, she works from home, her own business, so her schedule is flexible."

Pantera heard an announcement in the background.

"They're boarding, Tony. I have to go. Keep me posted on what's going on."

"I will. Sorry I had to lay this on you on top of everything else."

"I'm sorry I snapped at you. It's not your fault."

They disconnected, and Pantera returned to his work.

Blanton had been waiting for the next step in his plan, but what happened that morning caused him to alter his strategy. He had left a few bugs in Pantera's house to monitor what was said in there after removing the cameras and other equipment, and what he heard from Pantera's end of a conversation on the phone the night before when Pantera's ex had discussed her need to fly out of town made him smile. He'd wanted to set up surveillance in the home of Pantera's ex-wife to monitor what was going on there. The cameras would relay what they recorded in real time to the cloud where he could download it and enjoy it at his leisure, but he hadn't had an opportunity to install the equipment. Now, she would be out of town for several days, along with her husband and the two daughters. The house would be empty.

He even considered spending the night there but worried that his DNA would be left behind if he did.

He parked down the street from Pantera's and listened as Nancy Boyd arrived and dropped off the girls. He also heard that the little gifts he had left for Pantera to find were finally discovered.

Blanton scoffed at the idea that Pantera was supposed to be this great detective. He'd removed the surveillance equipment days ago, but Pantera had not seen the chalky dust that he'd purposely left as a clue. In fact, his daughter had to be the one to point it out to the so-called detective.

"Great detective, my ass," he said to the empty car.

He didn't want to be spotted by Detective Overmeyer, who was on his way there, so Blanton drove home. He would go to Charlottesville that night to install his equipment. It would come in very handy for what he had planned for Pantera's ex-wife and daughters.

Pantera managed to find someone at home at the other locations where people named Blanton lived. Crossing his fingers, he asked Harry, "You want to come with me to talk to the other two people named Blanton in the Richmond area that I know about?"

"First, I'm going to personally sweep your house for bugs to make sure all spying devices have been removed. You mind if I get a key?"

"I was going to do that myself when I get home."

"And have your daughters there watching while you check to see if the guy's still invading your privacy?"

"I hadn't thought of that."

"I did. Just give me your house key. Your place will be cleaned of anything we find before you get home."

"Okay, that sounds good," Pantera said. He gave Harry his house key, thanked him, and left the precinct for the first address. Neither of the Blantons would be home for long, and he needed to hurry.

Arriving at the first house, he went up and rang the doorbell. A man answered the door. He was about six feet tall and had an athletic build. Pantera wondered if he'd found his man.

"Eddie Blanton?" Pantera asked.

"Yes. You must be Detective Pondera," he said

"Pantera," he corrected and pulled out his badge to ID himself. "Do you have a minute?"

"Sure, but only a few minutes. I have to be at work at eleven."

"No problem." Eddie Blanton stepped aside and let

Pantera in. They sat in the living room just off the entry.

"What can I help you with?" Eddie asked.

"Do you know anyone by the name of Roxanne Beard?"

Eddie searched his memory. "Can't say that I do."

"How about Wendy Atwater?"

"No."

"Are you a beer drinker?" Pantera asked, considering the report of the video sent to Roxanne Beard.

"No, I don't drink alcohol."

Pantera wondered at his truthfulness.

"You mind if I look in your fridge?"

"What's this about?"

"Just a routine investigation. Again, do you mind if I—"

"As a matter of fact, I do, and not because I have beer in there. You want to search anything, you'll need a warrant."

Pantera doubted he would be able to get a judge to sign a search warrant based on such flimsy evidence.

"Fair enough. Can I ask where you work?"

"Crawford Health Spa. It's on West Broad."

"Can you tell me where you were Wednesday night?"

"What time?"

"Let's just make it the whole night."

"Well, I worked until seven that night. Stopped at my girlfriend's for dinner. She asked me to stay over. I didn't have to be at work the next morning, so I stayed."

"And what is her name, and where can I find her this morning?"

"This is something really serious, isn't it?"

"Her name and location?"

"Brandy Dillman. She works at Central Virginia

200

Realty as a secretary." Pantera could tell Eddie Blanton had decided he needed to do what he could to get himself out of being a suspect.

"Thank you," Pantera said, figuring he could either stay and ask more questions or verify the guy's whereabouts the night in question. If he did stay all night with his girlfriend, it wouldn't totally exonerate him since she might be a heavy sleeper, allowing him to slip out and back into bed without her knowing. However, it would go a long way toward removing him from the suspect list.

Pantera rose from his seat, and Eddie said, "Detective, if you want to look in my fridge, that's fine. I really don't drink alcohol. I'm a health nut. Just ask anyone who knows me."

"Thank you," Pantera said, and although he knew he would find no alcohol in the house if he were granted a search warrant, he took Eddie up on his offer. He was right. The refrigerator held fresh vegetables, milk, eggs, a low cholesterol margarine, bottled water, and several bottles of a protein shake sold in stores, along with a few other items, none of which would be considered bad for one's body. The fridge held no beer or other alcohol, not even a bottle of white wine.

Before leaving Eddie Blanton's house, he opened the internet on his phone and found the number of Central Virginia Realty. He wanted to call immediately after the door closed behind him when he left to prevent Eddie from being able to call his girlfriend and have her vouch for him if he was lying.

As the door closed behind him, he phoned. When the call was answered, he asked to speak to Brandy Dillman.

"Speaking," the pleasant voice on the other end said.

"Ms. Dillman, I'm Detective Tony Pantera with the Richmond PD. Do you have a second?"

"Sure." Her tone sounded worried and not as pleasant as before.

"I spoke to Eddie Blanton. He's your boyfriend?"

"Yes."

"Have you spoken to Eddie today?"

"No. Is he alright?"

"Yes, ma'am. He's fine. I just need to ask you a few things, if you don't mind."

"Okay."

"Were you out with Eddie on Friday night of last week at The Watering Hole?"

"The Watering Hole? What's that?"

"It's a bar in the city."

"A bar? Eddie won't set foot in a bar. He doesn't drink."

"Okay, thank you. Now, did he stay at your place overnight recently?"

"That's kind of personal."

"Well, he told us he did. I just want to verify the date. When was the last time he stayed over?"

"Are you sure you're a detective?"

"Yes, ma'am. I could stop by with my badge but to be honest, I need an answer to that question before I could get there. Time is important."

"Let me call Eddie to make sure you talked to him."

"Ma'am, I'd prefer you not do that. You see, I'm trying to verify his story without letting him speak to you first. I'm literally sitting in his driveway right now."

"What's going on?"

"Ms. Dillman, I promise if you'll answer that question honestly, it might keep Eddie out of trouble. We're searching for someone who matches his description. You're his alibi. Believe me, I'm not trying to pry into your personal business beyond knowing Eddie's whereabouts on a certain night."

"You better be telling the truth. I'm going to check up on this to make sure, and if some detective who doesn't know you're talking to me finds out someone with your phone number is pretending to be him, he's probably going to be angry about that."

"That's fine, Ms. Dillman. I really am who I say I am. My phone is issued to me by the department. If you would answer my question, I will get out of your hair. I won't ask for details or anything like that. What you do is your business since you're an adult and in a consenting relationship."

"Well, you talk like a detective anyway."

"That's because I am one."

She sighed heavily and said. "He stayed at my place on Wednesday night."

"Thank you, Ms. Dillman. You've helped me—and Eddie—quite a bit."

"May I ask just one more question?"

"What?"

He knew she would have a problem with this question and didn't want to give her a chance to talk to Eddie about it first, so he didn't ask. Instead, he said, "Actually, I think this one can wait until I see you face-to-face. I'll bring my badge. Will you be at work in a half hour?"

"You said you'd be out of my hair if I answered that last question."

"I know, but I really do have to stop by to ask this one. In any case, you'll be able to find out I am indeed a detective with RPD."

She sighed again, resigned to having to see him. "Fine, I'll be here. I'm at the desk when you walk in."

He drove to Central Virginia Realty and stepped

inside. The desk was empty, but within a few seconds, a beautiful young lady walked out and greeted him. "Hello, may I help you?"

He recognized her voice. "Hello again, Ms. Dillman. I'm Detective Pantera." He produced his badge and allowed her to inspect it thoroughly.

"Sorry about being difficult, but you can't be too careful."

"Believe me, I understand and commend you on your care. You are absolutely correct."

"So, what did you want to ask me, and I have a few questions for you, too."

"I won't be able to tell you about the case."

"That's not what I'm going to ask about."

"Okay, as long as you understand that I may not be able to answer your questions."

"Fair enough. Now what did you want to ask me?"

"Are you a heavy sleeper?"

She was obviously not expecting that question. "I can see why you didn't want to ask me that on the phone."

"I didn't think you'd answer until you could verify that I am a detective."

"You're right. I wouldn't have."

"So, are you?"

"Why do you want to know?"

"It has to do with the investigation, so I can't answer that."

"What? You suspect a heavy sleeper of committing some crime?"

"Could you just answer? Are you a heavy sleeper?"

"Yes, I am."

"So, Eddie could up and you wouldn't know it?"

"Did Eddie do something I should know about? Is he dangerous?"

"That's what I'm trying to figure out."

"Because that's sort of what I wanted to ask you. Should I be scared?"

"Has he done anything that suggests you might be in any danger with him?"

"Other than I'm not sure he's the faithful type, no."

"Do you suspect him of cheating on you? Have you caught him in lies?"

"No, it's just that he's—well—really good looking, and women are really—flirty—with him. I'm not sure he wouldn't, you know, take one of them up on their implied offers."

"Did you happen to wake up in the night and notice Eddie wasn't in bed?"

"No."

"I don't want to break up a promising relationship, Ms. Dillman. Unless you have reason to be afraid of him, I would say he's harmless because I have nothing to go on but a few things, and so far he's checking out as being in the clear. It's unlikely he would stay the night with you if he were planning to do what was done Wednesday night. I would imagine he would beg off with an excuse, so while it's theoretically possible he has committed the crime we're investigating, it's also very doubtful. I just need to leave my own mind open to the possibility, no matter how small, that he did sneak out, but at this point, I'd say it's less than a one-percent chance he did. I won't investigate him further unless I find another reason to."

"He seems like a really nice guy."

"He probably is. I came away with the same feeling, but I've known people who can fool others very easily. I'd just be aware of what he does and says about other people, especially people in subservient positions, like waitresses and the like."

The corners of her mouth turned up in a small smile. "Thanks."

"Is that what you wanted to ask me? If you should be afraid of Eddie?"

"Yes."

"I would say not until he gives you a reason to fear him."

"Thanks again."

They said their goodbyes, and Pantera left, heading for the last of the Blanton households he knew about. This house was in the Ashland area, north of Richmond. It would usually take him nearly a half-hour to get there, but traffic was particularly heavy on I-95 that day.

When he arrived at this Blanton residence, he found two sisters in their forties, both divorced and seemingly determined to stay that way. He spent less than five minutes with them and thanked them before heading back to the precinct.

When he arrived, Harry said, "We found a bug in your living room, your kitchen, and your bedroom."

"Son of a bitch!" Pantera said. "He's been listening in on my life, too?"

"Looks that way."

Pantera fumed for a moment, wondering what gems the creep had gathered from his eavesdropping.

"Nothing in the girls' rooms?"

"Nah. Apparently, he was happy just watching them."

"The asshole."

"We'll get him, Tony."

"You bet we will."

Blanton arrived at the home of Phil and Nancy Boyd around two A.M. that night. He unloaded his equipment, carrying it around to the back door. In his

206

previous recon of the house and property when he'd followed Nancy here from Pantera's, he'd seen that the Boyds had a lush lawn with no bare areas, other than the perfect circles of mulch around the bases of the few trees in the yard. He didn't bother with his special shoes because any prints that were made would disappear almost immediately.

After unloading, he drove a few blocks away and parked on a side street. Walking back, he began work on the back door's burglar alarm first. He was familiar with this model and had it disarmed in about twenty minutes. Then he picked the lock and was inside, slipping his shoes off to avoid leaving tracks in the house. He would leave no clues behind here, either now or later. Doing so would ruin his plans since this was where he would eventually confront Pantera.

After installing the cameras and testing them for focus and the ability to share the videos to the cloud, he left, walking the few blocks to his car. He grinned all the way back to Richmond. As far as the Boyd's neighborhood was concerned, nobody had entered or left. It was a nice suburban area where people were in bed no later than midnight and slept heavily until morning. They were certain of their safety and lived amid the usual stillness in blesséd ignorance of the evil that had visited in the night.

This was the focus of his thoughts as he drove and considered his next steps. Within a week, the entire Pantera/Boyd family would be dead.

And because of the genius of his plan, he would get away with it all.

TWENTY-SIX

When Pantera picked up his daughters from the Overmeyers', nobody felt like going out to Renaud's for dinner, so instead he stopped for pizza, a poor substitute for the cuisine of one of his favorite restaurants, but they had to eat something. None of them ate much of the pizza, only a slice each.

After dinner, Beth asked, "Dad? Why do people do horrible things like that guy did?"

He hadn't told them that this same guy had likely murdered someone and might be involved in more disappearances of young women, and he didn't want to. They were frightened enough that they'd been the victim of what they thought of as a peeper.

"There are a lot of sick people out there, honey. Some men—enjoy—looking at people going about their daily lives when they don't know they're being watched, doing the kinds of things everyone does when they think they're alone, like getting undressed to take a shower or bath or to change into pajamas."

"But why would he watch you, too, if he likes girls?"

"Well, we think he's someone we're investigating for another crime. He's spying on me because of that."

"What crime?" Andrea asked, her expression showing she suspected the worst.

"We found the same gypsum dust at other crime scenes. We think he left it on purpose so we'd know he was spying on his victims to learn their habits—that sort of thing."

"Victims of what?" Andrea asked, not to be put off.

"Baby, just leave it alone, okay?" he pleaded.

"No, Dad, we have a right to know."

"We think the same guy killed a local school administrator."

"You said 'victims.' That's more than one, Dad. What else do you think this guy did?"

Pantera took a deep breath and let it out slowly. "Before I tell you more, I want you to know that you are not his target. You two were like, I don't know, the cherry on top, an accidental inclusion in his spying on me. He may have known I have daughters who visit me frequently and figured 'what the hell' and set up cameras to watch you as well just for the fun of it—at least fun for him. I was the one he needed to watch."

"Why would he watch you?" Beth asked.

"Because I'm the enemy to him. He feels the need to know what I do when I'm alone. Perhaps he listened in on phone conversations, at least my end of them, to find out where we were in the investigation—or maybe just to learn more about me and what makes me tick." Pantera didn't mention the listening devices found in his home that day. As far as the asshole's motives for doing what he did, Pantera knew he was making suppositions with his daughters for their benefit since he wasn't totally sure why he was spied on. He just needed them to understand that they were collateral damage, not the target.

"Okay, we're not the targets. Now, what other victims?" Her gaze spoke of her determination to get the answers she needed.

"Two girls are missing. They were roommates. The odd thing is that one disappeared days before the other."

"Wouldn't that make us possible targets?" Andrea asked.

"It would if he hadn't also put cameras in my bedroom, too. You only visit every few weeks. I'm here all the time. It was possible he might have watched me for weeks before the two of you visited."

"Do you have any suspects?" Beth asked.

"Not yet, but I have some suspicions."

"Like what?"

"I think it might be a cop or someone else who works at the precinct where I work."

Andrea asked, "What makes you think that?"

"For one thing, whoever it is had access to my desk when I wasn't around."

"How do you know that?"

"I'd rather not get into that. It's only a suspicion. I don't have any other evidence that it's a cop, but the fact he had access to my desk makes me wonder."

"Are there any cops who don't like you?" Beth asked.

"I'm sure there are, but it's not like we're a couple of kids in the schoolyard trash-talking each other. With adults it's usually more subtle."

"What about that cop you had the fight with over what he said about people like me?" Andrea said.

"Well, we aren't each other's favorite person, but I don't think he could do something like this."

"How well do you know him?"

"Well enough."

"What's his favorite sports team?" Andrea asked.

"I don't even know if he likes sports."

She shook her head. "Yeah, you know him real well, huh?"

"I know him well enough to know he didn't do this." He watched her reaction, and it was obvious she didn't believe him. In fact, neither did he, not fully, but he wasn't going to tell her that. Still, it was worth giving it a cursory effort to rule him out. He did suspect someone in the precinct, and in truth if he went through every person individually, he would probably dismiss each one with no second thoughts because he believed he knew them well enough to decide if they could do something like this. In truth, everyone was capable of hiding their true selves to some degree.

Solving crimes was difficult enough without having to be a victim of one of the crimes. It was why he knew he would be taken off this case if Lt. Gariepy found out he'd been spied on. Gariepy had been out that day to attend a relative's funeral out of town and wouldn't be back for a few more days. He'd chosen not to mention finding the evidence in his home to anyone other than Harry to make sure he remained on this one. He'd sworn Harry to secrecy, which he'd agreed to reluctantly.

Andrea gave up her argument, and the girls watched some TV while Pantera studied the information they had on the Davis killing, as well as the disappearances of Roxanne Beard and her roommate Wendy Atwater.

Finally, Beth announced she was going to bed, but as she left she asked, "Dad? Is it possible there's another camera hidden in my room?"

"No. You're safe now."

"How do you know?"

"Because Harry swept the house today for anything, and it's clean."

When Beth left the room, Andrea turned off the TV and turned to her father.

"Dad?"

"Yes?"

"What if that man comes for you? What if he wants to kill you?"

"You don't need to worry about that. I can take care of myself."

She was silent for a moment. "That doesn't help."

He looked at her, and seeing her fear, he went to sit beside her. He put his arm around her, and she leaned into him, laying her head on his shoulder.

"Sweetheart, I'm a cop. It's a dangerous job. I've had close scrapes before, and I'll have them again. But believe me, my sense of self-preservation is strong. I don't do anything that could be considered rash or irresponsible in my job. I've survived this long because I'm careful. The only way he'd be able to kill me is if my death was the only way I could save you or your sister."

She reached around him and hugged him, burying her head further into his neck. "I love you, Dad. Please don't get yourself hurt."

"I love you, too, baby, and I'll do my best." He'd like to be able to say he would not get hurt, but she was old enough to know he couldn't promise that. He could only promise he'd try.

"I'm not a baby, you know," she said.

"Sorry. It's just something I say. To me and your mother, you'll always be our baby. We remember when you really were one, you know, and that image dies hard, and then only if you want it to, and I don't."

They were silent and stayed like that for several minutes until Andrea announced that she was going to bed. She kissed his cheek and left the room, leaving Pantera wondering how he could catch this creep who had destroyed his daughters' sense of privacy and safety, not only for themselves but also for him.

Finally, he put the file away. Nothing in there revealed the slightest hint who the creep was or where he could be found. He hefted himself from the sofa and went to his room. His first glance was at the vent where the camera had sat unnoticed for who knew how long.

At that moment, he realized he hadn't checked behind the vent to see if a gift had been left behind for him to find. He'd only been concerned about his daughters' rooms. He couldn't believe he had ignored the other vents in the house where he'd found the dust marking where the creep had been. He had been so preoccupied with what he found in the girls' rooms that what was usually automatic had been completely forgotten. Harry had checked for bugs, which was done with an electronic sensor, but he wouldn't have checked his vent because it was obvious the cameras had already been removed. Harry probably figured he'd already checked the other vents anyway.

Retrieving the stepstool, he moved the dresser out of the way and removed the vent. He froze when he saw the sheet of printer paper. It was face down, so he could not see the image, but he instinctively knew what it would be when he looked.

Lifting the paper, he saw himself and Lisa. They were in the middle of having sex. He was on top of her, but a clear image of her left breast could be seen.

When he checked the living room vent, he thankfully found nothing there, but then the asshole didn't need to leave anything else. He'd made his point.

Checking his watch, he saw it was nearly 10:30, too late to call Lisa. He would call her in the morning to let her know what had happened. It wasn't a call he looked forward to making, which was probably why he happily agreed with himself that it was too late to call her now.

Replacing the vents, he went to bed, but it was a long time before sleep finally came.

TWENTY-SEVEN

Pantera dropped the girls at Harry's on his way to work, picking up Harry to save him the trouble of driving to work himself.

When Harry was seated in the car, Pantera said, "I checked the other vents last night."

"You hadn't checked them before I got there yesterday morning?"

"Nope. Clean forgot in my anger over the situation."

"Did you find anything?"

"I found something alright."

"What?"

"A picture of me and Lisa in bed."

"Holy shit. Have you told Lisa yet?"

"Nope. I was going to call her this morning, but getting out of the house with the girls was hectic, and I didn't want to make the call in front of them for obvious reasons."

"So, when are you going to call?"

"As soon as we get to the precinct. I figured you could go in and I'll make the call."

"Sure thing."

When they arrived for work, Harry stepped out of the car and leaned down before closing the door. "Good luck. You're gonna need it. I'm not sure how she's going to take this."

"Neither am I, but she needs to be told."

"Agreed. See you when you finish."

Pantera sighed and called Lisa.

"Hey, sexy!" she said.

"You won't think so after you hear what I have to say."

"Oh?"

"Yeah."

"Are you going to tell me to get lost?"

"No. I'm going to tell you we were caught in the act."

"What does that mean?"

"Someone took video of us while we were having sex at my place. I found a picture that looks like a still from a video."

Silence met him.

"Lisa? You still there?"

"Yes."

"What are you thinking?"

"I'm not sure."

"Do you want to see me again? I'll understand if you say no."

"Of course, I do. It's not your fault. I mean, it wasn't you making the video, was it?"

"Of course not."

"Then don't blame yourself. Shit happens. I take it you don't have the video itself?"

"No. I'll explain how I found out about it when I see you again, which I hope will be soon."

"Will you be free this weekend?"

"As far as I know, yes."

"And the cameras are gone?"

"Yes."

"Then expect me Saturday."

"That would be nice."

"Can I stay the night?"

"If you want to."

"I definitely want to. Just no pictures or videos."

That made him smile. "It's a deal."

When he entered the squad room, he was in a considerably better mood than when Harry had left him in the car.

"It went well?"

"Better than expected."

"How so?"

"She doesn't blame me. In fact, she didn't sound all that upset about it. I mean, she wasn't happy about it, but she said, 'shit happens,' as if it weren't such a big deal."

"You're one lucky man, Tony Pantera. I hope you realize that."

"I wouldn't go that far. My daughters no longer feel safe, and I do have something of a stalker."

"We'll catch him," Harry said. "Count on it."

Pantera's desktop phone rang. "Pantera," he answered.

It was Sergeant Broadnax at the desk. "Hey, Detective. I got Lenny down here. Says it's about one of your cases."

Pantera sighed. "I'm a little busy right now. Can he talk to someone down there?"

"I'll do what I can." Sergeant Broadnax hung up the phone and said, "Lenny, Detective Pantera is busy right now. Can someone else take your statement?"

To Broadnax, Lenny took on an expression that was closer to having been told his dog had died. "But I did it!" he said. "He'll need to arrest me!"

"We can arrest you, too, Lenny."

Lenny's gaze shifted right and left before settling on his shoes. "I really want to talk to the detective."

At that moment, Vince Gordon, who had recently been promoted to detective, walked through the lobby. Broadnax knew Gordon was scheduled to get off work in about an hour since he was assigned to graveyard. Broadnax, who like most everyone there didn't like

216

Gordon at all because he was considered to have been promoted because he frequently kissed Chief of Detectives Childers' ass, decided to saddle Gordon with Lenny.

"Ah, Detective Gordon!" he called. "I have someone who needs to talk to you."

"Oh?" Gordon said as he approached.

"Yes, this is Lenny—what's your last name, Lenny?"

"Barstow."

"Lenny Barstow. He's here to confess to a crime."

Gordon had never met or heard of Lenny. He looked at Lenny now and said, "What crime did you commit, Lenny?"

"Those girls. I kidnapped them and killed them."

Gordon felt his scalp twitch. "Which girls?" Gordon asked as he led Lenny to the elevators, surreptitiously signaling another officer to come with them. There was safety in numbers, after all.

"I don't know their names."

Gordon looked disturbed by this news, and Broadnax smiled because Gordon's demeanor suggested he thought he might get credit for solving a double-homicide.

Gordon walked into the detectives' squad room with Lenny. He asked Lenny to take a seat while he talked to Lt. Gariepy about the situation.

Lenny complied happily while Gordon walked over to tap on Gariepy's door. Gariepy called out for him to enter, and he stepped inside.

"Lieutenant, I have someone here who wants to confess to a double kidnapping and murder."

Gariepy glanced at the man sitting at Gordon's desk. "I see you've met Crazy Carl."

"Who?"

217

"Crazy Carl. His real name's Lenny something."

"Barstow."

"Yeah, Barstow. He's what's known as a chronic confessor. He spends a lot of his time here confessing to one crime or another. He's mental, Gordon."

"Oh. Then he didn't kill two girls?"

"Anymore than you did."

Gordon seemed taken aback by the response at first. Then he glanced at Lenny before turning back to Gariepy.

"So what do I do with him?"

"Take his statement. It won't take five minutes because he's always a little short on details. Then ask him a question about the crime scene, something only the perp would know. Whatever he says, tell him he's wrong and be kind to him when you usher him out. He's a nice guy, just needs to confess to shit."

"I don't know anything about the crime scene."

"Neither does Lenny. Just make something up. Ask him how he got past the dog."

"Was there a dog?"

"Not that I know of. I don't even know what case he's confessing to this time. For all we know, he read or heard about something that happened in Chicago."

"He's confessed to crimes that happened somewhere else?"

"I don't think so, at least not yet, but there's always a first time. Just go easy on him and escort him out when you've shown him he couldn't have done the deed. He'll go peacefully."

Ten minutes later, Gordon had escorted Lenny to the front door. Turning, he looked at Sergeant Broadnax, who was chuckling.

"You make a collar on that double homicide, Vince?" Broadnax asked, laughing.

"Next time, maybe you could clue me in."

"Relax. He's the only chronic confessor we get here. He's harmless. Afraid of his own shadow. How long it take you to figure it out?"

"I went to Gariepy. He told me."

"Glad someone did. You mighta locked up an innocent man, but ol' Crazy Carl woulda loved it."

Gordon went back to the squad room.

Seventeen miles east of Richmond fertile farmland stretched for miles in all directions. Soybeans and corn were plentiful crops out there, and it wasn't uncommon for teenagers to wander between rows of cornstalks, aware that someone could be standing just feet away and not see them. The tall stalks that covered the landscape in places afforded privacy. Jimmy Wells and his girlfriend, Penny Halstead, were well aware of that fact. Whenever Jimmy was wanting some time alone with Penny, he would mention how the corn looked taller than it had just the day before. It was their signal. Soon after that, he and Penny would go "out for a walk."

Jimmy thought his mama didn't have a clue what happened on those walks, but she did. Many mothers would fret that their son might get a girl pregnant and have to marry her, which was the rule in their home. She and her husband, Robert, had probably said it a thousand times to Jimmy. "You get a girl pregnant, you marry her—no ifs ands or buts."

Her boy Jimmy was a wild one. For that reason, Loretta Wells wanted Jimmy to get Penny pregnant. It might be the only way he would settle down. She knew he was prone to taking off with his buddies and getting drunk, and she thought a family would make him more responsible, even if he was only seventeen. She herself had wed when she was sixteen and had her first son six months later, so she figured it was time for Jimmy . For his part, Jimmy was ignorant of this line of thinking from his mother. For Loretta's part, she would welcome someone else to help with the household chores. Robert was busy in the fields all day and the little ones weren't old enough yet to have more than a few chores. Jimmy was just plain lazy, so he searched for ways to get out of the work his mother needed him to do. Another pair of hands would be welcome indeed.

That morning after Penny arrived for her usual morning visit, Jimmy said to nobody in particular, "Dang, I think the corn's even taller than it was yesterday." Loretta sneaked a peek at Penny, who smiled with a happy glint in her eye. Five minutes later, Jimmy asked Penny if she wanted to take a walk. She agreed, doing a good job of pretending she really didn't want to but would if that's what Jimmy wanted to do.

They left the house and started walking along the mostly empty road that ran by the house. About a hundred yards from his front yard, Jimmy grabbed Penny's hand and tugged her toward the cornfield.

Plunging into the rustling rows of dry leaves, he laughed and was joined by Penny's equally exuberant giggles. After they were about ten feet into the rows, they fell to the ground and began to kiss while Jimmy worked at his belt and zipper and Penny did her best to tug her shorts and panties down.

As Jimmy began to kiss her neck, Penny screamed. She'd turned her head to one side to give Jimmy access to her sensitive throat and saw the body of a naked girl two rows away. Her head was sticking out from where it had been wrapped in something. An animal had apparently pulled the material aside to get at the girl's face. Penny scrambled up to a sitting position and faced a bewildered Jimmy.

"What's wrong?!"

"There!" she cried, pointing toward what she could now see were two bodies, not just one.

"Holy shit!" Jimmy said. Looking at Penny he said, "Get dressed! I gotta go get my mama!"

"You ain't leavin' me here with two dead girls!"

He looked around as if trying to find a landmark. Of course, there was none. "Well, someone's gotta stay here to help us find the bodies again by yellin' for us when we come back. I can follow a sound, but I'm not sure I can find this spot again. It would be too easy to miss."

"Well, I can follow a sound, too. You stay here! I'll be right back with your mama!" With that, she plunged into the surrounding stalks, heading toward the road, as if Satan himself were on her heels. As soon as she made it out, she began screaming for Jimmy's mother.

"Ms. Wells! Ms. Wells!"

Several minutes later, Jimmy heard them coming back down the road towards where they had first entered the rows of corn, their frantic conversations preceding them. He called out, "Over here!"

Seconds later, the two were plunging into the corn. His mother called out, "Yell again!"

"Over here!"

The two suddenly burst through the corn nearby and nearly stumbled over the bodies of the two girls.

"Holy Mother of God!" Loretta exclaimed.

"What are we gonna do?" Jimmy asked.

"Call your uncle."

"But he's a Richmond detective. He don't have any jurisdiction out here."

Her older brother had joined the Richmond Police Force about ten years ago. He was really her half-brother, but her father had adopted him when his mom married her dad.

221

"But he'll call someone who does. Someone who will do this right." Loretta said. "Besides, he'll be gettin' to his house soon himself and can stop by to help if it's needed. He's a detective in Richmond. Nobody out here's gonna turn that help down, even if it's only unofficial."

"I guess so," Jimmy said, pulling Penny into a hug to ease her shock from finding the two dead girls.

Turning to her son, Loretta said, "You might wanna zip and buckle up."

Jimmy looked down. In the turmoil, he'd forgotten to zip his pants or buckle his belt. The only thing he'd done was button the waist to hold his pants up. Penny blushed a deep red.

Five minutes later, Loretta was on the phone to her brother.

"Hey, Loretta," Vince said when she'd identified herself.

"Vince? You comin' home soon?"

"I'm about to leave."

"We found a couple of dead girls out here on the farm!"

Vince Gordon had been standing but immediately sat down as if his legs could no longer hold him up.

TWENTY-EIGHT

When Gordon arrived at his sister's house, the area was already swarming with sheriff deputies. The entire force must have been there. They were unused to homicide investigations, and it showed. He stepped up to an older deputy who seemed to be in charge.

"Hi, I'm Detective Vince Gordon with Richmond PD. Is there some way I can help out?"

The deputy, whose name tag read Morrison, asked, "What are you doing here? This isn't your jurisdiction."

"My sister's son found the bodies on their land. She called me."

"Oh." The deputy looked around as if trying to find an answer to Detective Gordon's offer to help.

Gordon spoke up before he could come up with an answer. "You guys investigate many homicides?"

Morrison looked at Gordon. "What do you think? This isn't Richmond." He looked around. "It's not even Louisa."

"I can help you in an unofficial capacity," Gordon said. "Just a consultant."

"Would you be charging for this consultant work?"

"Nope. I'll help out on my own time as a favor to my sister. Besides, I live just up the road myself. I'm just a concerned citizen with homicide experience."

Morrison held out his hand. "Welcome aboard."

Gordon shook it and smiled. "Have you removed the bodies yet?"

"No. I got some guys takin' pictures."

"Any footprints near the bodies?"

223

"None that I could see."

"Do you recognize either of them?"

"Not much to recognize. Animals got to 'em," he said. "Not a pretty sight."

"Never is," Gordon said.

"Still, it looks like they've been here at least a few days, and nobody around here has reported anyone missing. My guess is they're from Richmond."

"Well, let's go have a look," Gordon said and waited for Morrison to lead the way.

Gordon could tell that while Morrison knew he would have to contend with the bodies, he didn't really look forward to seeing them again. He couldn't blame him. He was a rural county's deputy.

"Is Sheriff Nichols coming out?"

"He should be here soon. He was in Fredericksburg visiting his brother. They went fishin' today," Morrison said, as if an excuse was necessary for the sheriff's absence. Morrison sounded almost resentful, as if he blamed the sheriff for being out of town, making him the lead investigator of a gruesome homicide scene.

When Gordon arrived where the bodies lay, he knelt beside one of the girls, a brunette. He recognized enough of what he could see of her face to know her from a photo he'd seen on Pantera's desk of a girl Pantera had said was missing. Pantera had taken the picture from the girl's home. Gordon had overheard Pantera talking about the case with Overmeyer.

"Yep, they're from Richmond, or at least this one is," Gordon said. He didn't want to call Pantera in but knew he would have to. A girl and her roommate had vanished. Now, he knew where they ended up, a place only their killer had known until his nephew had stumbled onto the scene when he and his girlfriend, Penny, were just looking for a place to have sex.

"I'm going to have to call another detective from Richmond. This was a missing person case he was investigating."

"Okay," Morrison said. "I'll call the sheriff and let him know."

An hour later, Pantera and Overmeyer arrived at the scene. Gordon had given him his sister's address so he could use GPS to find the place. It was truly in the middle of nowhere.

Pantera knelt beside the body of Roxanne Beard, wondering if he would have been able to save her if he'd taken her phone call more seriously. True, his hands were tied by the rules, but he could have at least visited the young man she feared to let him know they were aware of him. He didn't know if the perp had held her roommate, Wendy Atwater, prisoner until he had both girls, or if he'd killed her long before killing Roxanne. The autopsy would answer that question, along with a number of others that could help him.

He still needed to find this guy Blanton that she'd mentioned in her calls. He had Eddie Blanton as a possible suspect, but he'd been right when he told his girlfriend that he would likely not have stayed the night if he planned to sneak out that night to murder someone.

Something about this case made no sense at all. First, why was Davis's killer now killing women? Why would the perp spy on him and his family? What would he hope to accomplish with that? It's not as if he conducted the investigation out of his house.

This thought led him again to consider that someone at the precinct was guilty, but so far he'd not found anything that might link Davis with anyone there, much less either of these two girls. It was entirely possible that the stalker Roxanne Beard was afraid of had nothing to do with any of this. Odd coincidences happened, and this may be one of those. Perhaps he was on a search for an innocent man by trying to find the guy named Blanton, but he had no other clues as to the identity of the man who was doing this.

Was he dealing with someone who just enjoyed killing? Had this person recently moved to the Richmond area and was hunting victims there, and it was his bad luck to have drawn these cases?

His thoughts drifted back to how whoever this was had hidden cameras in heating and air conditioning ducts. Whoever this was, he'd managed to do that very early in his killing spree. Pantera figured he must have seen the name of the detective handling the Davis case in the newspaper and moved on from there to bugging his house. Davis's and Roxanne Beard's homes had been bugged prior to their being killed. Was the man planning to kill him now?

Pantera doubted it, mostly because he'd left pictures behind to taunt Pantera. He saw it as more of a cat and mouse game the killer was wanting to play, as if to tell Pantera, "I'm smarter than you." Serial killers could get off on that aspect of their crimes. They sometimes enjoyed gloating about their intelligence. Pantera had handled only one serial killer case before, and not that long ago, but that guy had considered himself sent by God as an angel of death. He was in a hospital for the criminally insane now.

It also occurred to Pantera that in games of cat and mouse, the cat felt the power to end the life of the mouse whenever he wished. Was it that way now?

And how did this particular "cat" know his daughters sometimes stayed with him? The cameras were set up to see the bed and its surroundings, knowing the most private moments took place in that area of any bedroom. He'd set up the cameras specifically to watch his teenage daughters in various stages of undress. Rage filled Pantera to think that this monster had watched them sleep.

"Whatcha thinking?" Harry asked from over his right shoulder. He was bending over and looking at the corpses of the two young women who had once been beautiful, but whose faces were now partially eaten by animals and birds.

"That we need to find this fucker before he does this again."

"Any ideas on how to do that?"

"Not yet, but nobody makes zero mistakes. Nobody. We just need to find where he made one."

"Sometimes one is all you need."

"Hey, Pantera. Overmeyer," a voice said from behind them. Turning, Pantera saw it was Detective Vince Gordon. He'd forgotten he was at the scene.

"Tell me something, Gordon."

"Yeah?"

"How did you end up part of this investigation?"

"My nephew and his girlfriend are the ones who found the bodies."

"Where are they?"

Gordon pointed toward the road. "Up by the road. They're with my sister."

"Where does your sister live?"

He pointed to the east. "About a hundred yards that way. She and her husband own this land. This is their corn crop."

As Pantera and Overmeyer walked out of the cornrows toward the county highway, Pantera thought how odd it was that the killer had chosen this plot of land to stash the bodies. Killers usually haunted only areas they were familiar with. How would the person who killed and dumped these girls like yesterday's trash know about this place? Was it sheer luck of the draw? Had he just driven until finding a suitable dumping spot before placing the girls among the corn stalks?

Or was he familiar with the land out here?

Gordon was following them, and Pantera turned to glance his way. Nobody cared much for Detective Gordon. Pantera's friend, the late Officer Sarah Tully, had been believed by most of the precinct to be first in line for that position, but Gordon had taken it instead. Tully had gotten drunk upon learning she didn't get the promotion and had gone home to be murdered. That night, she'd tried to entice Pantera to join her in her bed. He'd turned her down because he didn't want her to regret a decision she'd made while drunk and in a depression. He had spent months trying to convince himself he'd done the right thing, figuring she would be alive if he'd said yes.

Now, Pantera wondered if Gordon might be worse than a brown-noser. Whoever had killed Davis had access to Pantera's desk. And this perp seemed to be two steps ahead of Pantera and Overmeyer.

But the problem with this theory was motive. Why would Detective Vince Gordon want to kill an assistant principal, and why kill these two young ladies? Was it possible he was the worst of all serial killers? The ones who killed for no other reason than to kill someone?

As they stepped out of the corn, Pantera saw the woman who was probably Gordon's sister, along with her son and his girlfriend.

Pantera introduced himself and asked to speak to them one at a time in his car. As the sister walked with Pantera and Overmeyer, Gordon tagged along.

"Gordon, if you could, would you mind staying with your nephew and Penny? I don't want them talking to each other right now."

"Sure," Gordon said. Pantera noticed the resentment in Gordon's voice.

Pantera knew his reason for not to allowing Gordon to be a part of the questioning was lame, but Pantera did not want him there when he asked some of the questions. Being a detective, he might be able to figure out why he was asking them. He wasn't a very good detective, but if guilty, he'd figure it out easily.

After Loretta Wells sat in the front passenger seat, Harry climbed into the back and Pantera sat behind the wheel.

"Ms. Wells, this won't take long," Pantera began. He certainly didn't suspect her of killing anyone, but it was possible she knew more than she realized.

"Good, because I have things to do at home."

"Can you tell me what happened?"

"I was ironing. My son and his girlfriend had just stepped out to take a walk, but I know what they do instead. Don't take a genius to figure that out."

"Yes, ma'am," Pantera interrupted. He didn't want this to turn into a story of the difficulties of raising a teenage boy. "So you were ironing?"

"Yeah. I was ironing and watching one of my programs on TV when—"

"About what time was this?"

"It was maybe a few minutes before nine. I was watching an old Family Feud, and it was almost over."

"Okay, go on."

"Well, I was ironing and I heard Penny yelling for me like something bad had happened. I thought maybe Jimmy had been hurt or something, so I run out of the house and she says for me to come quick. They'd found some dead bodies in the corn."

She paused, as if that was the end of the story.

"Go on," Pantera urged. "What happened next?"

229

"Well, I run with her as quick as I could, and Jimmy had had the good sense to stay behind to help bring us to where the girls' bodies were because it's easy to get sort of lost in the cornrows. It coulda taken ten minutes to find 'em. Maybe more. So anyway, he calls for us and we follow his voice and there on the ground are the two girls, sorta wrapped up in sheets and stuff, with their heads stickin' out. It was plain to see they was dead."

"What did you do then?"

"I went home and called my brother. He's a detective on the Richmond Police Force." She said it with pride, as if she were talking to a couple of local rookie cops.

"Why didn't you call the local sheriff? He's the one who handles crime out here."

"You're here, and you ain't no deputy here."

"We're handling the case of the disappearance of the two young ladies you found," he said. "We're here in the capacity of that investigation, not to investigate the murder itself, at least not exactly. We're working with your sheriff's office."

"Well, anyways, I called Vince. He sounded like I'd told him we'd found a volcano on the property. He was in shock."

"Really?"

"Yeah."

"In what way? What did he say?"

"Mostly nothin' for a moment. Then he started talkin' about how awful it was."

Pantera glanced at Harry. "Okay, what happened then?"

"Well, he said he'd call the sheriff's office for me, which is what I wanted him to do. My husband was still in the fields and I didn't want to bother him none with this. It wasn't like he could do anything about it. So, anyway, Vince called the sheriff's office, and they came out here. The deputy in charge stopped by here and asked some questions like if we disturbed the bodies or anything. I told him we hadn't."

"When did Detective Gordon get here?"

"About an hour later than when we hung up."

"Did you touch anything at the crime scene? Did you touch the girls' faces or the stuff they were wrapped in?"

"No. I didn't want to look at 'em, so why would I touch them?"

"I understand."

Pantera glanced again at Harry then said to Ms. Wells, "Thank you, Ms. Wells. You can go home now and take care of whatever you needed to do."

"Thank you. What about Jimmy?"

"I need to talk to him. I'll send him home when I'm done."

"You got everything from me. I don't know why you gotta talk to him, too."

"Yes, ma'am. But we have to get everyone's story. It's part of the job. Your brother could vouch for that."

"Well, send him straight home. Don't let him walk Penny home. He'll be stoppin' on the way to take care of what he'd not been able to do before."

"Yes, ma'am," Pantera said, and she left the car and began walking home.

Harry climbed out and went over to where Vince Gordon was standing with his nephew and Penny.

"Could we talk to you now, Jimmy?" he said, and Jimmy followed him to the car.

"What can you tell me about what happened?" Pantera asked after Jimmy had settled himself in the front seat.

231

"We found two dead girls."

"Yes, Jimmy. I know that, but I want to hear everything, step-by-step. How you came to be there in the first place, what you did after finding the bodies— that sort of thing."

"Oh. Well, you see, Penny and me like to take walks in the cornfield," he said, blushing. Pantera figured he knew they didn't believe the two just enjoyed walking between the rows of corn and knew they had other things on their minds.

"Then we just came upon the bodies. We were just walking along and there they were."

"Okay, did you touch the bodies?"

"No. Their faces looked all eaten up, sort of. I knew they were dead, and I didn't want to touch them. Neither did Penny."

"What did you do then?"

"I was gonna go get my mom, but Penny said no way she was stayin' out there with the dead girls, so she went. I knew we'd have trouble finding them if we both left because every row of corn looks like the next, and it wasn't like we always took the same path."

"Okay. So what did you do while Penny went for your mom?"

"Tried not to look at those bodies, but I couldn't. It was like they drew my eyes to them."

"Okay, but you didn't touch them, right?"

"Said I didn't, and I didn't."

"How did your uncle come to be here?"

"My mama called him at work. Told him we'd found a couple of dead girls on the farm. I guess he called the sheriff." He looked at Pantera. "Next thing I know, the place is crawlin' with deputies. They're askin' questions and whatnot. I think the guy in charge thinks I mighta done it."

"Why do you think that?"

"Just his way of talkin' to me, like he don't believe me."

"It might be because you're not being honest about why you and Penny were in the cornfield," Harry offered.

Jimmy's head jerked around, and he looked at Harry. "What makes you think I'm lyin' about that?"

"First, you blushed when you said that you just liked to walk in the cornfield. Then, your mother tells us she knows what you and Penny go into the cornfield for." Jimmy blushed again. "It's okay, Jimmy," Harry continued. "We were all teenagers once, you know."

"Do you know what your uncle has been doing while here?"

"No. He's just been walkin' around and stuff. He's been back there to see the girls a few times, but other than that, I don't know. Why you askin'?"

"Not important," said Pantera. "Thank you, Jimmy. If it's any help, we don't think you had anything to do with this. It's the sheriff's case, but we have a lot of say in how everything goes down."

"Thanks," Jimmy said. "Can I go now?"

"Yes."

Jimmy left the car as if it had a contagious disease, and Harry walked over to Penny and asked her to join them.

When she was seated, Pantera introduced himself and Harry before asking her basically the same first question he'd asked Jimmy and his mother.

"Can you tell me how y'all found the bodies?"

"Well, me and Jimmy was goin' out to the cornfield." She ducked her head. "We like to, you know, make out away from everyone else."

Pantera was impressed that she hadn't tried to lie,

233

though she'd used a less sexual term for what they planned to do.

"Go on."

"Well, we had just lied down in the dirt and was kissing and all, when I turned my head and saw the two bodies lyin' close by. I screamed, and Jimmy sat up wonderin' what had happened. I pointed at the bodies but I didn't tell him I saw this crow on one of the faces." She shuddered. "It was awful."

The rest of her story matched Jimmy's, though she was a bit more observant about what they'd seen. Pantera noted her powers of observation were stronger than either Jimmy's or his mother's.

"How did Detective Gordon come to be here?"

"Ms. Wells called him. Said he'd know more of what to do since he's a detective and all. It's kinda funny because he didn't seem to take the news well at all, and I figured he would take it better than Ms. Wells or Jimmy."

"How do you know he didn't take it well."

"Well, when she told him we'd found the bodies, Ms. Wells sorta got concerned, saying things like, 'Are you okay, Vince?' and stuff like that."

Pantera exchanged a glance with Harry before asking Penny, "Did she mention what prompted her to say that?"

"No. She just told him how they was found by me and Jimmy, even though I'm actually the one who found them. Then she hung up and said he was on his way and would call the sheriff."

"What did Detective Gordon do after he got here?"

"I don't know. I try to avoid him. I didn't even want to stand with him, but you said for me to stand there, so I did."

"Why didn't you want to stand with him?"

234

"He's kinda creepy."

"How's he creepy?" Pantera asked.

"Like whenever I'm wearin' a dress, which isn't often but I do sometimes when I'm comin' from church or somethin' and havin' lunch with Jimmy and he's over for lunch, too, I can see him tryin' to look under my dress. That sort of thing."

"Has he ever touched you?"

Both Harry and Pantera could tell she then told her first lie. "No," she said, looking down at her lap.

"Thank you, Penny. You've been very helpful," Pantera said. "You're free to go now."

They watched her exit the car and join Jimmy, tugging his hand to get him away from Detective Gordon.

Harry spoke up. "You thinking what I'm thinking?"

"That we need to look into Detective Gordon?"

"That's exactly what I'm thinking."

"She lied when she said he hadn't touched her."

"I know." Harry took a deep breath and let it out slowly. "And the girls were found on land he's familiar with."

"Exactly. But first I want to ask Ms. Wells about her call to her brother."

Getting out of the car, the two walked to the nearby house. Pantera knocked on the front door, and Loretta Wells opened it.

"What is it now?" she asked, sounding annoyed.

"I have a few more questions about your call to your brother," Pantera said.

"What are they? I got biscuits in the oven and I don't want them to burn."

"Penny tells us that he seemed agitated when you told him about the bodies."

"Well, of course. Wouldn't you be?"

235

"She suggested he was taking the news harder than she expected him to—that both you and your son took it better."

"Why would she say that?"

"She said you told him—" He pulled out his small notebook and flipped to a page. "She says you asked him, 'Are you okay, Vince.' May I ask why you said that?"

"Well, he was quiet for a second, like he'd fainted or something."

"Does he usually take bad news like that?"

"Not really, but then I've never called him to tell him we found a couple of dead girls in the corn before. I guess he was anxious because someone who'd killed those girls had been that close to our house, like maybe he could come back and start in on us."

While her explanation of his upset was possible, Pantera was still suspicious of his reaction. If he'd been the person who hid the bodies there, possibly for later removal to a more secure place, he would have likely reacted exactly as he did. He hoped the coroner could give them at least an approximate time when the bodies had been left there.

"Thank you, Ms. Wells."

They left her and walked to Pantera's car.

"She's going to tell her brother you were asking about him," Harry said.

"Yeah, I know. Can't be helped, but maybe we don't want it to be. If he's guilty and thinks we're on to him, he may panic and do something without full planning. Maybe make a fatal error."

"You really think he might have done this?"

"Not sure, but right now, he's the best suspect we have. It's not as if he couldn't just pick the name Blanton out of thin air."

"Did Roxanne Beard say anything about this Blanton being older than she is by about fifteen years?"

"No, but it's not a certainty that she would have unless I asked specifics about him to investigate her complaint. She may think nothing of having gone out twice with an older guy."

They waited around for the crime techs and coroner to finish up before approaching them. "Find anything interesting?" Pantera asked the lead tech.

"You'll have to talk to the deputy to get a copy of our report," was all he said.

While Pantera talked to the tech, Harry went to the coroner. "Any clue on how long they've been here?"

"Well, one was placed here before the other. Days before. The brunette hasn't been here for more than a day or two. The other one, as much as five. I'll know more when I'm able to do the autopsy."

When Harry reported this to Pantera, they stared at each other for a moment, absorbing the meaning.

"That means he was able to find the exact place where he left the first body. The kids mentioned how one row looks like another. How did he know which row was the one where he'd left the first body?"

Harry stared at the rows of corn. Suddenly, his lips opened, creating a smacking sound of revelation.

"What is it?"

Harry paused a minute, looking down the rows to where they ended near the corner of the two highways that ran along different sides of the field, his eyes moving along them to where the rows were slightly trampled by the police and others moving in and out, a red marker flag sticking up in the dirt to mark the row where the bodies were found. "They were left between rows thirteen and fourteen," he said.

"What?"

Harry pointed at the corner of the cornfield to his right. "That's row one at the end." He counted rows, each planted in amazingly straight lines, stopping at thirteen. The bodies are between rows thirteen and fourteen. Unlucky thirteen."

"I'll be damned," Pantera said. "Good catch."

"Does that make me a better detective than you?" Harry asked with a smile.

"No, just a lucky one," Pantera answered, reflecting Harry's grin.

Two hours later, Blanton entered Pantera's home again. He had been up all night the night before and was tired, but he would have to do this now or never.

Blanton figured he'd have to come here again. He knew the detective would find the teasing clues he'd left behind in the vents eventually. Mostly, he was surprised the older daughter had been the one to see the telltale gypsum dust, which would lead Pantera to look behind the vents. After this, Pantera would have to sweep the house for bugs. The best part of all this was that Pantera would feel invincible against having his conversations listened to by someone else. He felt his house was now clean of eavesdropping equipment.

But Blanton was there to turn Pantera's feelings of safety into a lie. He reinstalled the bugs and left long before Pantera would arrive home that evening.

TWENTY-NINE

On their way back to Richmond, Pantera called the Chesterfield and Culpepper police to have them break the news to the parents of the two women that the girls' pictures matched two women who had been found dead and that he would contact them to arrange for positive identification. He could call Ms. Beard later to express his condolences, after they had been told in person by the Culpepper police. This was not the kind of news you gave over the phone. The call to the Beards was not one he looked forward to at all.

He would skip a phone call to Wendy's mother to express condolences. He would only give her the address of the coroner's office where the body could be identified, and he wasn't looking forward to even that. What she would likely say in response to the call would be depressing, and he was depressed enough because of what they'd found in the cornfield.

When they arrived at the precinct, Pantera stepped to Gariepy's office and knocked. He needed to see if someone could follow Detective Gordon to see what he could be up to. He knew getting Gariepy to agree was a long shot, but if he refused, Pantera had a backup plan, though even he had to admit it was a terrible one.

"Come in!" Gariepy called.

Pantera closed the door behind him as he entered and sat in a chair opposite Gariepy. "I take it this won't be a quick FYI thing?" Gariepy asked.

"Afraid not."

"Well, then, get to it. I have work piled up. Budget crap."

Pantera knew Gariepy hated budget issues more than just about anything else.

"I have a favor to ask."

"What is it?" Gariepy asked.

"I need someone to keep an eye on Gordon."

"Gordon who?"

"Detective Vince Gordon."

"Have you lost your mind? I know he's nobody's favorite, but why do you think we need to use manpower to follow him around?"

"It's possible he's the guy who killed two young women, Roxanne Beard and Wendy Atwater, a couple of ladies who were rooming together. Gordon may have been involved."

"And what crazy nonsense popped into your head that caused you to think this cockamamie thing?"

"It's a number of things, really."

"Then let's count them."

Pantera related all the reasons he thought Gordon could have had something to do with the women's deaths. In the end, he admitted it was only suspicion, but he felt they needed to pursue that line.

"That's it? He knows the area where the bodies were left? That's not much of a reason to go investigating a fellow detective."

"And he reacted rather bizarrely at the news the bodies had been found, not to mention his nephew's teenage girlfriend says he's, in her words, *creepy*. And both Harry and I agree she lied when she said he hadn't touched her."

"Okay, I'll give you that much, but it's not enough to suddenly pursue him as suspect number one in the case. I mean, it's entirely possible he reacted the way he did because two dead girls were found on his sister's farm. That's not news someone gets every day. It could fluster someone, especially someone like Gordon, who's a bit hyper anyway."

"Lieutenant, you know these perps like to drop off bodies in familiar surroundings."

"Fine, maybe you should do a door-to-door in the area to find out who might have done it. There aren't that many houses out there, so that shouldn't be hard, but I gotta tell you, if you do, I'll have to tell you you're wasting your time."

"That's your final answer?"

"Yes, Regis, it's my final answer. I don't need to phone a friend."

Pantera sighed and stood to leave. As he walked out, he said, "And just for the record, I don't think Regis hosts that show anymore."

"Get out!"

Pantera closed the door and walked over to Harry, who had a told-you-so smile on his face.

"I told you he wouldn't go for it."

"But I had to ask him first. Now on to plan B."

"Which is?"

"Mind if we stop by The Watering Hole on the way home?"

"The Watering Hole? What's that place have to do with plan B?"

"A request from me that model citizen Pete Bray do some tailing of one Detective Vince Gordon."

"Are you kidding me? Pete?"

"You have someone better?"

At that moment, Detective Crosswell walked in with Lenny.

"Yeah, like maybe Lenny here. He'd do a better job than Pete. Pete's a lush. He won't make it through one day without getting drunk. Hell, he won't make it through an hour. At least Lenny won't be stopping off at local bars to drink a brew before continuing."

"Pantera?" Crosswell interrupted. "Lenny says he needs to talk to you, and nobody but you this time."

"What is it, Lenny? We're kinda busy here."

"You need me to help you with a case, Detective?" Lenny asked, his eyes wide with excitement.

"Not today, Lenny. Maybe some other time."

"Oh," Lenny responded, ducking his head.

"Leaving him to you," Crosswell said and went to his desk.

"What do you got for me today, Lenny?" Pantera asked.

"I've been bad."

"Yes, well, what else is new?"

"No, really. I really did it this time."

"What did you do?"

Lenny pulled a cheap watch out of his pocket. "I stole this from Walmart."

"Which one?"

"Which one?" Lenny asked, not understanding.

"Which Walmart?"

"Oh, the one over on Sheila Lane, across the river."

"Why'd you do this, Lenny?"

"Nobody ever believed that I did anything."

Pantera picked up the watch. It was scuffed and the second hand wasn't moving. He tried to wind it but the fob was frozen.

"You didn't take this from Walmart, Lenny. You found it. It doesn't work." Pantera looked at it again. "From the looks of it, it hasn't worked in a while."

"It was like that when I took it."

"Lenny, really, we have a lot going on today."

"Then maybe I can help you, like Harry said."

Pantera glanced from Lenny to Harry and back, then said, "Maybe next time. I have someone to help."

"But Detective Overmeyer doesn't think he's reliable. I'll be reliable, Detective Pantera."

Pantera found it odd that he'd called Harry by his name one second before reverting back to 'Detective Overmeyer' in the next. He'd never heard Lenny call any detective by his first name before.

"Like I said, Lenny. Maybe next time."

"Okay," Lenny said, staring at the floor. "Can I use the bathroom before I leave?"

"Sure thing," Harry said and pointed down a hallway. "It's down that hall. Second door on the right."

When he'd left, Pantera said, "Well, it's quitting time. I'm heading to The Watering Hole for a drink if nothing else."

As they walked down the hallway, Pantera said, "You're right. I'm grasping at straws here, but what if Gordon is our guy and we don't take this opportunity?"

"Look, we can tag team some with the surveillance. We won't be able to watch him all the time, but at least we can keep some sort of eye on him. Maybe we can get lucky and catch him doing something that at least gets us the full-time surveillance from Lieutenant Gariepy."

"I guess you're right. It's about the best thing we can do under the circumstances. Hell, maybe Gariepy's right and there's nothing to warrant spending the time to follow him, at least until we have more to go on. I'm feeling stuck, and I tend to grasp at straws when I'm like that in a case."

"It's why you're good, Tony. You're always going down every avenue you can on a case, even if it leads down a rabbit hole."

Twenty minutes later, they walked into Pantera's favorite bar. Dean was behind the bar, as expected, and Pete was in his usual chair.

"Hey, Tony!" Dean said. "How they hangin'?"

"Can't complain," Pantera answered.

"Tony the Detective! He's grrrr-ATE!" Pete said and laughed at his joke.

"How's it going, Pete?" Pantera asked. Looking at Pete, he realized how insane his idea had been. Harry was right to call him out on it. He was getting desperate and he knew it. Perhaps taking him off the case would be the best thing.

Pete said to Harry, "How's the hairy detective?"

"Doing fine, Pete. You?"

"Hey, I'm breathin'."

Pantera did his best to relax and enjoy a drink, but only one. He was driving and would pick up the girls when he dropped Harry off.

The next morning, Pantera dropped the girls at Harry's again. Nancy had called and would be flying into Richmond that night, and he passed that on to Ashley and Harry. Ashley had not said anything, but Pantera knew she needed to return to her daily routines.

When they arrived at work, Harry stopped in the bathroom, and Pantera went to his desk. Opening his top drawer for a pen, he found a note that had been slipped inside. The note, which he handled by the edges, was printed on a sheet of printer paper. He would have it dusted for prints even though he knew they wouldn't find any.

When Harry walked in, Pantera said, "Look what I found," indicating the paper on his desk.

"Where did you find this?"

"In my top desk drawer."

The unsigned note was written in block letters.

I AM WATCHING. I AM WAITING. I AM YOUR IAGO, THE VILLAIN WITHOUT ANY

MOTIVE TO HARM YOU, BUT HARM YOU I WILL. WHY? BECAUSE I CAN. ALL WILL BE REVEALED SOON.

"Your Iago?" Harry asked.

"It's from Shakespeare. He was the antagonist in *Othello*. It's been said he had no motive to ruin Othello's life, but really, he was just jealous."

"So you think someone is jealous of you?"

"Could be. Or maybe this guy really has no motive other than he's capable of ruining my life."

"Any detectives who might be jealous of you?"

"Possibly. A couple, actually. Crosswell and Gordon."

"Anyone else?"

"You?" Pantera said, trying to lighten the mood.

"Why would I be jealous of you? I'm better than you at just about everything."

"Then find out who this is."

"Gordon worked graveyard the night before the girls were found. He left around 9:30 yesterday morning."

"We were still here," Pantera said. "Did he work last night?" They both looked at the schedule posted on a wall across the room.

"He did. His shift ended early at six this morning," Harry said.

"Who was here after we left?"

"Crosswell," Harry said. "He brought Lenny in to see you."

"Maybe we're thinking of the wrong creep."

"Crosswell? He probably knows less about Shakespeare than I do."

"I wouldn't let that check him off our list," Pantera said.

Harry sat at his desk and Pantera at his. Neither spoke for several minutes.

Harry said, "It says 'all will be revealed,' right?"

"Yes."

"Then whoever's doing this is planning on revealing himself soon."

"Maybe, maybe not. He could just be planning to do whatever he's going to do, thinking that might reveal his motives or something. Who knows?"

"I don't," Harry said, "but I wish I did."

"What about that guy you found named Blanton?"

"I still don't see him making a date to spend the night with his rather gorgeous girlfriend and sneaking out and taking a chance she'll wake up and find he's missing. I had the feeling she didn't trust the guy completely, which would spread into the romance department. She'd likely think he was out fooling around if she woke up and he was gone, and who'd blame her? Naw, I think if he was our guy, he'd wait until another night to kill Roxanne or make an excuse to get out of staying that night. It's not as if Roxanne Beard was about to leave town."

By the end of the day when Pantera drove Harry home to pick up his daughters, they were no closer to solving the case.

When they arrived at Harry's, Pantera thanked Ashley again for keeping the girls.

"It was no problem at all. I enjoyed an excuse to get away from work for a few hours each day, and the girls are no trouble at all." Ashley said.

On the drive to his place, Pantera asked the girls how their day had gone, but they were mostly excited about their mother's return that evening.

"I miss Dani," Andrea said, referring to her girlfriend.

246

Nancy arrived to pick up the girls shortly after seven. She signaled Pantera to come outside so they could talk.

"How's Phil's dad?"

"He'll be okay. He might have some problems with slurring speech, but it's as good as can be expected."

"That's good to hear," Pantera said.

"So what have you found out about this guy?"

"That he's elusive as shit and knows at least a little about Shakespeare."

"Huh?"

"Long story." He didn't want to talk to her about the note he'd found in his desk drawer, which would only cause more worry on her part.

"Are you getting close?"

Pantera considered the warning in the note. "Getting there. No telling how long it will take, though. The good news is that he probably has no idea where you live, but I think even if he knew your address, he'd ignore you and the girls. They were just in the wrong place at the wrong time. It's me he's after."

"How do you know?"

"Let's just say we have ample evidence to prove that. The girls were just collateral damage."

"Let's hope nobody else wavers into his field of view," Nancy said.

Gathering the girls and their belongings, she left, the girls hugging their father goodbye and thanking him for having them.

"Even if we did spend most of our time at the Overmeyers' place," Beth added.

After they were gone, Pantera fixed himself a drink of Writers Tears Irish Whiskey and sat at his piano, playing various tunes to relax. Between the whiskey and the soft melodies, his nerves stopped chugging in overdrive. He switched on a baseball game, grabbing a slice of cold pizza from the fridge to serve as a meager dinner.

THIRTY

Nancy thought about the situation with her daughters for most of the ride home. She would need to talk to Andrea and Beth about what had happened and what they knew about it, but she wasn't looking forward to it. She knew, however, that it couldn't wait until they arrived home.

"So, how did it make you feel to find out you'd been watched the last time you visited your dad?" she asked.

"That was creepy," Andrea said. "It's like I couldn't get comfortable. I always felt like I was being watched."

"Yeah," Beth added. "Seeing those pictures really creeped me out. It's weird knowing some guy has seen us naked."

"He needs to do more for security," Nancy said. "Letting the two of you visit him there makes me very uncomfortable."

"Mom!" Beth nearly screamed, "we can't stop seeing Daddy!"

"I know that, honey, but I want you to understand that every time you go there now will drive me insane with worry."

"Mom, Dad's doing something about this. He's getting more security for the house. He's as freaked out as you are about this."

"What kind of additional security?"

"Dad says he's going to put in cameras himself that will alert him whenever anyone comes to the front or back doors. He says alarm systems can be disabled, but

249

cameras set up outside make it more difficult to do that. He says he'll be alerted if someone comes close enough to a camera to spray paint the lens, even," Andrea said.

What Andrea was saying made a difference. If Tony put up cameras with an alert system, then maybe she was overreacting. All they had at their home was an alarm system. Tony was right, though. They could be disabled by someone who knew what he was doing. Perhaps they would look into something more like what her ex-husband was putting in.

"Will he have that installed before you visit again?" she asked Andrea, ignoring Beth's pleas for the time being.

"I don't know. You'd have to ask him. I just know he made the phone call to get it done, so I would think it will be in before then."

"Okay, if he's going to that much trouble and expense to protect you from the pervs, then that helps ease my mind."

"Why didn't you ask Dad when we were there what he was doing to protect us?"

"I needed to get your take on how it made you feel. Face it, girls, if you don't feel comfortable at his house, then every time you went to stay, you'd not sleep well or anything. You'd be a nervous wreck each time, and so would I. I just need to make sure you're safe when you go visit him. He deals with a lot of very bad people."

"We know, Mom, but he is who he is and he does what he does. It's not like anyone can change that."

"I once asked his parents to give him an annual allowance so he could quit the force," Nancy said. "They told me he'd never go for it, and of course, they were right."

"You asked Mom-Mom and Pop-Pop to do that?" Andrea asked, shocked.

"Yes. I couldn't go on wondering if he would never come home when he left for work."

"You loved Daddy a lot, didn't you?" Beth asked.

"I still do in a way," she confessed, "but not like a husband. More like someone who's a very dear friend."

"I think he still carries a torch for you," Andrea said.

"Why do you think that?"

"Because he's not really dated anyone since the divorce."

"There could be a lot of reasons for that. Maybe he's not found anyone he likes enough to date yet, at least not regularly. Or perhaps he just feels too busy to put in the time necessary to make a relationship work."

"Or maybe he still loves you," Andrea quipped.

Nancy looked over at Andrea and smiled. "Hey, I'm hard to forget."

Andrea chuckled, and Beth managed to join in, ending the tension that had grown in the car earlier.

Later, as Pantera was heading for bed, his phone rang. The 540 area code told him it was probably Roxanne Beard's parents.

"Hello?"

"Detective Pantera?" a weeping voice asked.

"Yes. This is Ms. Beard?"

"Yes. The local police came by to tell us today. They said you would need us to come identify the body?" He could tell she would rather be run over by a truck than do this.

"Yes, ma'am. I'm afraid you, your husband, or someone else close to her will need to do that."

"So it doesn't have to be me?"

"No, ma'am. They prefer a relative if we can find one, but it doesn't need to be you."

251

"I think my husband can be there tomorrow."

"Thank you." He gave her the address for the coroner. He waited for her to say something else, wanting to give her time to spill her grief.

"She sent me a picture," Ms. Beard said, "before she—disappeared."

"Oh?" He figured she might begin to ramble about something the picture reminded her of. Perhaps it was an old photo from her high school graduation or something.

"Yes, she was afraid of this one man she'd met and gone out with a couple of times. She said she ended it when he said some things that were—impolite."

Pantera froze. Did she have a picture of Blanton?

"When did she send you this?"

"It was in an email months ago. She was in the habit of taking a picture of any guys she went out with and sending them to me in case—in case something happened. She was cautious that way. I'm afraid the photo isn't a very clear one. Later she told me he turned out to be a creep. I only just thought about it before I called you. I doubt it will help, but would you like for me to send it to you? Maybe you can check him out?"

"Did she mention a name?"

"It's in the email, but I don't recall what it was."

"Was it something like *Blanton*?"

"Yes, that does sound like it. How did you know that name? Is he a suspect?"

"I'll just say he's a person of interest that we'd like to talk to. If you'll forward the email, I can see what we can find out. Having a picture of this guy would help tremendously."

"Okay, I'll go find it now and forward it to you."

"That would be greatly appreciated."

"I hope it helps, Detective. You've been nice to listen to me ramble."

"I wouldn't call it rambling, Ms. Beard."

"You're too kind. I'll forward that email as soon as I find it."

"Thank you."

Pantera paced for the ten minutes it took to receive the email. He figured she was having to search back in old emails from her daughter to find it. When his phone dinged that he'd received it, he opened the email and prayed this would help. It turned out it helped more than he'd ever imagined.

When he opened the photo on his phone, he stared at it for several seconds, trying to determine if it truly was who he thought it was. It was small on the phone, so he went to his computer and opened his email account.

Opening the email, he downloaded the photo.

He was sure of it now.

Roxanne Beard had taken a picture of her date. It looked as though it was taken without his knowledge. He appeared to be standing outside her door, and the picture was taken through a window. She had a fairly clear shot of the man's face, or at least the left side. Some may have called her paranoid, but in this case, she was right to be careful. The problem was she hadn't been careful enough.

The young man in the photo was well-known to Pantera. It was none other than Lenny, the chronic confessor.

For a few seconds he felt as though he couldn't breathe. Lenny? The man she'd described didn't sound like him at all. Lenny was shy, afraid of his own shadow. The man she'd described was self-assured, confident, and crude. Was it possible Lenny had an identical twin?

Or had he been fooling them all along?

Suddenly, everything clicked into place, and for a moment he had to admire the man for his cunning. Who

253

would be the one man they would never suspect of committing a crime?

A man who presented himself as an habitual confessor who confessed to every crime he could.

He realized now how little anyone really knew about Lenny. He was just Lenny, or Crazy Carl, a name used almost affectionately at the station, who would show up and take time away from their real job, solving crimes. Now he wondered how many of the crimes Lenny had confessed to were ones he'd actually committed. In a way, his method was genius. His mistake had been not knowing a girl he'd dated only twice had sent his picture to her mother.

He phoned Harry. Something like this couldn't wait until tomorrow to tell him.

"Hey, man. It's kinda late to be calling," Harry said as he answered.

"You'll thank me when you hear what I have to say."

"Oh?"

"Roxanne Beard's mother just emailed me a picture of the creep Roxanne went out with, the one who's been harassing her. It was in an email from months ago, and the name Blanton is mentioned in the email."

"We have his photo? That's great, Tony!"

"We have more than that."

"Oh?"

"I could tell you, but I want you to verify what I already know. I'm going to send you the email. Take a look at the photo and call me back."

"Sure. You mean you know who it is?"

"Yep. And you will, too."

Two minutes later, Pantera's phone rang.

"Holy shit!" Harry said. "It's Crazy Carl! Lenny!"

"Yep."

"But didn't you tell me the guy she described was all confident and stuff? Lenny doesn't sound like a lady's man at all."

"Don't you see? He's planned this. He confessed to numerous crimes so we'd never consider him a suspect."

"The son of a bitch. He played us."

"Yep," Pantera said. "But now we have the goods on him."

Their conversation continued for several minutes before they hung up, with Pantera's end of the discussion being uploaded to the cloud. The following morning, Blanton sat in his kitchen, listening to Pantera discuss how they were going to arrest him.

They would plant a news article of a crime they felt "Lenny" couldn't resist confessing to. As he listened, Blanton knew it was time to take the next step.

He would be going to Charlottesville that evening, where he would gain entry into the home of Pantera's ex-wife and her family.

After securing everyone with zip ties, he would call Pantera directly and invite him to join the party, warning him to come alone, assuring Pantera would follow those instructions by telling him what he would do if Pantera so much as told someone he was going to Charlottesville, even if he said nothing about going to his ex-wife's.

THIRTY-ONE

Pantera called Crosswell and told him what he'd learned. He needed an APB put out on Lenny. They had his picture from his driver's license photo. He instructed Crosswell to send a couple of units to the address on the license. They needed to act quickly on this.

Next, Pantera called Gariepy and filled him in. Gariepy was shocked at Lenny's plan and how nearly perfect it was. Pantera hung up from talking to him after telling him he'd keep Gariepy informed of what happened.

Twenty minutes later, Crosswell called Pantera. "He's not at that address. It burned down months ago. Never rebuilt. Arson."

Pantera was fairly certain who the arsonist had been.

"We need records on who last lived there. See if there is a forwarding address."

"I already have Gordon hunting that down," Crosswell said.

Pantera blushed remembering his most recent belief concerning the identity of their killer. And while it may be possible that Lenny was not the one to kill Davis and the two young women, the double personalities were a strong case against him, not to mention the nature of his relationship with Roxanne Beard. Now, he hoped nobody ever mentioned his suspicions to Gordon. Their relationship was strained enough.

"Let me know when you find something."

He disconnected the call and phoned Harry again, telling him about the possible arson.

"What do you want to bet our boy Lenny is also a firebug?" Harry asked.

"I don't know if he's a chronic one, but I definitely think he started this one."

"Think we'll be able to prove that in court?"

"I don't care as long as we can prove the murders."

Pantera managed to get a few hours of sleep before going to work the next morning, lying awake a long time before drifting off. The alarm sounded what seemed like minutes after he'd fallen asleep.

Quickly showering and shaving, he dressed and drove to the precinct, anxious to continue the manhunt for Lenny Barstow, aka Crazy Carl, aka Blanton.

When he pulled into the parking lot, another thought occurred to him. Was it possible that Lenny was a former student of Grant Davis when he was a teacher? Was there a distant grudge so strong he might have committed murder over it? The idea that a student might hold a deadly grudge against someone for that long had never occurred to him before, but now he realized that Lenny was young enough to have been a high school student when Davis was teaching but old enough not to have known him at Dunleavy High in Richmond.

When he arrived at his desk, Crosswell met him.

"No forwarding address on the tenant, but his name was Larry Briggs."

"LB," Pantera said. "It fits."

"You mean as in Lenny Barstow?"

"Yes." As he ran his ideas past Crosswell, Harry arrived and stood listening as Pantera finished.

"Where did he teach before coming to Dunleavy?"

"I don't know," Pantera said. "But I know several places to check for the answer."

Lifting the receiver of his desk phone, he found the number to Dunleavy High School and called. When he had the principal on the phone, he asked about Davis's previous school.

"Funny you should call today of all days. His son is here to get his father's personal belongings."

"He's there right now?" Pantera realized he'd forgotten to contact the son after not being able to for so long. It had been placed on a back burner with everything else they'd been doing.

"Yes. He's standing right here, in fact."

"May I speak to him?"

Pantera heard muffled chatter before a young man's voice said, "Hello, sir, this is Frank Davis."

"Good morning, Mr. Davis. My name is Detective Tony Pantera. I'm investigating your father's murder. Do you have a moment to answer some questions?"

"Yes, sir, but I was nowhere near here when he was murdered."

"I know, but I have some questions you might be able to answer that would help the investigation."

"Okay, sir. Ask away."

"Where did your father last work before coming to Dunleavy?"

"He taught math at my alma mater, Cantwell High in Alexandria."

"Thanks. What can you tell me about your father?"

"What do you want to know?"

"What kind of father was he?" Pantera had heard Grant Davis's ex-wife's opinion, as well as his daughter's. He wondered if the son's would agree with theirs.

"Not a very good one, I'm afraid, sir. My mother mentioned she'd spoken to you and I should expect a call, but you never called, so I forgot about it. If you know my mother's opinion of my father, you know mine."

"Okay, thank you. Now, do you recall any students he had particular problems with when he was at Cantwell?"

After a moment's pause, he said, "There was one. I remember this guy really hated my dad. We were on the football team together, and he blamed my father for having his scholarships canceled. He had dreams of playing in the NFL one day, but he was arrested for possession with intent to sell and blamed my father."

"He thought your father turned him in?"

"Not exactly. He thought my father planted the drugs in his locker."

"Did he?"

"I doubt it. This guy had plenty of enemies among the other students. Any one of them might have done it, but this guy hated my dad so much that he never thought it might be someone else."

"Would a student throw that much money into getting him?"

"Sir, there were guys at that school who would sell their mother to get Blanton. For a lot of them, a few thousand dollars would be pocket change."

"Do you remember the name of the guy who hated your father?"

"Yes, sir. Landruth Blanton. He hated his first name though. Always insisted on being called just Blanton. To be honest, I never blamed the guy for wanting to dispense with his first name. He swore he was going to change it as soon as he could legally do it."

Taking a deep breath, Pantera mentally kicked himself for not following up on his call to Grant Davis's son. He'd pretty well assumed he wouldn't give him much to go on since the mother and daughter hadn't, which had led to permanent placement on the back burner. He'd intended to contact him, but it had gone from a priority to a necessary follow-up he would eventually get to.

"Just curious. Do you think this Blanton was really good enough to one day play in the NFL?"

"Yes, sir, but without playing in college his chances were somewhere around zero."

"Do you know where Blanton is today?"

"No, sir."

"If I send you a photo of him, could you identify him?"

"Maybe. Depends on how much he's changed."

"I have your cell number. Is it still good?"

"Yes, sir."

"Thank you. You can expect my text in about one minute."

He disconnected the call and sent the picture. Moments later, he received a reply.

"That's Blanton in the photo."

After texting Frank Davis his sincere thanks, Pantera turned to Harry.

"We have a connection between Blanton and Grant Davis."

After he'd explained what he'd learned from Frank Davis, Harry whistled. "So, we have a motive for the first killing."

"And for Roxanne's murder, too, really. She spurned him, basically in his mind, she left him for another woman. Men with big egos can have a problem with that."

"What about the roommate? Wendy Atwater?"

"I suspect she was in the wrong place at the wrong time. Maybe came home and caught him installing or removing the surveillance equipment."

"That makes sense," Harry said. "Isn't it odd how you find one big clue and suddenly everything starts opening up, and you have mounting evidence?"

"Well, you know what he said in his note: 'All will be revealed.' I just don't think he had this in mind."

Turning to his computer, Pantera searched for any records on Landruth Blanton. A list of several crimes popped up from Alexandria, including an arrest for peeping in the windows of neighborhood homes. He was eighteen when he was arrested for possession with intent to sell. There were almost no details regarding the arrests, other than adjudication. He'd always received a slap on the wrist, except for the drug charge. He'd been found guilty and had spent time in jail over that one, apparently finishing high school while incarcerated.

Pantera printed the records and added them to his now growing file on the murders. He wrote "possible arsonist" in the margins. It was something he would use to try to get a reaction from Blanton when he had him in for interrogation.

"We need to plant the story," Pantera said. "Either we get extremely lucky and spot Blanton on the street, or we bait him into coming in to confess. I'm thinking the latter would be easier."

He and Harry spent the rest of the morning concocting a false news story about a home burglary. They included details they thought would entice Blanton to come in and confess. He'd never shown a tendency to confess to certain types of crimes or crimes with particular details, but they hoped adding that a non-working watch with sentimental value had been taken would be a final nudge. Other than a few particulars, there weren't many details about the crime, which was typical to allow the police to weed out confessions like Blanton's.

261

Next, Pantera called Bill Ledbetter, an editor with the Richmond Times-Dispatch. He knew Ledbetter from the "Purger" case he'd worked to solve last winter and felt he could get the paper to run the story in the city section.

When he'd explained why they needed the fake story planted, Ledbetter agreed, providing they could do an exclusive on the case once it was solved, highlighting the Times-Dispatch's role in bringing the killer to justice.

The story was scheduled to run in the next morning's paper, but Pantera would never see it.

THIRTY-TWO

That evening, Landruth Blanton drove to Charlottesville, parking in a commuter lot near I-64. He had all he needed in his backpack, along with a knife strapped to his thigh, and began walking the two miles to the Boyd residence. He would arrive before dusk. He didn't worry about his special shoes or swimmer's cap since Pantera knew who he was.

Before heading to Charlottesville, he had watched Nancy and the girls for over an hour on the cameras that were sending the images to the cloud and had finally grown bored since they were doing nothing worth watching. He wasn't sure what he was hoping to see, but it wasn't house cleaning and sitting around reading or watching TV.

As he approached the house, he saw Phil Boyd get out of his car and go inside, lugging a suitcase. Apparently, he'd come home from his trip. Blanton hadn't planned on that, but it wasn't a deterrent either. He'd just take care of Phil Boyd before dealing with the others.

He removed a pistol from his backpack, jamming it under his belt, and took the knife with a five-inch blade from the sheath he had strapped to the side of his leg. He'd not bothered to hide it as he'd walked through the streets to the house. Plenty of guys who went walking carried such protection. It was considered the smart thing to do with all the violent people running around, he thought, smiling at the irony.

Holding the knife to his side, he rang the doorbell, figuring Phil Boyd might still be the closest to the door. He was right.

Phil opened the door, apparently not worried that someone might intend to harm him and his family, and with a quizzical look of non-recognition, said, "Yes?"

"Oh, thank you," Blanton said. "My car broke down around the corner, and you're the first person who'd open your door to me. Could I use your phone to call AAA? My cell died or I'd use it."

The moment of hesitation was all Blanton needed. He knew Phil would be concentrating on making a decision about whether or not to let a stranger into the house, not bracing for an attack.

Blanton kicked the door, which flew open, knocking Phil onto his back.

"What the—?" he began, but was silenced when Blanton fell on top of him and jammed the knife as deep as it would go into the flesh between his ribs. He could feel the blade as it encountered one rib, sliding to one side and piercing the man's lung. Bright red blood began to run from the wound like a million ants escaping a fire inside their mound. Phil gasped and did his best to struggle, but Blanton ended that with another thrust of the knife, ending Phil's life with the razor-sharp blade. Blanton, now smeared with blood, stood and looked down at the man who was breathing seconds before.

"You'd have done better to stay another night where you were," Blanton said.

He heard someone in a nearby room. "Phil?" came a female voice. Suddenly Andrea Pantera stood in the doorway that led from the entrance hall to the rest of the house.

When Andrea screamed, Blanton slammed the front door to block the sound while simultaneously whipping the .32 caliber Smith and Wesson from his belt and pointing it at her.

The shock of seeing the gun silenced her screams. He heard footsteps racing toward them, and both Nancy Boyd and Beth skidded to a stop beside Andrea, taking in the scene with horror-filled eyes.

"Now, if everyone is quiet and cooperative, nobody else will get hurt," he said as calmly as possible.

"Who are you?" Nancy asked, beginning to cry.

Blanton pointed the gun more in her direction. "I thought I asked you for quiet."

She clamped her mouth shut.

"Please don't hurt us," Beth said, beginning to cry.

He pointed the gun at her with one hand and held a bloody finger to his lips. "Shhh."

She tried to be quiet, doing her best to stifle her sobs of fear and grief.

"Now, everyone move into the kitchen."

The kitchen held a breakfast bar that split the room. A small dining area made up one side of the room and the kitchen itself lay on the other. He made the girls stand in a corner of the dining area on the other side of the small dining table.

"Don't move from where you are unless I tell you to. Understand?"

They nodded.

He told Nancy to lie down on the linoleum floor of the kitchen side of the breakfast bar and put her hands behind her back, reminding her that cooperation meant she and the girls would live through this ordeal. He wasn't being honest, but of course he wouldn't tell them that, though he might take Andrea with him for some added fun before killing her and disposing of the body.

"Beth," he said, "come here—slowly."

She did as she was asked, as he knew she would.

Handing her a zip-tie, he said, "Do you know how to use this?"

She looked at it and nodded, tears continuing to slide down her cheeks.

"Good. Wrap it around your mother's wrists and pull it tight. I want to see the flesh squeezed around the tie so I know it's tight enough.

"I'm sorry, Mommy," she said, crying.

"I didn't ask you to talk," he said, and she said nothing more.

He watched as the flesh on Nancy's wrists were squeezed by the plastic tie, forming a crease that ensured that she would not be able to slip out of the binding.

"Good job," he said to Beth. Indicating that Beth should follow him, he walked to where Andrea stood trembling with a mixture of fear and loathing.

"You're the guy who spied on us at my dad's, aren't you?"

He grinned. "Yes, and you have a very sexy body, Andrea." Then he slapped her with his open palm. "Now, do what I said and shut up." She glanced down at the gun in his hand and winced.

Blanton handed a zip-tie to Beth. "Same thing. Just as tight."

He watched as Beth cinched the zip-tie around her sister's wrists. Again, the flesh bulged from where the tie wedged into the skin.

Making Andrea lie on her stomach, he told Beth, "Now, I'm going to have to use the zip-tie on your

266

wrists. I want you to understand before I do that if you run or resist in any way, I will have to either shoot you, or—if you somehow manage to escape, which is almost impossible—I will shoot your mother. Do you understand?" He started the zip-tie a few notches to make a circle of plastic binding.

She nodded, the sobs still coming, though he could see she tried her best to stop them or at least keep them as quiet as possible. That was good. It meant she was determined to do everything he said, regardless of what it was.

"Stand with your back to me and your hands behind your back," he said. She complied, as he knew she would, and he placed the circle of the tie around her wrists and cinched it tight.

Nancy and Andrea were on their backs, making it nearly impossible to stand because they couldn't use their hands or arms, so he felt safe.

He made Beth sit at the small dining table. He would need her to perform one more task.

First he took out his phone and logged into his cloud. Opening an icon, he listened while Pantera wordlessly went about what sounded like making dinner. Pantera said nothing as he worked. The only sound was that of the pans clanking.

Nancy's purse was on the breakfast bar and he walked to it. Searching for a few seconds, he found her phone, which he needed for this call. It was locked, of course.

"What is your code for opening your phone?" he asked Nancy.

She didn't answer, and for a moment, he wondered if she'd fainted.

Stepping to where he could see her eyes, which were open, he pointed the gun at her "The code?" he said with the tone of someone tired of a lack of cooperation, though there had been nearly none.

"2-3-8-4."

He pondered the meaning of the code until he realized it was alphabetical, not numerical. "Beth," he said. "How clever of you."

He punched in the code and the phone woke. Opening the contacts list, he found "Tony."

He walked to Beth and said, "I'm going to call your father. When he answers, you're to tell him he must come here. Can you do that?"

She nodded. He knew the girl would not be able to keep from crying as she spoke to her father. He counted on her fear and how that would sound.

"Then, once your father hears you, I will take over the call. Do you understand?"

She nodded.

"Tell me what you are supposed to do."

"I have to tell him to come here to my house."

"The exact words I want you to say are, 'Daddy, you must come here right now.' Can you repeat that to me?"

"Daddy, you must come here right now."

"Good. Do you have permission to say anything else?"

"No."

"Very good."

Blanton pressed the button to call Pantera. When Pantera answered, he said, "Hey, Nancy, what's up?" Blanton's phone on the breakfast bar echoed the words.

Blanton held the phone for Beth to speak into it.

"Daddy, you must come here right now."

He loved the fear and crying in her voice. It would make Pantera do anything necessary to keep her safe.

He held the phone to his own ear in time to hear

Pantera say, "What?!" His voice registered his shock at the words and their tone.

"Good evening, Detective," Blanton said.

"Blanton," Pantera said. "Or should I say Landruth? Or maybe Lenny?"

"I know you know who I am," Blanton said. "Don't say another word, unless I ask you a question or I'll shoot Beth square in the face."

Pantera was silent.

Blanton waited a beat. "Good. I'm going to give you some instructions, and they must be followed to the letter. First, don't fuck up and think I won't know if you make a plan with anyone to storm your ex-wife's house, which I might add belongs solely to her now since her husband is dead in the entry hall."

"Phil's dead?"

"Did I ask you a question?" Blanton paused again.

"You are to come here immediately. I don't care what excuse you make up, but if you tell anyone where you're going, your family won't be alive the second I know. Am I clear on that detail?"

"Crystal."

"Good. Then when you get here—absolutely alone—you are to park in the driveway and come to the back door. It will be unlocked, so you can come in. If you go to the front door, you and your family will suffer the consequences of your decision to do what you want instead of what I want. Do you understand?"

"Yes."

"I know how long it takes to get here from your place. No stops along the way. One more warning about bringing reinforcements. You do, and your family dies. Are we clear?"

"Yes, we are clear."

"Don't fuck this up, Detective. If you do, even if

269

it's not your fault, you won't like what happens."

He hung up without waiting for a response. He had at least an hour to kill—no pun intended, he thought to himself and smiled. After fixing himself a sandwich and Coke, he moved Nancy and her daughters to the living room, making them lie on their stomachs.

He analyzed why he wanted to kill Pantera as much as he did. Pantera had never really done anything to him, but he represented all that Blanton hated. He had the power of the badge, like the cop in Alexandria who had arrested him despite his pleas he'd done nothing wrong when the drug dog found the drugs he still believed Dipshit Davis planted in his locker.

Davis must have been in league with the cops, using dope they'd already confiscated to frame him and ruin his life. It wouldn't be that hard to do.

He figured Pantera had done similar things, so he would get revenge for all the poor souls whose lives were ruined by Pantera. Killing the man would make him feel better, so killing him was necessary, but he would take his time.

Then he'd kill Pantera's ex-wife and the younger daughter before taking off in Pantera's car to retrieve his own, with Andrea bound and gagged in the back seat.

THIRTY-THREE

Pantera grabbed his gun and a bottle of water. The fear Blanton had caused in him had made his mouth feel as though he'd put the nozzle of a hair dryer in it and turned it on. Stepping outside, he called Lisa, whom he'd invited over for dinner earlier that day.

"Hey, sexy! I'm nearly there."

"How far away are you?"

"Two minutes. No more than three." she answered.

He thought about it and decided he could wait that long for her to get to his house, where he could tell her face-to-face what had happened. He would be speeding on I-64 with his bubble light flashing, so that gave him an extra ten minutes at least. Without betraying his distress, he told her he would see her when she arrived.

He took out the small notepad he used at crime scenes and jotted a few notes, tearing the small piece of paper from the spiral binding. He would give this to Lisa when she arrived.

It had startled Pantera that Blanton was aware they knew about him. It demonstrated that Blanton was still able to monitor what happened in his home. He doubted Blanton was able to eavesdrop on the squad room, so his home was the only place left. Pantera recalled he had been home when he talked to Harry on the phone about what he'd discovered.

He assumed Blanton was telling the truth about Phil. Pantera had no idea when he was supposed to arrive home, but he figured he wouldn't have been far behind Nancy.

Lisa's car pulled into the driveway. She was all smiles until she saw Pantera's face. The worry must have been visible.

"What's wrong?" she asked as she climbed out of her car.

He quickly explained how Blanton was holding his family hostage and was threatening to kill Beth if he suspected reinforcements were coming.

"Oh, my God! What can I do to help?" she asked.

"I need you to call Harry. Read this to him," he said, handing her the small piece of notepad paper.

She glanced at it. "Are you sure?"

"No, but I have no other choice."

She hugged him, and he was surprised at her strength as she held him for several seconds. Finally, he pulled away. "I have to go. I'm more or less on a clock."

"Be careful, Tony."

"I'll do my best."

As he drove, he thought about a number of things: the fact his ex-wife had lost her husband to senseless violence, the frightened look on Lisa's face when he drove away that said she feared losing him, the words he wanted to say to his daughters. He'd told Andrea and Beth he loved them many times, but the idea he might not have another chance to do that weighed on him, making him hope and pray that he would be able to tell them again. Thousands of times, in fact.

He received a text from Harry: "I'm on it." He wondered how the conversation between Harry and Lisa had gone. Had Harry questioned the instructions? It would be normal to do so, given the circumstances.

Once on I-64, Pantera put his bubble light on the roof and sped toward Charlottesville, weaving through the traffic with little difficulty. His heart seemed to race faster with each mile.

Lisa sat in her car before leaving, thinking about what had happened. She'd not met the Pantera daughters yet, and the thought that a madman might kill one or both of them made her want to kill the man called Blanton. She looked down at the note again. Tony's ex-wife's address was on it.

There was something Tony didn't know about her, and this gave her pause. She'd held this detail about her life back because she wasn't sure how he would take it. Now, it made her wonder about something else and whether she was being fair to him by holding back. It was a small thing, really, but now it bothered her.

She read the note again. After the address in Charlottesville, it read, "Nancy and girls held hostage by Blanton. Phil dead. Come alone. Enter back door 10 minutes after I text the word *now*, which I'll do upon arriving. Use lights and siren, just not on approach. Haul ass and don't be late."

Harry had asked how long it had been since Tony left, and she'd told him, "Ten seconds before I called you."

"Is he sure? No cops?"

"I asked him the same thing. He said he had no other choice."

"I'll have to hurry. Talk to you when we get back."

If you get back, she thought.

Starting her car, she drove toward I-95, praying things would turn out well.

As Harry merged onto I-64 from I-295, he felt his heart sink. Brake lights gleamed as far as he could see in the distance. His bubble light was already on, and he moved onto the shoulder, flipping the switch to activate the siren. When a pickup truck moved onto the shoulder as well to try to bypass the lanes of stopped traffic, Harry moved to where his car was riding the man's bumper. The driver, seeing the flashing lights and hearing the siren, stopped, thinking he was being pulled over for driving along the breakdown lane.

Harry edged his way into the traffic again, moving along now at under five miles-per-hour to get around the stopped truck. Harry glared at the man as he passed him, giving the man his middle finger. As soon as he was around the truck, he sped up again along the side of the highway. As he reached the accident that was the cause of the traffic jam, he saw that three heavily damaged cars blocked two of the three lanes. An ambulance was parked in the breakdown lane. Harry again had to edge himself into the lane of traffic that was slowly passing the wreck. As he drove by, a state patrolman glared at Harry, obviously wondering who Harry was and why he was using his siren and lights to speed down the shoulder to get around the accident.

As soon as Harry cleared the mess, he sped up to nearly ninety miles an hour. Tony would be depending on him to enter the house at the appointed time. Now, he wondered if he could get there in time to park on the next block and rush to the house without being seen. It wasn't as if he could come to a screeching halt in front of the house without being noticed.

Pantera prayed that nobody else would be hurt when he finally arrived. He had encountered the wreck as well, but had been able to get around it faster than Harry had because the wreck had occurred only ten minutes before he had come upon the traffic jam. He'd considered calling Harry to suggest he take an alternate route, but he wondered if his car could be bugged. If Blanton had placed a listening device in the car, he would be killing his family with a call. He figured Harry would get around the mess the same way he had.

His nerves were on edge, and he jumped when his phone rang. The car swerved a bit before straightening. He took a deep breath to calm himself before answering the call.

"Pantera," he answered.

"Tony, it's Harry. I was slowed down by a wreck. I just wanted to let you know. I'm flying as fast as possible to get there."

Pantera had to be careful what he said. "That's fine, Harry. We can talk tomorrow about it. I gotta get somewhere right now. An important appointment. I'm running a little late because of a wreck on 64. Had to use my lights and siren to get around it, in fact."

Pantera knew Harry would understand why he was talking this way, almost in code.

"Okay, I get it. I'll see you soon. Maybe we could fumigate your car tomorrow."

With that Harry clicked off. Pantera tossed his phone into the passenger seat and sighed. For the first time, he wondered how many would die today because he was certain Blanton wasn't finished with the carnage.

About forty minutes after getting past the wreck, Pantera was finally arriving at his exit. His tires squealed as he exited the interstate, taking the off-ramp curve a little too fast.

His bubble light was still on, and the blue beams lit the dusk with an eerie glow. He wouldn't use his siren. Phil and Nancy's house wasn't that far from the highway, and he didn't want to try and gauge how far he had to be from the house to turn it off. Besides, traffic was light this far from central Charlottesville.

When he was about a quarter mile from the Boyds'

275

home, he turned off the bubble light and drove to the house. He'd been instructed to park in the driveway. He would have parked on the next block and walked, but he feared that upon seeing him entering without parking in the driveway, Blanton might shoot Beth. He would still have Andrea, Nancy, and him as hostages, so shooting one daughter would not be a problem for Blanton.

Pulling into the driveway, he saw that the house appeared dark. No lights were on inside the house, and for a moment, Pantera wondered if Blanton had taken Nancy and the girls and left.

Or maybe he had killed them all before leaving.

Pantera's years of training and encounters on the job could not prevent the onslaught of near panic that rose within him. He'd been trained to know that his life depended on thinking clearly in the most chaotic moments, but he'd never been trained for this, where he had a personal stake in keeping his ex-wife and daughters alive with his actions. The thought that he might have driven here only to find them dead made him wonder if he would be able to handle the discovery. He'd learned that sanity was fragile, and despite his insistence that he could take anything and survive it mentally, he realized now that he'd been wrong. He wasn't sure his psyche could handle such heartbreak and prayed he wouldn't have to find out if it could.

He texted Harry the word Now before getting out of the car. He didn't wait for a reply.

As he began to walk around to the back door, he realized the house itself felt dead. A home where people lived seemed to ooze life from its frame. This house felt as dead as the elm leaves that carpeted his yard in November.

When he arrived at the back door, he found it was not only unlocked but slightly ajar. Now the house seemed malevolent, as if it was something dead that ate the living. It felt like a monstrous thing that needed a morsel to finish off its dinner, and he was the perfect dessert.

I've been waiting for you, that door said. *Pay no attention to how it seems more like a mouth than a door. It's only a door. A portal into your past—and your future. Come inside. I have something for you.*

As he touched the door, it moved open almost as if it really was something eagerly waiting to devour him. He stepped inside, glancing left and right before entering to be sure Blanton wasn't waiting just inside to knock him out or shoot him.

The back door led into a combination mud room and laundry room. The washer and dryer sat in the shadows like sentinels that were now on break, so who came or went was none of their affair.

The kitchen lay just beyond the next door, and Pantera peered around the corner of the doorway before entering. More appliances sat in silent darkness. Not even the stove's clock was on, and Pantera realized Blanton had turned off the house's power.

He was still afraid of what he would find in the other rooms. Would their bodies be in plain sight? Or had he killed each in their bedrooms, possibly posing them in lewd postures? What if they weren't there at all and he was searching an empty house? What then? Would he call again with a new address? What if he never called again and his family disappeared for months or years—or forever?

Pantera wouldn't put anything past the bastard. He thought of Blanton as pure evil, as if Satan himself had created his own version of Adam. He'd dealt with pure evil before, and the lengths to which people like that would go were immeasurable.

277

He eased into the spacious den beyond the kitchen. It was lit only by the moonlight coming through the thin curtains that covered the large front window. He saw nothing there. He looked toward the doorway to the entry hall on the opposite side of the room. Was Phil's body in there, or had Blanton been lying to ratchet the tension up a notch, making Pantera more prone to mistakes or miscalculations?

He paused there, straining to hear something, but the house was as silent as death.

Then moving to the foyer, he could see Phil's body lying in a pool of blood. Blanton had been telling the truth.

Pantera crept to an open doorway that led to a hallway. Down that hall were a guest bedroom and bathroom, along with a library and a home office.

He stuck his head into the bedroom before walking into the bathroom across the hall from it. Both were empty.

Pantera moved along the hallway, pressing himself against one wall, his gun drawn and ready for use.

Sticking his head into the office, he could see nothing. There were no windows, so the room was too dark. Listening, he heard nothing, so he moved to the library. One small window in a far wall provided enough light from a nearby streetlamp for him to see well enough to know the room was empty.

Looking back up the hallway and seeing nothing, he risked taking out his penlight. Leaning against the doorjamb that opened into the office, he pointed the light into the room and flicked it on. Nothing.

Nobody was downstairs. Switching off the penlight, he moved along to the stairs, glancing at his watch. Harry would arrive soon if he managed to get there on time. Pantera wanted to encounter Blanton—if he was there—before Harry arrived. He wanted to be able to mask any sounds Harry might make while creating enough noise that Harry wouldn't have to do what he was doing, perform a slow room-to-room search.

He crept up the carpeted stairs, stopping at the top to listen. The house was still silent, and he began to decide Blanton had taken Nancy and the girls somewhere else, probably to a place Pantera would never find. A despair he had never felt began to settle on him.

A small window at one end of the hallway provided enough moonlight to see, though only barely. He dared not use the penlight, since it would easily mark his location should Blanton step out of a room and shoot.

He could see the doors to the girls' rooms were closed. The master bedroom door was open slightly.

He went there first, creeping up to the open door and sticking his head in. There were several windows here, so he was able to see clearly that nobody was in that room. Stepping to the master bath, he peeked inside. Again, nobody was there. The feeling that he was in an empty house multiplied.

Moving across the hall, he opened the door to Andrea's bedroom. As he did, he looked into the darkness. The moment Pantera's head was fully into the room, a bright flash of light, like a flashbulb, blinded him. He felt a blow to the back of his head and everything went dark.

Harry drove past the house at normal speed to prevent suspicion in case he was seen and noticed Pantera's car in the driveway. Other than that, the house looked empty. The same thoughts that had occurred to Pantera about what this might mean now caused Harry to wonder as well. None of the possible outcomes of

279

finding the house empty of living people were good.

Parking on the street at the next corner, he climbed out of his car. A woman walking her small dog on a leash noticed him.

"Excuse me, can I help you?"

"No, ma'am. I'm fine," Harry said, moving toward the Boyd home.

"But you're parked in front of my house."

"I apologize ma'am. I'm on official business," he said, taking out his badge and showing it to her.

"Oh, dear. What's happening?"

"I'm sorry ma'am, but I don't have time to talk to you now."

She spoke again, but instead of acknowledging her, he kept walking. He moved along the street before detouring into the Boyds' backyard, feeling the woman's eyes on him.

Approaching the back door, he stopped when the lights suddenly came back on, lighting several windows on both floors. Either Pantera had the situation in hand, or Blanton did. He waited to see if he could figure out which one before entering the house. A light from one of the upstairs rooms went out, and Harry knew. Pantera wouldn't be bothering to turn off lights. Blanton had control of the situation, which likely meant that Pantera was a hostage now.

When Pantera's eyes opened, the lights were back on and his hands were bound behind his back. Blanton was standing over Beth, who was sprawled on the floor nearby, her hands secured by a zip-tie behind her back. The man was smiling, as if he'd just completed an amazing trick.

"Welcome back, Pantera," Blanton said. "Glad I didn't kill you. In the end, you might be the only one left alive, except for me, of course. But that will depend on you and whether you follow my instructions."

Pantera said nothing at first, choosing instead to take stock of his situation. He knew Harry would be here soon, if he wasn't already inside the house.

He went for the movie cop response since he figured that's what Blanton expected and he didn't want to disrupt Blanton's expectations for now. "You'll never get away with this, Blanton. Everyone knows about your confession scheme—a scheme to get away with murder. But then, you haven't gotten away with anything yet, have you? We know you killed Grant Davis, a revenge plot you'd apparently worked on for years. We also know you killed Roxanne Beard and Wendy Atwater, and dumped their bodies in a cornfield. You won't be able to get away with any crimes now."

"At least, not in Richmond," Blanton said. "Who says I'm ever going back there?"

"Every police station in the country will have your picture by tomorrow."

"That's fine. I can survive. I'll be forgotten in a month or two. I'll just be a picture of some guy in Richmond."

Taking out a pistol, he aimed it at Pantera. A small cry was heard from across the room, and Pantera recognized it as Andrea's voice.

Then Nancy was speaking. "Please don't do this."

"Do what?" Blanton asked. "Kill your ex-husband or rape you and your daughters?"

Pantera felt the rage rising in him.

"We've got all the time I need or want," Blanton continued. "Everyone who knows anything about me being here at this house is either dead or in this room."

A small popping sound came from outside the room. Immediately, Pantera knew what had caused it.

Harry's knees could use some physical therapy, and one of them had popped at the worst moment possible. They had joked about it many times, but now it wasn't a joke. It might prove deadly.

Blanton's head jerked toward the door. In two steps, he was there and stepped outside into the hallway before he rushed toward the stairs. A gunshot reverberated through the upstairs, and Pantera heard the unmistakable sound of someone falling down the stairs, feet striking the wall as Harry tumbled.

Pantera's rage peaked as he prayed Harry was alive.

Stepping back into the bedroom, Blanton said, "I really must invest in a silencer. That was loud. If it brings cops, it won't be good for you."

"Or you," Pantera said.

This time, Blanton aimed the gun at Beth. "This one is worthless to me. Too young to fuck. I didn't even enjoy seeing her naked." He looked over at Pantera and glanced at Nancy. "I should just kill her now. One less person to worry about."

"Kill me instead," Pantera said. "Leave my daughters alone. They've never done anything to you."

"True, but it makes me happy to think of killing them in front of their parents."

"What do you have against me, anyway?" Pantera asked. "I was just doing my job."

Blanton shrugged. "You're a cop. Do I need more?"

"Are you going to kill every cop you meet?"

"No, but a few along the way wouldn't be bad."

"Someone probably heard that shot. The cops will be here in a few minutes."

"Maybe. But I'll negotiate my way out of this. I have a cop hostage, along with a woman and two teenage girls. They'll be handing me my freedom on a silver platter."

"Don't count on it, Blanton. It would be better if you gave yourself up now. More killing won't solve anything and will only serve to get you life in prison without parole."

Blanton smiled. "You think I'm an idiot? I'll get that just on the killing of that fuck, Davis." He looked down at Beth before looking back at Pantera. "So, you see, Detective, you're dealing with a man who has nothing to lose but his freedom. That would make me the most dangerous adversary, wouldn't you say?"

"Yes," Pantera said, "but one who the entire nation will know to watch for."

"Whatever," Blanton said and pointed the gun at Beth, who lay sobbing on the carpet of her bedroom.

Everyone in the room jumped from the sound of the shot, squeezing their eyes shut from the reverberating blast.

Pantera forced his eyes open and saw something he couldn't believe. Blanton lay on the floor next to Beth, much of his head missing. Blood was quickly pooling beside where he lay dead.

For a moment, Pantera thought that Harry had survived the gunshot at least long enough to make it to the door of the bedroom, take careful aim, and shoot. His entire face went slack from the shock of seeing Lisa step through the door, a .32 caliber Glock G32 pointed at Blanton's corpse.

The mist of Blanton's blood still hung in the air. Pantera could both smell and taste it. He looked at Beth and saw that she was covered with blood splatter. Looking down, he saw he was as well.

"What the hell are you doing here?" he asked.

"Saving your family—and you, too, apparently."

"How's Harry?"

"Breathing, but I don't know for how long."

"Get something to cut my ties!"

Nancy spoke up. "There's a knife in my bedroom in the far bedside drawer. Phil kept it there for protection."

Pantera said nothing about how much protection it had been. Doing so would be cruel and pointless.

Returning with the knife, Lisa cut everyone loose, starting with Pantera.

He immediately jumped to his feet, ignoring the dizziness and cramps that threatened to stop him from reaching Harry. He stumbled down the hallway and nearly fell rushing down the stairs, grasping the banister to prevent him from tumbling down the carpeted stairs to land on Harry's body.

When Pantera knelt beside his partner, he felt his neck for a pulse. One registered, but it seemed weak.

Running to the house phone in the den, he quickly dialed 9-1-1. When the operator answered, he said, "Officer down!" He continued by supplying the address. Within four minutes, an ambulance had arrived, along with several police cars.

As Harry was wheeled out, Pantera asked, "Will he make it?"

"Don't know," came the reply. "He's lost a lot of blood, but we'll do our best."

After he'd given his statement to the Charlottesville detective, he found Lisa, who had just finished doing the same with another detective.

"I'm glad you came," he began, "but I'm not sure what the hell just happened. Why did you come here?"

"Tony, I joined the Marines out of high school. I'm an expert marksman, but beyond that, I was so good a shot that I nearly made the Olympics in the ten and twenty-five meter pistol competitions. I also worked for the D.C.P.D. for three years. I didn't like the work, so I quit for a more peaceful library job. I never mentioned it because I didn't want to have you take me to a shooting range and have your fragile male ego challenged by me. That's not conducive to having you continue to want to see me, at least not early in the relationship."

"You were never going to tell me?"

"No, I would have told you eventually, after we had learned enough about each other for something like that to be an outing we did for fun and not a competition."

"Well, I'm glad you made it here."

"So am I. He was about to shoot Beth. She's the younger one, right?" He nodded. "You might have been next."

"I don't know about that. I think he wanted me to watch him rape Andrea and Nancy before he did that. Or maybe he would just leave me with the memories to destroy my life."

"What did he have against you?"

"He said it was just because I'm a cop, but I don't know if that's true. We'll probably never know. But never having anything to do with him other than taking his bogus confessions, we haven't had any interactions. He may have just had it against me that I represented the law to him. He was as crazy as they come."

"And brilliant," she said. "It was quite a plan. Confess to crimes to become known as a confessor while committing crimes you confess to."

Pantera changed the subject. "I need to call Ashley."

"I already did," Lisa said. "She'll be here as soon as she can. Well, she'll be at the hospital anyway to be with Harry. Certainly no reason to come to this house of death."

"Speaking of death, I need to talk with Nancy and the girls. Nancy lost her husband in this, and the girls lost a stepfather they loved."

"Okay. I think I'll find a decent motel, get checked in, and go to the hospital."

"Sounds good," he said. "I'll be there as soon as I can get away from here."

"Shall I make the room a double?"

"I was thinking of driving home tonight."

"You shouldn't try to drive back to Richmond. Besides, you'll want to see Harry when he wakes up."

"I hope he does," Pantera said, looking at his lap.

"He will," she said, hoping she was right.

He kissed her briefly on the lips. "Thank you, Lisa."

"You're welcome, Tony. So, a double it is?"

"Sure. I'd probably fall asleep at the wheel."

"You might go clean yourself up. You have blood all over you," she said.

He looked down at himself and saw the blood splatter. "You're right. Excuse me," he said. Stepping out to his car, he took out the bag he always kept in the trunk in case of emergencies. He walked back into the house and into the guest bathroom. He changed his clothes and cleaned up, washing the blood off his face and hands.

Meanwhile, Lisa checked with the detective who had taken her statement.

"Will I be charged with anything?" she asked.

"No, ma'am. I highly doubt it. If it were up to me, you'd get a medal."

"Thank you."

"So, I can go now?"

"Sure. We have your contact information. Nice shooting, by the way," he said as she left, waving at him over her shoulder.

Pantera sat with Nancy and the girls for about an hour until they decided to leave and stay at a hotel.

"I'm not sure I can ever come back inside this

house," Nancy said, and Beth instantly agreed. The tears had dried up from exhaustion, but the sadness remained.

"I know I can't," she said. "Even if I do, I can never sleep in that room again."

"I know, baby," Nancy said.

Her own tears had finally dried up as well. She had to be strong for her daughters' sake. Someone would have to handle the aftermath of this—the funeral arrangements for Phil, the counseling they would all likely need, the sale of the house none of them ever wanted to see again.

She looked at Pantera. "Will Harry make it?"

"They don't know yet."

"You'll let me know?"

"Yes."

"Even if it's bad news, Tony. I can handle it."

"I know you can."

He said goodnight to Andrea and Beth, holding each in a tight hug for nearly a minute.

THIRTY-FOUR

When Pantera finally arrived at the hospital, he was directed to a small room where family and friends could wait. When he entered, Ashley was already there with Lisa beside her. Ashley, with red eyes, stood and hugged Pantera, sobbing into his shoulder.

"Have you heard anything?" he asked Lisa.

"Not yet."

Pantera sighed with cautious relief. He'd been afraid Ashley's tears came from the news they might have received.

He held Ashley while she cried. The door opened, and Harry and Ashley's daughter, Chloe entered. She attended UVA and had probably arrived before anyone, including Ashley. She carried a cardboard tray with three coffees.

"Oh, hi, Detective Pantera," she said. "Mom told me you'd be here, but I wasn't sure when, so I didn't get you a coffee. Sorry. I can go back if you want one." Her eyes were red from crying.

"That's okay, Chloe," Pantera said. "I can get my own if I want one later. I'm fine for now."

"I'm just trying to keep myself occupied with something so I don't have to—" She burst into tears. Lisa stood and did her best to comfort her niece. All of the women were crying, and Pantera was doing his best to maintain control. Harry was more than his partner. He was a good friend, one of the best that Pantera had ever had.

He needed to call Gariepy and fill him in on what

had happened. He hadn't before because he knew Gariepy would order him to stand down and let the Charlottesville PD handle it, which Pantera would not have done. As they say, he thought to himself, sometimes it's easier to ask forgiveness than permission.

A sleepy Gariepy answered his phone.

"This better be important," was his greeting.

"You know I wouldn't call you, especially at this time of night, if it weren't."

"What is it, then? Good or bad?"

"Both."

"Of course," Gariepy said with a sigh. "Give it to me."

He filled him in on the night, ending with Harry's surgery.

"Will Overmeyer be okay?"

"We don't know yet. I'll call as soon as I find out something. He's still in surgery."

"Shit."

"You can say that again."

They ended their call with Pantera telling him he would be in as soon as he could make it back to Richmond, but he'd need to see Harry before leaving Charlottesville.

Nearly two hours later, all conversation had ceased as they waited to hear something. It was approaching two AM. Fatigue made the time creep along.

They all jumped when a phone in the room rang. Pantera took this as a good sign. If the news had been bad, the doctor would have told them in person.

Ashley lifted the receiver. "Hello?"

She listened, and they all could see the joy spreading on her face. They all looked at each other and smiled, sighing with relief. The sudden good news had left them all both buoyant and exhausted.

Animated conversation filled the room.

"He's going to be okay!" she said. "He'll be in the hospital for a few days while he recovers. Then he'll be coming home!"

She hugged Chloe and they cried, but this time it was from relief and joy.

"When can we see him?" Chloe asked.

"Probably not until tomorrow," Ashley said. He's in recovery now and will get a room once he's out. We can stop in tomorrow morning."

As they talked, Pantera could feel the adrenaline rush begin to dissipate. It had been a difficult night, and he needed a shower and a bed.

Ashley followed them to the hotel, and Chloe returned to her dorm. After Ashley paid for a room, she said goodnight to Pantera and Lisa, thanking them for being there for her.

When Pantera and Lisa entered the room, she turned and kissed him passionately.

"Oh, honey, I'm too tired," he confessed.

"Me, too. I just wanted you to know how much I appreciate you."

As he lay there trying to sleep, Pantera considered how wonderful Ashley was. She hadn't blamed him for what happened to Harry. He would have to ask her why one day.

He also thought about Lisa and her kiss as they entered the room. She was special, too. As he drifted off, he thought how he would have to take her target shooting. She could probably help him improve his aim.

The following morning, Pantera made love to Lisa after they both slept in. As they lay in bed afterwards, Lisa's phone rang. It was Ashley, who was already at the hospital visiting Harry. Based on Lisa's end of the conversation, Harry was asking about Pantera, wondering when he and Lisa would be by to visit. Pantera called out in a voice loud enough for Ashley to hear, "Tell him Gariepy expects him back to work tomorrow!"

Lisa chuckled at Ashley's reply. When she disconnected, she said, "Ash said to tell Gariepy to go fuck himself!"

When they walked into the hospital room, Pantera smiled at Harry, joking about the tubes running into and out of him. "You look like Frankenstein's monster," he said.

"Beats looking like the monster's bride," Harry croaked.

After they chatted for a while, a nurse came in to shoo them away. As they left the room, Pantera took Ashley aside.

"I have to ask you something," he said.

"What is it?"

"You don't seem upset with me that I nearly got Harry killed."

"I'm not."

"Why not?"

She thought for a moment. "Are you blaming yourself?"

He considered her question and realized he was. "Yeah, I guess I am."

"Don't."

"Ashley, I—" he began, but she cut him off.

"Stop! Let me ask you one thing."

"Okay."

"If Chloe and I were in the same situation as Nancy and your daughters, and Harry asked you to help, would

291

you? Even if you knew there was a 100% likelihood you'd be shot?"

"Of course, I would."

"That's why I'm not upset."

"But his being there did nothing. It nearly got him killed is all."

"I'm not sure about that. From what you say, Blanton was seconds away from shooting Beth."

"And?"

"Harry's being shot took time away from Blanton's actions. It interrupted his plan, and he had to take care of Harry before continuing, which would start with shooting Beth. Those few seconds allowed Lisa to get to the bedroom before he fired and made the difference between Beth being dead or alive."

"You don't know that."

"But it's a definite possibility, wouldn't you say?"

He looked at her. She smiled at him and he returned the smile. "I guess you're right."

"And you'd do the same thing for Harry. Frankly, if he hadn't gone to help you, I might have divorced him."

"What?!"

"Because he wouldn't be the man I married. He wouldn't be the man who would risk his life for others. He'd have to quit the force at the very least."

"Ashley Overmeyer, you have an odd way of looking at things."

"No, I don't. I have the right way of looking at things. The only way if you ask me."

He hugged her goodbye and promised to have them over for dinner as soon as Harry recovered enough. "And bring Chloe when you come over," he said. "She's a wonderful young lady."

"You have a couple of wonderful young ladies as daughters, yourself," she said.

Lisa followed Pantera to his house so he could change into his typical work attire. When she left, he promised to call her that evening. As she climbed into her car for the ride to her home, he said, "Would you and your girls like to join me and my girls for a week at the beach?"

"When?" she asked, smiling.

"The week of July 17."

"I'll check and see," she said.

"Where are your girls, by the way? You didn't leave them alone, did you?"

"Don't be silly. They're with my mom. She lives in Fairfax."

"Good place to be, I suppose."

"As good as any." With that, she started her car and drove away, blowing him a kiss.

THIRTY-FIVE

Nearly two weeks later, Andrea and Beth arrived for a visit. They would be leaving for the beach in another two weeks. That evening, they went to see a Richmond Flying Squirrels minor league baseball game and fireworks for the fourth.

On the way to the ballpark, they visited the man whom the girls were starting to call, "Uncle Harry." He was home now, and much improved. He would be starting back to work in just a few days. Arriving at the ballpark, they sat in their seats along the left field foul line, and Pantera leaned toward the girls. He needed to ask them about having Lisa join them on their beach trip.

"Before the game starts and we begin focusing on that and the food vendors, I need to ask you both a question."

The girls stopped their chatter and turned to him.

"I'd like to have Lisa join us for our beach trip, if it's okay with you two."

They both grinned. "You mean the lady who saved us?" Beth asked.

"Yes."

"Sure, why not?" Andrea said. "After all, if it weren't for her, we'd not be going to the beach, right?"

"I guess not," Pantera answered.

"There's one thing I need to know, though," Andrea said.

"What's that?" Pantera asked.

"Will you two be sleeping in the same bed?"

"That's a rather personal question, but since the answer will be obvious, yes, we will."

"But Dani and I can't sleep together?" Her grin told him she was half joking—but only half.

"That's different. When you're an adult, you can make those decisions for yourself."

"That's only three years, Dad."

"Yes, but it's my last three years of being able to tell you what to do in cases like this, and I'm not giving those years up."

She smiled and sighed, indicating her next comment was not serious. "Okay, I suppose you two can sleep together."

"Can we stop talking about people sleeping together? It's creepy talking to Dad about that stuff," Beth said.

"I agree," Pantera said. "No more talk today about 'that stuff.' We have a baseball game to watch."

They enjoyed the game and conversation as they watched the Squirrels beat the Somerset Patriots 4-3. The Squirrels scored two in the bottom of the ninth to pull out the victory.

As they waited for the fireworks to be set up, Andrea said, "Dad?"

"Yes?"

"Do you love Lisa?"

"I'm not sure yet. I have feelings for her, but love is something that develops over time. At least that's what I believe."

"You don't believe in love at first sight?" Beth asked, disappointed.

"I believe in a strong attraction at first sight, but love? Not really. That first attraction is usually physical and involves what you so eloquently called 'that stuff' a couple of hours ago. There may even be strong attractions to someone's personality or other qualities, but love takes time. Love takes seeing people at their worst and still loving them. That's not something that happens when people have known each other for only a few minutes, or even a few weeks."

"So you don't love her?" Andrea asked.

"Well, let me put it this way. I love a number of things about her, but there are a lot of things I still don't know. The same goes for her. There are a lot of things she doesn't know about me."

"Like what?" Andrea asked.

"Like things I'd rather not talk to you about."

"Like how you're still in love with Mom?"

He was surprised by this question, not only because it came out of the blue, but also because it was mostly spot on.

"What makes you think I'm still in love with your mother? I care deeply for her. You can't live that long with someone and not feel something for them, especially when the parting was amicable."

"What's amicable?" Beth asked.

"Friendly."

"Oh."

"Anyway, my question stands. What makes you think that?" he asked Andrea.

"Because you can still get nervous when you're around her. How you look at her sometimes, like you wish you two were still together. That sort of thing."

"Sweetheart, your mother and I will never get back together again. For one thing, she doesn't love me anymore, regardless of what you think I feel."

"I'm not so sure, Dad. She asked us about how much we knew about Lisa. How you felt about her. That kind of thing. She looked—I don't know—interested in you again."

"She's just keeping tabs on me. Making sure I don't f— mess up."

Andrea grinned. "You almost said the F-bomb!"

"And you're getting a little too smart for comfort."

"So you and Mom might get back together?"

He looked into her eyes that were hopeful yet knowing that the hope was an empty one. "No, honey. We're not. Your mom is just being a mom."

"But you were her husband, not another one of her children."

"I bet your mom would disagree with you on that in a number of ways."

This made the girls laugh, and Pantera used the moment to change the subject.

"Who's up for some nachos and a drink?"

"ME!" they both said, grinning.

As he ate his nachos and drank his beer, Pantera thought about what Andrea had said. He had to admit it was intriguing that Nancy would be asking about Lisa. He wasn't sure how to feel about that if she were considering trying again.

The date for the beach trip finally came, and Pantera picked the girls up from their house early that afternoon. Nancy was preparing to sell the home she'd shared with Phil. Andrea's girlfriend, Dani, was there as well. They would be staying at Pantera's house that night and going to the beach the next day.

Lisa arrived that night with her daughters, introducing them to everyone, and Beth began to giggle almost uncontrollably when Lisa set her suitcase in her father's bedroom. Andrea took Beth aside to talk to her, and calm was restored.

Dani was fine with sleeping on the couch, saying she understood the separation while claiming her own mother let her and Andrea sleep in the same bed when Andrea spent the night.

"But she's, like, really liberal," Dani said.

"Well, I'm liberal, too, but not that liberal," Pantera said.

The next day, they drove to the beach and checked into the three bedroom condo on the water, where they would enjoy their week.

Pantera was nervous about spending that much time with Lisa. Would it end their relationship? Make it stronger? What if it had no effect? What would that say about them?

He decided to talk to Lisa to see what she was thinking about this.

After they had checked in and the girls changed into swimsuits before rushing to the beach, he fixed Lisa and himself a drink, asking Lisa to join him on the balcony.

As they drank and chatted, he watched the girls as they lay in the sun, occasionally running into the Atlantic for a swim before returning to lie on their towels and work on their tans.

Finally, he asked, "Are you as nervous as I am about spending a week together?"

"A little. Why are you nervous?"

"I'm worried that either something will happen or nothing will."

She laughed. "That's an odd answer, but I understand it completely."

"I'm afraid of change," he said. "I like the *status quo*. Change makes me nervous."

She turned to him. "Do you mind if I try to give you some advice about that?"

"Sure."

"Tony, change is as inevitable as the sun rising. Sometimes it's good—a sunny day like today. Sometimes, it's not—storm clouds everywhere. Life's a crapshoot. We're all on borrowed time, even those of us who've not had close brushes with death like you and me." She looked out at the beach and added, "And your girls. Might as well enjoy every day you can and accept the good with the bad."

"I know what you say is true, but accepting it is not that easy for me."

She leaned toward him and kissed him. Sitting back again, she said, "Let's just take it one day at a time and see where life leads us?"

He shrugged. "I guess I have nothing better to do."

She laughed and said, "What a romantic thought!"

He grinned sheepishly. "Sorry. I'm not what you'd call a romantic guy."

"I disagree. There's plenty of romance in you. It just needs to stop being afraid of itself."

He smiled, raised his glass in a toast, and said, "To not being afraid."

She clinked his glass. "Yes, to the impossible—or at least the improbable."

Pantera sat there as she went back inside to make more drinks, thinking of what she'd said as he looked down at his daughters. They were so close to being adults that it frightened him. It was just another part of life that scared him. Lisa was right. Change was inevitable, and he would have to live with whatever changes came his way. It didn't matter if they were changes in his own love life or changes in the dynamics between himself and his daughters.

She joined him again on the balcony, and asked, "So, what's on the agenda for tomorrow?"

"I don't know. Perhaps we can play it by ear."

She grinned and raised her own glass in a toast. "To playing it by ear."

He clinked glasses with her.

"Yes, to the inevitable," he replied and drank.

ABOUT THE AUTHOR

Charles Tabb is an award-winning author whose short stories have appeared in various literary journals. His other novels, including the literary bestsellers *Floating Twigs* and *Finding Twigs*, are available at charlestabb.com/books. He lives with his wife, two horses, and two dogs near Richmond, Virginia. When he is not writing, he enjoys traveling, visiting with friends and family, and reading.

If you enjoyed this book, please write a short review on Amazon and/or Goodreads. They are greatly appreciated by the author and potential readers.

You may find more about the author by going to charlestabb.com, where you can also sign up for his monthly newsletter or just enjoy browsing his website. An accomplished speaker, he is available for speaking engagements, either in person or virtually on Zoom. Virtual appearances at book clubs are free. You can reach him by visiting his website and clicking "CONTACT" in the top banner.

Made in the USA
Las Vegas, NV
24 August 2022